Aventurine on the Bailgate

Also by Anne Britting Oleson

The Springs

Aventurine and the Reckoning

Aventurine on the Bailgate

AN AVENTURINE MORROW THRILLER

Anne Britting Oleson

Encircle Publications
Farmington, Maine U.S.A.

Encircle editor: Cynthia Brackett-Vincent
Cover design: Deirdre Wait
Cover images © Getty Images

Published by:

Encircle Publications
PO Box 187
Farmington, ME 04938

info@encirclepub.com
http://encirclepub.com

This book is for

Deirdre Wait,
who willed it into being;

and for

Joan Connor,
because it took so long
to discover that we were always
meant to be friends.

Part I:

Cathedral

One

Her footsteps echoed on the stones of the passageway from the cloisters. Her perspective shifted, although she kept her eyes on the central pillar of the chapterhouse, visible through the open doors at the end of the corridor. With each step, she could feel her body becoming stranger, until—and she couldn't quite understand how this was happening—she could *see* herself walking. She could see her shoulders drawing back, see her chin lifting, her gaze steady. At the same time, it wasn't an out-of-body experience, for she was fully aware of, and inside of, the body that walked, that stared.

She felt cold. She rubbed her arms, beneath the jacket she wore over the flowered dress. The world around her seemed to expand, the echoes deepening until they felt like the ringing of Old Tom, the tower bell.

Then she passed through the giant doors and into the chapterhouse. Slowly she approached the central pillar, its base surrounded by a couple of low tables. She let her eyes climb upward, toward the ribbed stone ceiling. *Vertigo.* Staring upward made her dizzy; she was made anxious by the realization that so much of the weight of that stone was balanced and carried by the pillar, reaching its ribs out to the sloping walls. She could imagine the strain shouldered by the stone, and her eyes searched in vain for a meter, such as the one she'd seen in Worcester Cathedral, gauging any movement caused by that strain. She closed her eyes, waiting for the crack, the shake, and the roar as

1

the stone dome, built some thousand years ago, collapsed under its own weight and crushed her.

The clearing of a throat behind her snapped her eyes open again.

Neil.

But of course it wasn't Neil. Neil was dead, had been for months. She had seen him die.

Slowly she turned.

It was the Cathedral tour guide.

For a moment the circular room spun, became a vortex, and she was spinning around the pillar. The sweat broke out along her upper lip and at her hairline.

Neil, falling. To his death.

No. Neil, falling, after his death.

There was a roaring in her ears. She groped blindly for something to hold onto.

"Miss?"

There was a hand on her elbow.

"Sit here."

She felt the stone seat behind her legs, and sank onto it.

"Lean forward. Put your head between your knees."

She did as she was told. She opened her mouth and gulped down the cold air. Convulsively. Her arms hung down, and after a moment she grasped her ankles, feeling a strange comfort in their boniness.

Aventurine hadn't meant to spend so much time in the Cathedral. But as luck would have it, when she approached the scaffolding at the west front, the skies opened up, as though with the wrath of God. She hurried in under the shelter, and into the entrance. All outside sounds were immediately muffled. She had her omnibus ticket, for the castle and Cathedral both, and when she showed it to the ladies at the counter at the rear of the nave, they waved her toward a knot of people beyond the pillars.

"You've come at a lucky time," one said, handing her a brochure.

"The floor tour's just begun. You won't have missed very much at all."

So Aventurine slipped into the back of the group, who were listening with various levels of intent to an elderly man wearing a blue sash across his chest, under his suit jacket. The dim light glinted off his glasses as he spoke of the history of the Cathedral and its several builds and rebuilds since the Normans, his hands gesturing toward the soaring heights. She looked around furtively at the other members of the tour: a couple her age, and another, much younger couple who were holding hands. A woman wearing a headscarf and sunglasses despite the dimness. A mother and father with a teen who seemed engrossed in the guide's words, and two younger children who did not; the parents themselves looked as though they'd already spent a long day listening to competing demands and were breaking under the strain. Two other men who might have been in their thirties, one of whom narrowed his eyes as though trying to catch the guide in some grave historical error.

And me, she thought. A frenetic non-writing writer—the kind who was courting insanity, if Kafka was to be believed. A middle-aged woman who had supported herself with her writing all her professional life, and who couldn't manage to string a decent coherent sentence together lately, no matter how hard she tried.

Not since Shep's disappearance. Not since Neil's death. Not since Paul—she caught her breath and squeezed her eyes shut for a moment—had learned the truth of his parentage. Paul, avoiding them all, and fleeing to Italy with his friend Lance.

The group moved forward, the tour guide indicating the tomb of a bishop, or an archbishop—she couldn't quite hear him, but whether that was the echoing nature of the place, or her inability to concentrate, she wasn't sure. She hung back at the edge of the pack anyway, scanning the arches and the statuary and the tombs for something that might catch her imagination, that might dislodge an idea. Any idea. The autumn sun shone through stained glass soaring overhead, and splattered the ground around her with precious jewels. She leaned down and put her hand on the cold stone, trying to capture the spark of peacock blue, but it only flitted onto the back of her fingers, mocking her.

"And here," the guide said, lifting a hand toward two sarcophagi on the other side of a wrought-iron fence closing off an archway, "are the tombs of Katherine Swynford and her eldest daughter Blanche."

Here was something. Aventurine sucked in a breath and moved closer to the fencing, laying a hand on the iron, colder than the stones had been. The sound she made, or her movement, had attracted the tour guide's attention, and he turned to her now. His brows lifted, as though surprised that, among this group who seemed marginally interested but not overly knowledgeable, his words had elicited more than a nod from his audience.

"You know of Katherine Swynford?" he asked. He held his hands together before him, almost reverently. "The mother of the Beaufort line? John of Gaunt's third wife?"

She was aware of eyes turning toward her.

"Mistress before wife," she corrected, looking at the dark stone, imagining the woman inside, long turned to dust.

If it had been a test, she would have passed on the first question.

"That's right."

There was a pause. The man too ran a hand along the iron bars, but familiarly, as though in greeting. Perhaps he did it every time he led a group by here. It was an interesting thought, a glimpse into character. He seemed to be waiting for her to offer more.

"De Roet before Swynford," she added. Her eyes were drawn to the intricate carving. From that woman had come the woman in the tomb beside it. From that woman eventually descended Henry Tudor. Standing here, she could imagine that Katherine de Roet Swynford's death was more recent, had not happened 600-odd years previously. She felt the ghost of a grief for a woman she hadn't—couldn't have—ever known. *One of the Badass Bitches of Britain,* she thought, and felt the corners of her lips turn upward.

The guide smiled. "Do we have a fangirl here?"

Aventurine couldn't help but laugh then at the incongruous term from the elderly man's lips. "You might say that." Still, she didn't really know enough about Katherine Swynford; perhaps she should start reading up. One never knew where inspiration would come from. "She was Geoffrey Chaucer's sister-in-law, too."

His smile grew wider, and he nodded—but the rest of his charges were becoming restless, and the two small children had begun to tug at their parents and whine. He gave her a last smile—a rather sweet and intelligent look, she thought, and a gratified one—before waving his group forward. She glanced back once at Katherine and Blanche before following toward Bishop Hugh, and the Imp.

Aventurine was unable to make out the Lincoln Imp, billed as the culmination of the tour, until the guide flipped a light switch to illuminate it. She leaned back on her heels, hands clasped. She felt both unimpressed and impatient with herself for being so judgmental. Someone, hundreds of years ago, had carved the little devil as either a warning, or a joke, and she found herself unable to imagine the reaction of the parishioners who would have been looking up to it.

"Thank you all," the guide was saying now, holding up his arms in benediction. "It has been a pleasure to show you the treasures of our Cathedral proper. If you have time, and if you have interest—as some of you have—" and he looked directly at her— "in Katherine Swynford, be sure to stop in the Medieval library, on the other side of the cloisters, to have a look at the Swynford Jewel, on temporary loan to the Cathedral until November 25th, thought to be Katherine's birthday."

After a quest to find the ladies' room, Aventurine had sought out the Medieval library. She found the carved stairway near the tea room, and followed it upward, until she reached a timber-framed room with heavy standing desks along one side. Where the chained books were to be read, she surmised, and wondered how the ecclesiastics would have been able to read anything in the dimness before electric lighting. At the other side of the room were solid display cases, but one was made more prominent by the librarian standing vigilantly beside it.

Aventurine crossed to have a look.

"The Swynford Jewel," the librarian breathed. His voice was pitched low, but the architecture of the room would have deadened any conversation anyway. "Have you come to view it?"

"The Cathedral guide suggested I should."

"Ah. Henry, I expect." The librarian chuckled.

The display case was heavily glassed, but inside, on a bed of black velvet, a startling trinket took pride of place. It looked to be a charm of some sort, to be worn on a chain around a woman's neck. It was in the shape of a book, of gleaming gold. The pages lay open: one with an image of a haloed saint holding a swaddled child, the other with a glittering many-faceted ruby inlaid in it. An overhead light blazed off the stone, making it look as though it were glowing with some pulsing energy.

"Who is the saint?" Avi asked, peering more closely.

"Careful," the librarian warned quickly. "Too close, and you'll set the alarm off. Then the whole place will be rushing with security."

"Really?" Aventurine looked around quickly, for the security system, the blank black eye of the camera.

The librarian shrugged his shoulders under his dark suit. "Probably, though it might take them awhile." Again he chuckled. "Don't tell anyone I said that." He cleared his throat. "The saint is thought to be St. Margaret of Anjou. She's the patron saint of childbirth and pregnant women. This looks to be a jewel that was made for a wealthy woman, possibly as a gift to be worn as a talisman during her pregnancy."

Aventurine smiled wryly. There should be, she thought, a talisman for *not* being the mother of a grown child in his early twenties. "Tell me about this piece. Why is it the Swynford Jewel? What connection does it have to Katherine Swynford?"

She looked down again into the case, at the saint, and at the blazing red of the stone which might have been the color of a mother's heart, or the color of the blood she shed to bear a child. Hugh Swynford's child? John of Gaunt's child?

"It was found during work on the Chancery, which Katherine Swynford rented, in which she lived with her family and servants. The level of debris surrounding it, and other material in the area in which it was found, indicate that it would have been contemporary to her. The style and the level of decoration also date it to that period."

"It's lovely," Avi said, knowing that that assessment fell well short of the mark. Imagine being a woman who would wear such a thing. Imagine being a man who would give a woman such a thing. A woman who was bearing, or who had borne, his child. A boy, most likely, because it would have been an extraordinary Medieval man who would be so excited about a girl child. She smirked at her own cynicism.

Even Shep was excited about a boy. The thought was a sudden stab to the gut, unexpected and unwelcome. She inhaled deeply, looking down once more at the Jewel.

After a moment, Aventurine realized that she was still sitting, head between her knees. She closed her eyes and opened them again. The roaring in her ears faded slowly. The pillar rose above her, then spread into its arches overhead. She could hear sounds from beyond the chapter house, echoing voices, the booming of a door closing. Inside this beehive, nothing stirred. She shook her head. She wasn't passing out. No one spoke. The stone upon which she sat was cold.

Slowly she straightened, sensing a strange *deja vu*.

The elderly tour guide sat on the stone bench close by along the circular wall. Not far from the door. So engrossed had she been, inhabiting her progress toward the pillar, that she had walked right past him and never noticed: had he been a wild animal, she would have been easy prey. As it was, he sat next to her with his back straight, his hands on his knees. She noted again the blue sash, wondering what it signified: an order of some kind? A guild of Cathedral tour guides?

"I didn't mean to startle you," he said. His eyes were brilliantly blue, to match his sash. "Are you all right?" His smile was calm, concerned. Slightly curious. For a moment she imagined the shade of Katherine Swynford gliding in to take the seat on his other side. No doubt she would slip her ghostly hand into his. He seemed comfortable, as though he came into the chapter house after every tour to recharge for the next one. Perhaps he did. She half-smiled at her own fancy. He was watching her still.

She shrugged, made mildly uncomfortable by his unwavering gaze. "I was looking at the pillar." She felt a sudden wave of exhaustion wash over her. She leaned back on the stone seat.

For a moment they were silent. Somewhere towards the cloisters, a child shouted indistinctly, to be answered by another shout. Footsteps echoed in the corridor outside, then trailed away again.

Aventurine cast a furtive glance at the guide. He was contemplating the pillar, or perhaps the stained glass beyond; the sun had come out again, fitfully, and jewels littered this stonework at their feet, as it had in the nave earlier. If they stayed, as the sun lowered in the sky, the jeweled light would crawl upward and over them. Even now, though, the blue sash he wore under his coat shimmered richly. She looked away before he saw her glance.

"Tell me," he said quietly at last, "what were you looking for in our Cathedral?"

8

Two

—————

Aventurine had booked the hotel on the Bailgate for two weeks. An anonymous room on the first floor, done in a tasteful yet somehow characterless grey palette. Nothing too jarring; nothing too exciting. Just what she thought she needed, to order her mind; perhaps it would soothe her enough that she could put pen to paper, or fingers to keyboard. The double window between the bed and the bathroom door overlooked the courtyard behind the pub: round wooden tables, brightly colored umbrellas, some still furled. She leaned against the window frame, looking down on the foreshortened customers taking advantage of the unseasonable warmth. A man passed beneath her, a pint in each hand, then disappeared under one of those umbrellas. A woman in an optimistic sunhat, reading a book, lifted a stemmed glass to her lips. This would be Aventurine's life for two weeks, walking the city, coming back to the top of Steep Hill before dinner, to stand here imagining herself into the worlds of those people below.

If she could.

If she were still capable.

Aventurine threw herself across the double bed. The high ceiling, with its discreet sprinkler system, mocked her, and she put an arm over her eyes. She felt like weeping, and chided herself for that pointlessness. It wouldn't help. It would make her head ache, her eyes red, her nose run. It would not help her overcome this writer's block.

9

How long since she had thrown open the cover of the laptop, eager to type out the words of her newest work? How long since there had *been* a newest work?

She took a deep breath, trying not to shudder.

Of course she knew how long. She knew exactly how long. To the day. To the hour, almost.

She turned her head and looked at the desk on the far side of the room. The desk upon which she had laid out the computer, her notebooks, her pen. Her recorder and her phone perched atop the stack of printouts, interview transcriptions Linda had typed out for her. All she needed to get started. A start she had not been able to make even after getting back her stolen materials.

Write the article, Micheline had suggested. *Start small.*

Even her twin had not really understood, and that, in a way, was shocking. And more distressing than Mick would ever understand.

Genevieve, of course, had not said a word about it. The way she had tilted her head in the Facetime call, however, the way her gaze had sharpened as Aventurine attempted to explain the block—Genevieve knew. Even though such a thing would never have happened to her, Genevieve had the power of imagination to understand.

A couple of weeks. When Aventurine had made the initial reservation, she had seen it as an opportunity: time to get back to work without interruption. Now she saw it as a sentence.

She wouldn't cry, she told herself sternly. She wasn't a cryer, not really. But she was so tired, so *tired* of being trapped inside herself, with words that wouldn't form, sentences that wouldn't be written, ideas that never came to fruition. So tired of the sudden shattering of her life. Shep. Mick. Neil. Paul. *Oh, Paul.*

It wasn't crowded—still early yet for the evening diners and drinkers, even if the warm weather had not been such a surprise. Aventurine ordered a pint of 49 Squadron and carried it back through to the garden, where she found a table near the rear fence. The afternoon was still bright; she wore her sunglasses and hat against the glare. She'd brought a book, and now she opened it—the perfect disguise— and pretended to read while people-watching.

If she glanced up to her left, she could see her window. She looked around for the woman with the wine glass, and found her seated back-to a couple of tables down, holding a book and wearing the sunglasses and hat just as she was. This woman, however, appeared really to be reading. The wine glass was nearly empty; and as Avi watched, the woman lay the book face-down on the table, then gathered her glass and purse to go inside to the bar for a refill.

There was a candle in a glass holder at the center of the table. Aventurine dug in her purse and found one of her sister's lighters; with some maneuvering, she was able to light the candle without burning herself or setting the table on fire. It would be quite some time before the evening drew on enough for a candle to be effective, but the tiny guttering flame somehow made her feel more at home. More hopeful.

The Man on the Bridge. She turned back to the first page, knowing she had not been at all paying attention to the words, and that was sacrilege. It was her favorite of Stephen Benatiar's novels, a story of transgression and redemption, and she determined to pay it the attention it deserved. She sipped her pint and settled in.

John and Oliver were flirting in the bookstore when she heard the first *no*. The second was more forceful, and she looked up.

It was the woman with the wine, over to her right. She had returned, and held her book again in her hand, but someone had joined her at the table. Aventurine looked over the top of her own book, her eyes narrowed. A dark-haired, handsome man: he had settled into the chair opposite that woman, and now leaned forward, his hand on her arm. Familiarly. Aventurine didn't like the feel of the situation. It was, she realized, too close to home.

The woman jerked her arm away, nearly upsetting her wine glass.

There was something about the man and his deceptively small actions that made Aventurine cringe. The subtle power moves. Her stomach was in knots. She felt her grip on her glass tighten; her knuckles, when she glanced down, had whitened. Slowly she let go of the pint, and straightened her fingers.

His voice? She couldn't distinguish his from the hum of the other people on the terrace. Was he pitching his voice purposely low so that no one would overhear?

Perhaps it was the way he leaned forward again, reaching that familiar hand this time to the woman's hat brim, as though he would take it from her head. The woman put up her own hand sharply to stop him, and at the same time pulled back in her chair.

Don't give him any ground, Avi thought desperately.

He didn't look at all like Neil. But his demeanor was very much like Neil's. Avi put her hand on the blue aventurine bracelet Genevieve had sent her for her birthday, trying to draw strength from it. Courage. The woman at the other table might need strength, might need courage, at least from the looks of things. Avi had moved beyond cringing: her skin was crawling.

Neil was dead.

"No," the woman said again. Her back was straight, and her voice, though low, was forceful and carried.

The man reached for her arm again.

Abruptly the woman pushed away from the table, snatching up her purse and spinning toward the rear gate. Aventurine tried to catch her eye behind the sunglasses as she rushed past, hand holding her hat in place, but was unsuccessful. The man now clambered to his feet, to follow.

Avi moved without thinking. She stood quickly, awkwardly blocking the space between tables. She felt the man's hand at her shoulder, an attempt to shove her aside, and she jerked her own purse strap, pulling her chair over. She tumbled, exaggerating her fall, grabbing at the man's arm and pulling him down with her.

"Oh," she exclaimed, trying to right herself, but instead shoving the chair into the man's leg so he went down to a knee again. He cursed, scrabbling at the chair, the table. She strained her ears over the noise to hear the rear gate to bang shut. "I'm sorry. So sorry!" In climbing to her own feet again, she managed to knock over her pint with such force that the beer splashed on his sleeve and down his pant leg.

"Fucking bitch! Watch what you're doing!" His eyes passed over her, unseeing, as he tried to make out where the other woman had gone.

By the time he'd regained his feet, several seconds had passed. But was it enough? *Please have gotten away,* Avi urged the woman silently. At least out of the car park, around a corner. Somewhere, out of sight. The man dashed through the gate, slamming it behind him.

Someone helped her to her feet, someone else righted her chair and handed her the purse. From inside the bar, a waitress came with a cloth and a mop.

"I'll get you another," the waitress offered.

Aventurine smiled shakily. "No worries. I was just going in to order my dinner." But she suddenly had no appetite. All she could see, in her mind's eye, was the man's hand, reaching, familiar and possessive. Striking out, like a venomous snake.

After a dinner she only took a few bites from, and another pint she drank way too fast, Aventurine returned to her room, concentrating on her path: through the dining room, up the stairs, and along the maze of corridors circling around in their confusion, until she came to a door, the number on which matched the one of her key. She still felt shaken, could feel a hand on her arm as though she had been the one accosted. She let herself in, and then, wary, checked and double-checked the lock behind her. For a long moment she leaned against the door, not reaching for the light switch. She'd left the window open to let in the unseasonably warm air, and now the evening breeze lifted the curtains gently. The air was cooling as the night drew on. A swell of laughter from the terrace below jolted her.

In her pocket her phone buzzed. She blinked rapidly and fumbled for the light switch. When she drew out the phone, she saw the text notification: Micheline, her twin sister, at home, anxious, wishing

13

only to be somewhere in Italy with Paul and Lance. She dropped the phone and watched it fall, as though in slow motion, to the grey carpet and disappear under the bed.

She finally managed to flick on the light, and then blinked, feeling lizard-like. Slowly she moved to the mirror over the dresser and leaned forward to peer into her face. The lines around her eyes were more pronounced now than she remembered: when had that happened? Tonight, now, her pupils were wide—perhaps the shock of the encounter with the two strangers. Her bottom lip was still full—*delightfully inviting,* Gio used to say, tracing his thumb along it. The dimple in her cheek appeared when she smiled or laughed, neither of which she felt inclined to do right now. She ran her hand up into her hair, naturally blond, kept short and low-maintenance; Micheline had taken to dying hers, complaining that the color was growing dull.

Aventurine turned to look down at the phone, partially obscured by the bed's dust ruffle. *Micheline.* She needed to talk to her sister. And tell her—what?

Call me. Just the two words, when she retrieved the phone and clicked on the message icon.

"What's wrong?" Mick asked.

Avi took a long time to answer, crossing to the window to look down at the garden again. The fairy lights strung along the fence top, and wound through the potted shrubs, twinkled with a merriness she resented. The umbrellas were only shadows now, and the few remaining people seated under them were more so. There was no point in asking how her sister could know anything was in fact wrong; she always did. They had never read each other's thoughts, but there was still the finest filament of feeling that stretched between them.

"I need to tell you this," Avi stumbled. The words tumbled out: the woman with the hat and sunglasses. The man who appeared, and who gave Aventurine the creeps with his possessive familiarity.

The first and then second *no,* and the force bordering on desperation in the woman's voice. The fleeing, and Avi's attempts at foiling the pursuit. As she listened to herself, she despaired of conveying the feeling that had permeated the encounter—the feeling that welled in her a sort of *deja vu,* or that the woman had been reliving an ugly part of Avi's own life.

There was a long pause over a cell connection that crackled in her ear. Then a whisper from Micheline. *"He's dead, Avi. Neil's dead."*

"I know. Don't talk about him. Don't let's even mention his name." *Pretend he never reappeared in your life,* Genevieve had ordered. *Pretend he's someone you forgot twenty-five years ago*

"But that's why you're upset."

"Yes."

"He didn't look like—him."

"No. Younger. Better looking. Better cared for." Aventurine tried to reassemble her scattered perceptions. "There was more money there. But it was the attitude. The privilege. Like the woman owed him something, and he could—and would—have it from her, whatever her wishes were."

"But you saved her."

"I *hope* I saved her. I hope I bought her some time. Slowing him up like that was the only thing I could think of to do." Avi sighed. She looked again down into the rear garden of the pub, and the shadows that passed back and forth beneath her like a tide. On the one hand, she wondered what their stories were; but on the other hand, she didn't want to know. She didn't want to become involved, and something told her that she already was, though she couldn't quite identify how. Surely she'd never see either of the strangers again.

"You did *good,* Aventurine," Micheline said reassuringly. "You did what you could."

That was the frustrating part. "But was it *enough?*"

"There's no way to know. You probably will never know."

"But Micheline," she protested. "I can't help it. I feel like that woman is in danger."

Three

A venturine slept later than she intended, and realized, upon emerging from a hot shower, that she had missed breakfast down in the dining room.

It hardly mattered, she thought, as she pointedly ignored her computer, closed on the desk, and pulled on jeans and a light sweater. She scrabbled on top of the dresser for the blue earrings that matched the blue aventurine bracelet, and frowned at the bags under her eyes as she leaned toward the mirror to slide the French wires into her earlobes. She looked tired. She felt hungover, despite having only drunk a bit more than one pint. *Lightweight,* she hissed at her reflection, then slapped on some lipstick, grabbed up her purse and jacket, and headed out.

She hadn't really taken the time to explore the castle, so she headed along the Bailgate to the top of Steep Hill and turned right. The sun was shining weakly, and it was cold and damp under the archway. She bought herself another ticket inside the prison building, and opted for one to the wall. Restless, that's what she was, and if she stopped moving, she'd start worrying herself into knots about the woman, and more, about the writing. The not-writing. She sighed and took herself to the wall entry, where she smiled half-heartedly at the two guards who took her ticket and ushered her through the turnstile.

"Cheer up, love," the younger advised. "The walls aren't anyplace for a sad person."

How to tell him she wasn't sad? That word didn't even come close to the mess she *was*. She felt herself on screech, and it wasn't even eleven in the morning. The constant feeling as though she were going to cry, just below the surface—the feeling that always needed to be tamped down and chained away. Instead she only smiled again, and mounted the spiral stairway.

There was a slight breeze on the wall, and Aventurine pulled her jacket more tightly around her. She opted to turn to the left, to make a counterclockwise circuit. Up here the warmth of the sun seemed to be making little headway against the breeze; when she looked down into the bailey, the leaves on the trees were just barely turning. To the other side, the buildings of old Lincoln, some hundreds-of-years-old stone and brick, others postwar. An interesting juxtaposition, as most of this country was an interesting juxtaposition, layer upon layer of time and human attempts to leave a mark. She turned and leaned against the parapet, gazing toward the Cathedral. Maybe she'd go back later today, sit beside the sarcophagus of Katherine Swynford and try to commune. She looked across the roof, to the tower that housed Old Tom, and thought about being up there on the roof tour, looking back toward here. Maybe she'd see herself. The utter fancy of the thought twisted her lips in a sort of grimace, and she straightened against the wind and walked on.

Very few other people were up on the wall walk; high tourist season had long since passed. Aventurine moved slowly around and up onto Cobb Hall, still looking down into the streets and alleyways, thinking about the woman from last night. Had she gotten away? Avi searched the rooftops, trying to pick out the hotel, but the buildings of the Bailgate crowded around where she thought the car park might be, so there was nothing to be seen of a possible escape route anyway. Had that woman had a car? Had she run toward it, clutching her hat, then leapt inside to squeal away? Or had she been on foot, and running—to who knows where? Out the back, across the neighboring lot, down the street past the school and the Victorian water tower, and toward the laundromat the desk clerk had suggested to Aventurine when asked? From up here, the entire hilltop appeared a maze. She thought about descending into the bowels of Cobb Hall, but decided against it, moving instead onto the long straight stretch towards the bath house, and the west gate beyond the courts.

A third of a mile, all the way around, she read from the brochure, and laughed wryly to herself. Like doing a forced march along the York walls with Genevieve, only on a smaller scale, and alone. There was nothing on her agenda, since she could not bear to go back to her room and stare at the blank computer screen. She could just keep circling, physically, as her thoughts circled in her brain, and at least get in some exercise. Instinctively she reached for her phone and opened the camera app, snapping a few pictures to aid her memory, should some impulse to write miraculously appear.

Aventurine stopped again at the west gate, to lean against the parapet and consider the street below. Cars and the occasional delivery van threaded their way past, far beyond the faux drawbridge, and she watched them idly. Off to the right, a building dark with age sported a sign for a pub, and she wondered whether she might try to find it for lunch later. It was while she was considering that the movement of a taxi caught her eye, pulling up to the pavement below. A woman emerged, leaning back inside to pay, and then the cab drove off again. The woman adjusted her hat with one hand, and then looked around quickly, almost furtively, before spying a car further along. As she approached it, the passenger side door opened; she climbed inside, and the sedan slid away from the curb.

Even from this angle it was impossible to mistake: Aventurine had first seen that hat from above, yesterday afternoon, looking down into the beer garden from her room on the upper floor. Straw, blue crown, wide light-colored brim.

Aventurine breathed in deeply, first in surprise, and then in near-relief. The woman from the hotel. Still wearing the hat, and, from this distance, it looked like the same clothes. Arriving in a taxi, leaving immediately in a waiting car: obviously planned.

Whoever she was, it appeared she was effecting her escape.

Four

Maybe it was coincidence that had her walking up Steep Hill at precisely the time that the tour guide from the Cathedral was coming down later that afternoon. Or maybe it was destiny. Maybe it was the flash of the blue of the sash across his chest that caught her eye and made her look twice. Maybe it was his slight stumble, his hand flailing for a moment, the other hand going momentarily to his forehead before he righted himself.

She crossed the cobbles hurriedly and lay a hand on his arm. "Hello," she said.

For the slightest of pauses, he scanned her face, before a smile of recognition appeared—a smile that didn't quite reach his eyes. "Ah," he said. "My American friend."

Something told her that mentioning his momentary weakness would not be welcome.

"I was just going in to have some tea," Avi said instead, indicating the sign overhead. "Perhaps you'll join me? That is, if you're not in a hurry."

For a moment he looked as though he'd fob her off with some excuse, but then he glanced at the windows of the tea shop and seemed to change his mind. "Do let's. It would be my pleasure."

The bell over the door tinkled cheerily as they entered. A teen-aged girl in a frilly apron approached. "Two?" she asked.

"Please."

She led them toward the back and up a small flight of stairs to a table tucked into a corner. Once seated, Avi could see over the rail to the tables below; only a couple were occupied. She turned her attention to the menu the girl handed her. She still wasn't very hungry, but to quote Genevieve Smithson, she might have been a bit peckish, at this point in the afternoon. Perhaps her appetite was coming back, since she knew the stranger from last night was on her way to safety.

"Darjeeling and a fruit scone, I think," Avi said. "Jam and cream?"

"Same for me," her guide said, "except for Assam, if you would." He hadn't looked at the menu at all. The girl smiled and slipped away back down the stairs.

"And now," he said, holding out a hand, "I expect I should introduce myself. Especially if we are destined to continue meeting. Henry Hallsey. And you are?"

Aventurine gave him her hand. His grip was firm, though his skin was dry and papery. "Aventurine Morrow."

His fine silver brows lifted, and he nodded, as though in affirmation. "Aventurine Morrow," he repeated. "Your book jackets don't do you credit."

Avi always flushed when people recognized her. Even after all this time. She just couldn't get used to it, though it was incredibly gratifying. "Thank you. That's kind of you to say."

When the waitress returned, she set the tray down and transferred cups, saucers, and two small teapots: one painted garishly as a merry-go-round, the other predominantly green, save for the image of Hamlet, holding aloft the skull of Yorick.

"I knew him well," Avi murmured.

"Such fatalism in Shakespeare," Henry observed dryly. He thanked the waitress for the plate of scones, then flipped his napkin out and draped it across his lap. His pale blue eyes followed the waitress back downstairs, then wandered toward the windows at the front of the shop, overlooking Steep Hill. He offered nothing further, and Aventurine didn't, either.

Instead she poured a bit of tea into the cup before her, checking the color to be sure it was brewed enough.

"Milk?" Henry asked, holding up the pitcher.

"Not for me, thanks. I take it straight up."

"Ah, yes. I remember now."

She slewed her eyes toward him quickly. "What? We've never—"

Henry held up a veined hand. "Your book. The one about that musical group? You wrote about black tea there. And how they made fun of you because of it."

A Year in the Life of Mobius. She had written about how the band had told her she'd never be mistaken for a Brit, drinking tea like that. Of course, they'd also told her she'd never be mistaken for one of them, as they usually drank real ale, and plenty of it, and she definitely couldn't keep up.

Your book jackets don't do you credit. Right.

"You read *A Year in the Life.*" Stupid thing to say. He'd just about admitted it.

"My daughter Nicola had it on her bookshelf." He shrugged, but then his eyes trailed away toward the window again. The cobblestones were in afternoon shadow now. "I found it highly entertaining. Somehow heartwarming, and heartbreaking at the same time." He smiled gently. "They were trying so hard, those young people. Weren't they?"

"They still are." Aventurine's answering smile was fond.

"You asked me yesterday," Aventurine said, once the scone was finished; there were still crumbs on the plate, but Henry Hallsey and his old-world manners made the idea of gathering them and licking them from her dampened fingertips seem *gauche,* "what I was looking for in the Cathedral."

Henry dragged his attention back—he was definitely preoccupied. His eyes kept flickering toward the front windows and the street. "I'm sorry. That was presumptuous of me."

She shook her head, leaned forward with her chin on her fist.

"Oh, no. I didn't mind. It was such an interesting question, and I was taken aback. I mean, I could have answered it on any one of several different levels."

He seemed not to have heard. "It's just that there was that something—familiar—about you, and the way you were entranced by the chapter house. Even before that, when you knew about Katherine Swynford. The interest—it reminded me in a way of my daughter."

"Mr. Hallsey—"

"Henry," he corrected automatically.

"Henry, then. What's wrong?"

Aventurine regretted asking almost as soon as the words were out, and was surprised. This reticence was new. After all this time of interviewing strangers, of asking probing questions, the shyness was surprising and uncomfortable. The old brash Aventurine seemed a lifetime ago. No wonder she couldn't write a damned thing.

"Nothing is wrong," he said quickly. Too quickly.

Avi turned her attention to her tea, emptying the last drops from the Hamlet teapot into her cup. She waited.

Henry couldn't stop himself, as she knew he wouldn't be able to. "It's just that Nicola—"

"Your daughter?"

"Yes, my daughter. Nicola. She's—missing."

Avid looked down at the film on the surface of her tea, then pushed the cup away. "What do you mean, missing?" she asked slowly. The anxious feeling was back, the feeling of being on full screech. She found herself scanning the room quickly.

Henry looked toward the window with his thousand-yard gaze, as though searching for a figure walking purposefully along the cobbles. As though thinking would conjure up his daughter. He shook himself. "I'm sorry," he said. "It's probably nothing." He set his teacup down, and it rattled against the saucer.

Avi frowned. When he saw her looking at his shaking hands, he busied them with the napkin in his lap.

"It's obviously upset you, so it's not *nothing*."

22

But Henry only shook his head again. He lifted the last bit of fruit scone to his mouth, and chewed as though chewing cardboard: no enjoyment, all work. His swallow looked painful. "No, really. I can't be bothering you with this foolish worry. You don't even know me."

Aventurine placed a hand on his arm, then drew it back quickly. "You asked me what I was looking for in your Cathedral. I didn't have an answer for you. Maybe this is my answer. Maybe I was supposed to run into you, so I could offer you my ear. Or my help, if that's warranted."

For a long time he studied her face, his pale blue eyes slightly filmy. "I'm not even a religious man," he murmured after a moment. "You'd think I would be, guiding people through a Cathedral, of all places. So pompous of me to ask you that question."

She waited. Not certain of what to say, but saying nothing frequently had an effect.

Finally he dropped his eyes. He poured the remainder of his tea from the pot into his cup, then sat back without drinking it as well.

"Nicola always phones on Wednesday evening. Ostensibly it's to remind me that we have a standing date for breakfast on Thursday morning." His lips curled into a half-smile. "It's her day to go in late to work. We've done it nearly every Thursday morning since—her mother died." His voice trailed off. His meaning, however, wasn't hard to ascertain.

"She didn't call you last night." It wasn't a question.

Henry shook his head. "No. I was surprised, but I didn't really think much of it. I mean, I don't *need* the reminder. If anyone is forgetful, it's Nicola. I figured she probably had a date or something." He shook his head again. Now that he was telling her, all his reticence had disappeared.

"But that's not what happened."

Henry held out his hands. "I don't *know* what happened. What I do know is that I went along to meet her at the restaurant as I always do, and she never arrived."

"And she didn't call?"

"And she didn't answer when I phoned her cell."

Avi sat back, thinking. "And the restaurant—where's that from here?"

"It's in Nettleham, not far from where she lives." When she still looked puzzled, he waved a hand. "About three miles from here. I drive in, and she walks. She doesn't drive a car right at the moment." Henry's hands were still shaking when he picked up his teacup, so he abandoned it again. "I waited. I phoned a few times. She never answered." His words were more puzzled than frightened, but perhaps that was just his way of keeping his anxiety at bay: to look at the situation as a problem needing to be solved.

"What did you do then?"

He looked embarrassed. "I didn't know what to do. I mean, if she had had a date, and perhaps they had gone back to her place—"

Aventurine nodded. She could imagine the embarrassment. More, she could imagine Nicola Hallsey's embarrassment, when she and her erstwhile lover were interrupted by the advent of her father.

"I've been at the Cathedral since noontime," he continued. "Worrying. I'm trying to not worry. Nicola is an adult, after all." He smiled self-deprecatingly. "She has her own life. She's lived on her own for nearly twenty years, since university. I'm afraid that since my wife's death, I've let Nicola coddle me. Not a lot, just this weekly check-in. I pretend to need it, because, selfishly, I want it. I was lonely. I wanted some of her attention."

Aventurine thought she could understand that. Loneliness. Her own had lessened over the years; she allayed the occasional feeling that threatened to overwhelm her with a quick crash-and-burn affair, and then moved on. Like the one she had shared all those summers ago, and occasionally since, with Gio Constantine. She felt herself blush a little at the memory. Had she a living father, she probably wouldn't want him barging in on the morning after either.

Avi brought herself back with a jerk. She looked again into Henry's blue eyes. "You've called her since you got off duty?"

24

He nodded. "Just a bit ago, but there's still no answer. The call went straight to her voicemail."

"Maybe her battery is dead," Avi suggested. Trying to sound reassuring.

"Perhaps it is." He grasped at the idea like a lifeline.

"You could drive over this afternoon, or early this evening," Avi added. "Even if she was entertaining a friend, they'd probably be done by now." She realized, after she'd said it, just how crude that sounded to her own ears, but fortunately, Henry either didn't pick up on the unintended innuendo, or he was too much of a gentleman to admit it. *Entertaining. God.* It was all she could do to keep from dropping her face into her hands from shame.

Henry nodded again, pushing his tea away. He signaled the waitress, who appeared with the tally. Aventurine reached for it.

"No, no, my dear," he said, covering the slip with his hand. On his ring finger, a wide gold wedding band shone dully. "This one is my pleasure."

"But—I invited you," Aventurine protested.

"Please, my dear." His tone was firm. From his wallet he extracted a couple of notes and set them on the table. Then he stood and held her chair as she got to her feet. They descended the steps together, then went out onto the street. "My car is up beyond the Cathedral," Henry said, indicating the way up Steep Hill. "Could I give you a lift anywhere?"

"I'm staying up on the Bailgate," Avi told him. "I'll just walk with you until then, shall I? But you have to promise me you'll let me know how you fare at Nicola's." She drew out the notebook from her purse, scribbled her cell phone number on a page, then tore it out and gave it to him. "I don't even know her, but I'm worried about her."

The anxiety gnawed at her all the way back to the hotel.

25

Five

When Aventurine entered the hotel, the sky was clouding up, and the wind was picking its way sharply along the Bailgate. She pushed the heavy door shut behind her and paused a moment to get used to the dimness. Two tables in the far corner were occupied. She peered around the bar into the dining room, which appeared empty.

"What'll you have, love?" The counterman, she knew, was called Pete. He had a shaved head which almost glowed in the dimness, and his muscled arms stretched the short sleeves of his shirt beyond the possible.

Aventurine scanned the pulls. "Adnams? What do you suggest?"

He made a face, considering. "You don't like the pale ales." He knew that after how many nights? He was good. "You might try this Southwold bitter. You like bitters?"

She nodded. "A pint, please. And I'll probably have dinner in a bit."

He knifed the foam and nodded. "I'll run you a tab."

Aventurine took the glass to the table beneath a light near the front window. From the front pocket of her purse, she drew out the new book she'd bought down in the high street, to take the place of the one shed finished the previous night. *The Women of Blackmouth Street,* by Thea Sutton. She'd been attracted by the atmospheric black and white cover. Now she sipped the bitter and cracked open the book.

No sooner had she done so, than her cell phone buzzed. A text. She slipped it out of her purse and looked at the message. From Genevieve Smithson.

Don't drink too much. After dinner, write the first sentence. And then send it to me.

Talk about the Badass Bitches of Britain. How did Genevieve know where she was, sitting in the gloom of the bar, drinking a pint? It was almost as though the old woman were a spy. Avi smirked at her own joke. And she was to send Genevieve a sentence, as though the old woman was some battle ax of a teacher, waiting to mark up her work with a red pen. Aventurine set down the pint, and typed in a quick reply.

Don't you trust me?

The answer was immediate. *No.*

After a dinner of joules mariniere and a baguette for sopping, Aventurine mounted the stairs to her room. There had been no further texts from Genevieve. She wandered the room, getting herself a drink of tap water—not very nice—and looking out the window into the empty terrace, where the umbrellas were furled and the rain had begun. At last she opened her laptop. Then she took a deep breath and pulled out the chair. When she had settled, she opened a new document. The cursor blinked at her, an accusing eye. She willed her hands to lift from her lap again, and her fingers to situate on the home keys.

Another deep breath. She closed her eyes and typed, not opening them again until she hit the period key with her right ring finger. Then she read:

Genevieve Smithson killed her first mand when she was sixteen, stabbing him in the throat.

"Mand" was underlined in red by the spell checker.

Screw it, she thought to herself. She appended the document to an email, addressed it to Genevieve, and clicked send. Genevieve had demanded a sentence. She hadn't demanded it be edited. It was an ARC: advanced review copy. An unedited draft.

Feeling elated at the success of the single sentence, she stripped off her clothes and fell into bed. It was one more sentence than she had written in ages.

She fell asleep almost immediately to the sound of the rain on the roof overhead, and didn't wake up again until the sun rose the next morning.

Aventurine hadn't heard the message notification from her phone, but when she took it off the charger, she saw the text from Henry Hallsey.

Nicola wasn't home. She still doesn't answer her phone.

Six

Aventurine had arranged to meet Henry after he had finished his last tour at the Cathedral at three. Impatient, she waited outside the shrouded west entrance until he appeared, pulling on a rain jacket over his suit. He looked tired, pronounced bags under his eyes. As he came out onto the cobbled way, he wiped at his nose with a handkerchief; seeing her, he quickly thrust it into his pocket.

"Good afternoon, Aventurine, my dear." His voice sounded tired, too. She wondered how much sleep he had managed the night before. His text had been time-stamped near midnight.

"Still no word?"

Henry sighed, looking up for a moment at the uniformly grey sky. "Still no word." He coughed slightly, and indicated the way back along the Exchequergate. "Let's walk out this way."

In her presence, he seemed to try to straighten his back, to cover up his worry. Avi supposed this was his version of the stereotypical stiff upper lip, his interpretation of keeping calm and carrying on. She bit her lip, wishing he didn't feel as though he had to hide from her, but realizing that it was his nature to continue that hiding. She fell into step beside him, her hands in her pockets.

"Have you figured out why you came here, to the Bailgate?"

The quick change in topic took her by surprise.

When Henry walked beside her, he leaned forward slightly, his hands clasped behind his back. Today, despite his jacket and tie, he seemed somehow unkempt, as though his heart wasn't in his usual dapper appearance. Even the question seemed half-hearted, as though he only asked it to keep all the other questions at bay. Questions like *where was Nicola?*

She humored him. "Apathy," she said. The word came out in a tone far more raw than she intended.

Henry's brows lowered. With a glance at her, he jerked his head in the direction of the Magna Carta. "Let's go in here for a pint, shall we?" he suggested.

She followed him in. Henry ordered a G and T at the bar, and Aventurine a half of the Hobgoblin Ruby. They seated themselves at a tall two-top near the window, where they could watch the foot traffic turning into the Exchequergate from Steep Hill. The cobbled street outside was grey under the clouds, but still thronged with people. Avi could tell the difference here between the kinds of passersby: the tourists, who held big carrier bags over their arms, and who walked in clumps with their eyes on the Cathedral tower; and the natives, hunched against the wind, hands in coat pockets as they moved purposefully toward the Close. She wondered fleetingly what she looked like, walking along the streets, feeling neither one nor the other.

"What is it you can't bring yourself to care about?" Henry asked. He squeezed the lemon into his glass, took a sip from his drink, then wiped at his upper lip with a napkin. He waited.

Avi let him steer the conversation; perhaps it helped in his distress? Today it was her turn to look out the window. "I haven't written," she said slowly, "for months." Even saying the words felt crippling.

"And you're courting insanity?"

She almost laughed. But the sound caught in her throat. "Anybody who tells you that writer's block isn't real doesn't know what they're talking about."

Henry dipped his head. "Don't credit me, Aventurine. That's Nicola quoting Kafka. She says that all the time."

As do I. Bells and whistles. She felt the chill snake itself down her spine, but she ignored it, and pushed the conversation toward Nicola. Gingerly.

"You said there's been no word from her."

Henry looked away. "I don't want to get into her private business."

"You're not. You're her father and you're worried. She's behaving in an uncharacteristic way."

He shrugged, clearly uncomfortable.

Avi took a deep breath. "Have you contacted the police?"

Henry looked absolutely horrified. "Oh, I couldn't. She'd never forgive me."

Aventurine pressed. "Henry. What if something's happened? What if she's hurt?" Something niggled at the back of her mind, but she ignored that, too, her attention on the old man.

He turned agonized eyes on her.

She relented, but only a little bit. "How about work?" she asked after a moment. "You said Thursday was her late day, isn't that right?"

Henry nodded miserably.

"Did she show up to work yesterday?"

"I—I—don't know."

"And today?" When he said nothing, she tapped the table before him with a nail. "Call them."

He reared back. "And say what?"

"Ask to speak to her. If she's not there, ask when they expect her back."

He looked doubtful.

"You do it, or I will. If she's there, she's going to be a bit weirded out by a stranger calling. If she's there, you can just ask for a rain check for the breakfast she missed."

Henry's hand was shaking as he drew his phone from his pocket. He fumbled with it, turning it in his hands until he poked the screen with a finger. He pressed it to his ear, glaring.

"Yes. This is Henry Hallsey calling for Nicola Hallsey. Is she in, please?" There was a pause. "No, that's all right. Could you tell me when you expect her in? Oh. Oh, that's fine. Thank you very much."

He set the cell phone on the table before him and slumped in his chair.

"She's not there." Aventurine leaned forward and ended the phone call.

"No."

"She didn't come in to work yesterday."

"No."

"And what did they say about when she'd return?"

"The woman I spoke to said she had called to take a few days off—she was owed some holiday time, and decided to take it." Henry shook his head, as though attempting to clear it of the confusion. "She had to take care of a family emergency."

Now, it was Aventurine's turn to be surprised. "A family emergency?"

"I'm her only family, Aventurine. Both her mother and I were only children, so there are no cousins. I'm her *only family*. And I haven't had anything that vaguely counts as an emergency in ages."

"And it was really her, the person who called in?"

"The receptionist didn't say otherwise. And everyone in the main office knows everyone else. It would have been odd to them had anyone else called."

Aventurine frowned, picking up her half pint absently. "What do they do for work?

Henry shrugged, distractedly, looking out the window seemingly without seeing anything. Except, perhaps, his missing daughter. "They're a security company. They provide alarm systems for establishments around greater Lincoln, and for homes as well." He tapped a decal on the glass beside him. She squinted, trying to read it backwards. *Apex Security and Alarm,* she finally deciphered. "They have technicians, of course, who travel about and install and maintain the systems. They have people to monitor the systems. The front office, where Nicola works—she works in billing and traffic and whatnot—has only ten or a dozen people." He took a sip from his gin and tonic, grimaced, and pushed it aside.

"It's strange, though, isn't it?" Aventurine mused. "That she would lie about her reasons for taking off." *Taking off.* The anxiety was back in force. "Has she done this before?"

Henry drew up as though thoroughly insulted that Aventurine should suggest such a thing. "Never. Our Nicola is a most reliable young woman. This is so unlike her."

"All the more reason for you to contact the police."

He looked torn.

"Aren't you anxious?" The question was rather mean of her. Of course he was anxious. Even now his fingers twined together, his knuckles whitening with the force of that. "Look. I'll go with you."

Henry looked up now. When he took up his drink, he downed half of it before answering. "You know what they're going to say."

"I know. But don't you think you have to at least be on record with this?" When Henry didn't answer, Aventurine reached out to place a hand on his sleeve. "I'll go with you. Really. *If* you want."

She felt as though they were balancing on a precipice. She held her breath, waiting to see on which side Henry would come down.

At last he nodded. One small movement of the chin, so small that it seemed he was hoping she'd miss it and he could take it back. He drank the rest of his G and T quickly.

Aventurine pushed back from the high top. "Okay. We can go right now. Do you have a picture?"

One of the last times she and Micheline had traded places before the pregnancy was as freshmen in high school. Since Micheline had always favored green and Aventurine blue, they had simply raided one another's closets. In classes they had sat in one another's seats, and in the hallway, lingered at one another's lockers. It hadn't been difficult; no one, not even their closest friends, had twigged it. And there wasn't even a payoff: it wasn't as though one had a geometry test that the other wouldn't be taking in another period; it wasn't as though they didn't earn similar grades anyway. It was just out of boredom. It was something to do.

Avi thought of this now as she held the picture Henry had passed to her in a shaking hand. Staring at the wide face beneath the blonde cap of hair, the green eyes with their direct expression, the smile that hooked up at one corner, as though unable to disguise the sense of irony. The dimple in the left cheek. Avi had the reeling thought that somehow Nicola Hallsey had joined the party late, but had claimed her place as a third in what had always been a party of two.

"*This* is Nicola," she said. She could not shift her eyes from the photograph. Her voice sounded strangled to her own ears. She half-expected Henry to admit to some mistake—*oh, no, sorry, that's not my daughter*—and hand over another photograph, of someone with dark hair, perhaps, someone with blue eyes, or brown.

Henry smiled down at the picture. Nicola was in three-quarter profile, caught as though in the middle of a mildly amusing conversation; a wind was lifting the hair slightly from her forehead, that hair that shone like spun gold in the sunlight. "Yes. She looks rather like her mother here." There was the smallest tinge of sadness in his words.

Aventurine opened her mouth, then closed it, the words difficult to form. After a moment she tried again. "Henry. *She looks like me.*"

Seven

At the station the duty officer took the report, but as they had expected, was not overly helpful. They'd keep a lookout, he said, have someone maybe stop by Nicola's cottage for a wellness check—but she was an adult, and she'd only been gone, as far as they knew, since Thursday morning, Wednesday evening at the earliest. *Give 'er a few more days, and she'll turn up.* Aventurine and Henry left the station frustrated. They headed back up Steep Hill together, and parted at the Magna Carta.

"Call me if you hear anything," she said. She shifted on the cobblestones as though on quicksand; she still felt the uneasiness in the pit of her stomach that had only been strengthened when she had held the photograph of Nicola. With Henry's permission, she had taken a picture of it with her phone.

"Yes," he said, looking around the street as though his daughter might mysteriously appear. "Yes, I will. I'll keep trying to call her." Then he turned back. "I'm not on the rota for tomorrow. I'll go by her cottage. Will you come?"

"I don't know what help I'll be," she protested.

Henry seemed at a loss himself. "I don't either. A different pair of eyes? Maybe you'll see something I've missed. I'll come for you at ten, if that's all right? At your hotel?"

They agreed, and she watched his back, stooped a bit more than it had been, until he disappeared through the Exchequergate. Then she turned her steps onto the Bailgate, her throat thick with foreboding. She wouldn't think it. She wouldn't. It—all of it—was coincidence. *Coincidences.* That was all.

What few leaves there were up here were swirling along the cobblestones, whispering as they headed downhill, telling secrets in a language she didn't understand. Above Steep Hill, the late autumn sky was a darkening blue, shadowed with clouds. The afternoon had drawn on to early evening, and was considerably cooler: a weather change. Between the storefronts which lined the street, the wind tunneled, and stung.

In her pocket, the phone vibrated. She ducked into a doorway, out of the way of any foot traffic, and now she leaned against the wall to answer. Micheline.

"Are you okay?" they both asked at the same time. Then they both laughed nervously.

"I dialed. You answer the question first," her sister ordered.

"I'm not okay," Avi said slowly. "Not really. I think I might be losing my mind."

Anyone else might have cracked a joke, but not her twin. "What is it?"

How to explain? Henry, Nicola—the whole serpentine confusion. And the part that she dared not give voice to, not yet.

"I'll send you a picture."

She opened the photo app, then forwarded the copy of Nicola's photograph.

"Look. I'm nearly to the hotel and it's getting cold. I'll call you back when I get inside and up to my room. You'll probably have the picture by then, and it might make a bit of sense to you. Or not."

"Avi—"

"Give me ten minutes."

36

Her phone was buzzing again before she hit the last turn in the hallway. She wrenched the key around in the lock, dropped everything on the desk before closing the door, and pulled the cell phone from her pocket.

"Avi, who the hell *is* this person?"

Micheline sounded as shaken as Aventurine felt.

"Her name is Nicola Hallsey. Ring any bells for you?"

A long, indrawn breath over the phone. "Should it? I mean, is it supposed to?"

Aventurine flopped onto the bed and threw her arm over her eyes. "I don't know. I just wondered if—in all your genealogical research— you had come across any Hallseys. In the family tree. I mean, she could be a throwback. Hell, *we* could be throwbacks. For all we know, Nicola and we could have a common great-grandparent or something." Since Shep's death, Mick had taken up and abandoned any number of hobbies to distract herself. The genealogy, though, seemed to have stuck.

There was the sound of pounding on a keyboard. *Rage typing*, Avi had always called it, but in this case, it was more like *anxiety typing*.

"It's weird. Look at her. She could be one of us. She could be—our triplet?"

Between them the awkward knowledge spread thin, of the intricacies of family trees, the secrets they held about parentage. Genetics. DNA. Secrets the two of them knew all too much about.

"She's younger, though," Avi said after a moment. "By about ten years."

A long pause. She knew that Micheline was looking at the photograph she'd sent; she could feel her sister's intense study.

"She's us, ten years ago. Just look at her."

"That's exactly what I felt when her father handed me her photograph."

"Whoa. Hold on. Back this train up. You know her father?"

Carefully, Aventurine related the story of her initial meeting with Henry, trying to recall every word, every impression. Micheline, of course, would want every detail.

"This woman, this Nicola Hallsey, though. She's missing?"

"And Henry is very worried, though he tries to say he doesn't want to intrude into Nicola's life. Her not calling him, though, and not meeting him for that long-standing breakfast date—it's totally unlike her, he says." Avi told her about the police and their non-response, as well as the *family emergency* for which Nicola had taken time off.

"That's really weird, Avi," Mick breathed. "But what's even more weird is the fact that you—that we—look so much like this woman, and he never mentioned it."

Henry's reaction, when she had pointed the resemblance out in the Magna Carta, had been a bit surprised. "Oh, she does, now that I look at you both together," he'd said. He seemed embarrassed. "I hadn't really thought about it, except perhaps in a superficial way. You know—*she's got hair like Nicola's.* That sort of thing." He had shaken his head. "I just always think of her as looking like my wife did, when we met." Again, the glance between the photo he'd held in his hand, and Aventurine, seated across from him. "It *is* rather odd, now that you mention it."

"But it's uncanny, Avi," Mick insisted. "And what are the chances? That you would end up in the city where she lives. That you should meet her father. I know she's younger than we are, but if she's not our long-lost triplet, she could be our sister."

The silence fell between them—not the silence of people having nothing to say to one another, but the silence of people who have far too much to say.

"Do you think–Dad—?"

Aventurine squeezed her eyes closed. Their father had loved their mother, she was certain of that. So much so that he had insisted Micheline be named after her. Surely he wouldn't have had an affair, wouldn't have cheated on a woman he loved that much? But at the same time, Henry Hallsey seemed to have loved his wife very much as well—would he have, had she been unfaithful to him? Of course, that would mean that he would have had to find out. And then there was the matter of proximity—somehow the parents had to have been in the same room with each other. Aventurine wracked her brains, and it hurt.

"Was he ever here?" she managed at last. "Did he ever visit the UK? Lincoln? I'm trying to remember whether there had been any business trips. Any vacations. Because there's that matter of a couple of thousand miles between them."

Micheline gasped. "You're not really considering this."

"I don't even know what I'm considering." The fact remained that Nicola looked enough like them to be a sister. "That's why I wondered whether you found any Hallseys in that family tree of yours."

"And yours."

"And mine. I'd rather think we were cousins, even distant cousins, than think Dad would ever have illegitimate children floating about in the world."

"A sperm bank? Maybe he donated to a sperm bank?"

"And ended up donating to someone on another continent."

Micheline's sigh was enormous, and Avi could picture her squeezing her face in her hands, much as Avi herself was doing now.

"Listen," Aventurine said, tired of the way her brain was fizzing. She struggled to sit up. "I think I need to eat something, or I will pass out. Go look at your genealogy notes. Oh—" Avi slapped her forehead, as she remembered. "That DNA test. Whichever one it was. Did you finally take it?" They'd discussed it in passing ages before, and had decided against it then, in order to avoid upsetting Paul—though, Avi had argued, she and Mick were identical twins, with identical DNA. Thanks to Neil, of course, all that worry had become a moot point anyway.

"I did. I took both of them, to see who I could find out there in the forest. I'm still waiting for the results."

"Well, when you find out what strange birds are in our family tree, let me know, will you? There might be an answer to this puzzle."

"But not an answer to the puzzle of the missing Nicola." Mick clicked her tongue; there was an undertone of anxiety to her tone. A familiar anxiety.

"Not an answer to that puzzle, no." Aventurine stood. Her spine cracked and popped. The room was shadowed now. She turned on the bedside lamp.

"Well, you damn well better keep me posted about that particular mystery. I need to know."

She had to be going crazy then, Aventurine told herself as she ended the call, because even Mick hadn't given voice to the thought nagging at her. She backed off and let it swirl to the surface: Nicola had gone missing, at just about the same time the woman from the beer garden had fled.

Eight

In the morning, the wind still blew, the street was still slicked with dampness, but the rain from the night was over. Autumn was creeping toward winter. After her breakfast, Aventurine returned to her room and opened the laptop. One sentence. That's all she needed. *Baby steps.* She stared at the one she had written at Genevieve's command. What sentence would follow that?

She spaced down a few lines and wrote something only tangentially connected.

Genevieve Smithson was born neither Genevieve, nor Smithson, but if she told you what the name on her birth record actually was, she'd have to kill you.

She fired that one off in an email.

The response was immediate. *That's two.*

At ten minutes to ten, Aventurine went back downstairs, carrying her coat, to wait for Henry. She was unsure whether he'd come to the front or the back, but it was too cold to wait outside anyway, with the wind blowing grit along the pavement, and whistling overhead around the chimneys. She was staring out into the street when Pete appeared behind the bar, a lemon and a lime in each hand.

"Message here for you, love," he said. He set the fruit down before extracting a slip of paper from his pocket and sliding it across the gleaming wood, along with a key on a fob.

Depping this morning for an ill guide. Leaving you the key. Still no word.

There was an address on the paper.

"Everything all right?"

She looked up, frowning. "Yeah. Yes. Thanks." Drawing out her phone, she opened the maps app and plugged in the address on the Nettleham Road. Fifteen minutes to walk there. She left the app open, pocketed the key, and stepped out into the wind, pulling her coat on.

Aventurine kept her head down, and turned up the volume slightly, so that she could hear the voice cues in the map. Through the Newport Arch, the passageway of which smelled like dead leaves and urine. Then a right onto Church Lane, and finally a left at the hospital onto the Nettleham Road. There were still some leaves on the trees here, but they rattled and whispered: they wouldn't be there for long. Around her feet, the leaves which had already given up swirled and crunched.

The cottage turned out to be the second in a row on the left: a grey stone that appeared to shimmer, otherworldly, in the wet morning light. The front door was painted a deep blue, almost the same color as the beads on the bracelet on her arm; beside it, a single window, with two on the floor above. Aventurine glanced over her shoulder furtively, as though she were a housebreaker—which was absolutely ridiculous, as she had the key in her hand. She was relieved to see no one else in the road. She let herself in quickly, and shut the door to lean against it. Thinking of Genevieve, she turned and locked it again.

Aventurine looked around curiously, but with an underlying feeling of guilt. Trespass. "Hello?" she called, and her voice echoed in the way of voices in long-uninhabited spaces. She shivered and checked the locks once more, then pocketed the key.

The overwhelming feature of the front room was the bookshelves. Every available stretch of wall was covered in bookshelves. Between the window and front door, beneath and above the window itself. Along either side of the woodburning stove, which was recessed into the wall to the left. The room held a loveseat and two wing-backed chairs grouped around a coffee table, on which books were piled. A book lay face-down over the arm of one of the chairs.

Aventurine felt a shock of *deja vu*. It was almost like a homecoming, walking into this room. It was like walking into her own apartment back home on the Back Bay.

On the wall above the woodburner was a single framed photograph, of Henry Hallsey and the woman who was, presumably, his wife. It might have been taken twenty years ago, from the looks of Henry's face: he was probably in his early fifties. He was still recognizably dapper, and from the way he was gazing down at the woman beside her, obviously madly in love. Avi felt a twinge, and stepped closer.

The woman was undeniably beautiful, with that classic bone structure that never ages, and the slight porcelain glow of skin that every woman wished she could age into, or hold onto. Her hair was pulled back into a chignon, but it was recognizably blonde, not yet turning to silver. *She looks so like her mother,* Henry had said about the photograph of his daughter; so much did she, to him, that he had not noticed that Nicola looked so much like the woman who had been sitting across from him at that time. That, Avi supposed, was what came of being the man who looked down at this woman as Henry was doing in this photograph of the wall. The woman, she thought, didn't look much like either Aventurine or Micheline at all. So where had Nicola's looks—her face, her hair—come from?

She shook herself and stepped away from the framed photo.

A door in the far wall led into the tiny kitchen; the window over the sink would let in the afternoon light. To the right, the small refrigerator; to the left the stove. Sink at the far end. Not enough room here for a dining table. There was a clean plate in the strainer, along with a knife and fork. A teacup and saucer stood in the sink, a skim of tea on both.

A tiny room debauched off the kitchen, and here was the dining table, big enough to seat two people, though they'd probably be bumping knees as they ate. Only one place had a mat, free of crumbs, though the indent of the plate remained in the soft green material. Another bookshelf took up the wall space beyond the table. This one, like the shelves in the living room, was crammed full.

The door into the minuscule back garden was locked. Outside was a little glass table with a pair of wrought iron chairs. On the table, a pot of petunias desperately needed deadheading, but it was probably too late in the season to try and save them anyway. It had probably been something on the list of chores for the weekend, and now the weekend was here, but there was no sign of the inhabitant of the little house.

Aventurine turned back to head up to the stairs. On the second, no, *first* floor—she quickly corrected herself, remembering where she was—she found the front room, though it was the larger of the two bedrooms, being used as an office. A long library table stood before the windows, with a MacBook Air closed in the center. More bookshelves here, full, and books in piles on the floor. A file cabinet. A yellow legal pad on the desk to the left of the computer, with a single pen lying atop the scribbles, and more pens in a cup on the window ledge. Aventurine half-expected to find a small voice recorder amongst the tools, and was both disappointed and relieved to find there was none. Still, the clutter here indicated a place for real work.

In the bedroom to the rear, the bed was made, the curtains open, the slippers lined up neatly on the rug. The sink in the bathroom was dry and clear of smears of toothpaste or makeup. The towel hanging next to the shower was dry. Feeling like a voyeur, Avi opened the medicine cabinet over the sink, and found a package of Paracetamol, along with some foundation, lipstick, eye pencil, and blush. Makeup basics, for those few-and-far-between special occasions: Avi knew that drill oh, so well.

Frowning, she returned to the office and slowly lowered herself into the chair, a high-backed black leather affair with surprisingly good lumbar support: the chair of someone who might need to sit in it for a while and wanted to be comfortable. She looked out the window at the cottage across the road, a narrow stone facade similar to this one; the windows opposite had the draperies drawn—a closed eye. Nothing to be seen there.

When she lifted a hand to open the laptop, Aventurine saw it was shaking. The knot of guilt made itself felt, low in her gut. She didn't think she'd ever opened someone else's laptop without permission. It felt like a violation of privacy, of an implied trust, something she knew so very well. Instead of lifting the screen, she dropped her face into her palms, overwhelmed by the queasiness crawling up from her stomach into her shoulder blades and upper arms. She knew viscerally what that violation felt like. Wasn't this the same thing Neil had done to her?

That was silly. Of course. Henry Hallsey had asked her to have a look around. He wouldn't have done it if he hadn't been desperate. Avi saw again in her mind's eye his shaking hand, heard his quaking voice. His daughter was missing, had been for days. He had asked her for help.

She straightened and lifted the lid of the laptop.

It was password protected. Of course it was. On a whim she placed her index finger on the small black key in the corner. Sadly her likeness to Nicola did not extend to fingerprints.

Aventurine stared at the screen. The lock screen was set to the same photograph that hung in the front room downstairs. She found herself looking again at the younger Henry Hallsey, and the woman with chignon and sparkling eyes, who had both hands wrapped around his upper arm, and who was leaning into him. Possessively? Not, that wasn't really it. Comfortably. As though she knew his every shape, his every movement, his every mood. His wife. She didn't look like a woman who had had an affair, who had passed off a child as his. Aventurine remembered the way Henry had stumbled over the word *wife* Thursday in the tearoom. His late wife, someone he missed very much. Nicola Hallsey's mother. Avi studied them both, wondering at the nature of a couple who had remained married, devoted, for ages, and whether these two had actually been what this photograph would have her believe.

She shoved the thought of her father away quickly. She couldn't face the other side of that equation right now.

Aventurine shook her head, trying to rid herself of speculation along those routes. She needed to find a clue as to Nicola's whereabouts. Was she safe? If so, why didn't she contact her father? Could she and the woman from the hotel terrace actually be the same person? Avi turned to the computer again. She wondered if Henry knew the computer's password, or if he knew his daughter well enough to hazard a guess. She wondered whether Nicola had made a note of the password somewhere. Slowly she opened the middle drawer of the library table. Pens. Stamps. A small pocket notebook with a cover decorated with images from New Orleans. She drew it out, flipped through the pages: lists, a phone number, a couple of email addresses. On one page, a word and a number combination which looked like a possibility. She typed it in, carefully, making sure of the capital letters and the numbers. *Serendipity1983*. Nothing happened. She tried again, in case she'd made a mistake. Still nothing.

Avi slumped back in the chair. *Serendipity*. It was the name of her favorite song by Mobius, from their first album. Which had not come out in 1983—but perhaps that was Nicola's birth year? She added that to the list of things to ask Henry.

But where had Nicola gone? Everything at the cottage was neat and orderly, as though she'd simply popped off to work Wednesday morning, fully planning to return.

Aventurine's eyes strayed around the room. In the corner opposite the door stood a wardrobe, dark and heavy, the doors neatly closed; atop it was a small red suitcase, which looked suspiciously like her own small blue one. She pushed out of the chair and crossed to pull the suitcase down. When she unzipped it, she found it empty save a matching red canvas Dopp kit. She opened this to find it full: toothbrush, toothpaste, disposable razor. Makeup—a few basic items, duplicates of those in the medicine cabinet in the bathroom.

She rocked back on her heels. Nicola clearly had not meant to be away for long. She obviously had not planned a trip to a remote location. Otherwise, this bag and this Dopp kit would be with her there instead of here. For the first time, she felt vaguely sick about Nicola. Gone since Wednesday, it was beginning to look like—but without taking enough clothes and things for three days. Had she gone off on an assignation, as the police seemed to believe, surely she would have at least brought a few changes of clothing: one could only stay so long in bed with a lover before having to get up at least to eat. The longer Nicola stayed out of touch, the more it looked like she was in danger.

Aventurine dropped her head into her hands once again.

I think the woman might be in danger.

Now she left the suitcase on the floor, returning to the chair and slumping into it. She had said those words, just the other night, on the phone with Micheline. But she and her sister hadn't been talking about Nicola then, surely? They had been discussing the woman in the rear terrace at the hotel, and the man who had inspired in Aventurine that sense of foreboding, or that sense of flashback. Mick must have been thinking about the coincidence last night, just as she had been, just as she was doing now. Two mysteries, two women, too many parallels to be ignored. Those two things had to be connected.

Could it be that the two women were the same?

Aventurine closed her eyes and tried to think back through the sequence of events in the beer garden. How she had noticed the sunhat from above, the book, the glass of white wine. The woman had not seemed to be waiting for someone, and yet, the next time Aventurine had seen her, the man had joined her at the table. He had been forceful; she had been resistant. The only time Avi had seen her face, the only flash, she had been wearing sunglasses and had her hair tucked up under that sunhat. Whether that had been Nicola, Avi couldn't really say. She tried to shift her focus. What had the woman been wearing? A dress, with a light jacket over it, to stave off the cooling autumn afternoon air. What color? What pattern? But the details escaped her.

Biting her lip, Avi got up to open the wardrobe, but even as she did she knew it would be fruitless. There was no dress in there that she recognized, and if that had actually been Nicola, and she had not returned home Wednesday, the dress wouldn't be in there anyway. Still. In the wash? Avi took a quick look into the bedroom for a laundry hamper, but did not find anything that cued her memory in there. She trudged back to the office and dropped into the computer chair.

Before her, the computer screen, not having the password input it had requested, had returned to black. Aventurine tapped the space bar to make the family photograph reappear. There was Henry again, gazing adoringly at Mrs. Hallsey. Someone—Nicola?—had taken the photograph at the perfect time, the adoration of the couple so obvious, the light shimmering, the love of the photographer for the subjects without question.

Nicola's parents. Nicola, who had got up Wednesday morning, had a bit of breakfast and some tea in the morning, had presumably gone off to work, *perhaps* had stopped into the pub afterwards—and then, nothing. She had simply disappeared.

Without having said anything to her father, her only close relative. According to whom, this behavior was a definite aberration. Again, Avi could see Henry's distress, forced down behind his natural reserve, but leaking out in his shaking hands, his lowered voice. *This just isn't like Nicola.*

But what was Nicola *like?*

Slowly Aventurine descended the stairs to the living room and slid into the nearest chair. Other than the books in their careless pile on the table before her, and the one that lay open over the chair arm to her right, nothing seemed out of place or disturbed here, either. Nicola Hallsey might just have stepped out to visit the shops, or to go to work. There was no sign of struggle, no sign of departure in haste.

Aventurine picked up the book. She already knew what it was, having recognized it by the cover. Her own book from several years ago. *A Year in the Life of Mobius.* With a finger between the pages to hold the place, she turned it to look at the front of the dust jacket. Mobius, a photo taken from the rear of a festival ground, the sea of fans dark, and the brilliantly lit stage showing a slightly blurry but wildly colorful band. Peter held his hands high over his head, while Linnie waved with one hand, the other still holding her fiddle beneath her chin. They all looked so young. Avi peered closer, as she always did when she stumbled across this dust jacket, to the rear corner of the stage, where she herself was a dark smudge beyond the sound bank. That summer, that wild and crazy summer, where she ended up doing double duty, as writer and roadie. She touched their spotlight-blurred faces, Linnie, Peter, and the rest, fondly. She missed that summer. She missed the band, even their cranky road manager Ruth.

The book cover was intact, but worn around the edges, the way they become when read and re-read. Nicola had either read this book several times, or had bought it used. She'd apparently lent it to her father as well, and the fact that Henry had read it—and had remembered parts of it—spoke volumes about his interests and personality. Aventurine felt gratified, but at the same time somewhat strange. That the Hallseys had apparently known about her for some time before she had known them. And even if Henry hadn't immediately twigged her resemblance to Nicola, surely Nicola had?

She still didn't know Nicola, Avi reminded herself. That was why she was here.

Aventurine flipped the book to see what page Nicola had left off on. Somewhere in the middle chapters. She read a paragraph or two, feeling the weird out-of-body experience she always did when reading the published version of her books. *I wrote that.* She couldn't quite believe it, even after all these years; couldn't quite believe that she was making a living—and a fairly comfortable one at that, with the help of her financial advisor—writing books. It was all she had ever wanted to do. Which is why it was so painful to be stuck like this. Stuck. As she had been since the night on the York walls, when Neil had died.

Aventurine closed her eyes tightly, trying to get away from the visceral memory she carried of the rain, the dark, the hush—until the hollow sound of that blackthorn walking stick against Neil's skull. At least she was no longer having the nightmares. But she was still haunted. She thought of her nephew Paul, and how he had taken it; surprisingly, after his delicate angry balance, after his father's death, he seemed to have gathered himself and soldiered on, off to Italy with Lance. Avi wished she could do the same.

Just as he'd done when they were young and starting out, Neil had rocked her professionally—not just personally—and she couldn't seem to find her feet again.

Damn you, she thought, surprisingly close to tears.

When she left the cottage and headed back along the Nettleham Road, she took the book with her.

Nine

"Did you find anything?" Henry asked when he at last picked up the call.

"Have you heard anything?" Aventurine countered.

Somewhere along the line there was a scrape of a chair, and a sigh. Henry must have taken a seat to answer the question.

"Nothing," he said. "Not a damned thing." He didn't even bother to ask her pardon for his vulgarity; Avi knew how upset he must be. "I've called several times. It goes straight to voicemail."

"Listen, Henry." Aventurine cleared her throat. "Listen. I know this is hard, but have you tried calling area hospitals?" She knew he hadn't.

"*Hospitals?*"

Hospitals were certainly better than morgues. But she didn't say that.

"In case she's had an accident. In case she's been admitted somewhere, and hasn't been able to tell them who her next of kin is."

"Yes. Yes, of course."

"And no, I didn't find anything helpful at her cottage," Avi said. "I really didn't know what I was looking for. There were no notes, nothing obvious like that, nothing saying *I've gone to London for a couple of days.* Nothing at all." She wondered whether she should tell him about the small red suitcase atop the wardrobe in the office. She wondered whether she should tell him that she'd stolen a book out of Nicola's house. Even more, she wondered whether she should tell him that there was a possibility that she had actually seen Nicola on Wednesday evening—and possibly again, on Thursday morning.

"All right." Henry sounded as though he were steeling himself for an ordeal. "I'll get off the line with you and call the hospital. Thank you for all your help."

"And check in with the police—"

But the line had already gone dead.

After a moment, Avi realized that she was playing with the blue aventurine bracelet Genevieve had given her, spinning it around and around her left wrist. It occurred to her now, as she looked at the beads, just how much she would welcome a long conversation with that woman. How much she actually missed those mornings she had spent in the dim front room of the house in York. The old spy would know how to listen, sitting still and straight in her high-backed chair, only her glacial eyes moving. Then she would order the facts, pulling each strand of the story out into a logical progression, making the connections between the seemingly disparate events. How she missed Genevieve's incisive intelligence, her ability to recognize patterns and see past distractions.

Avi reached for her phone, but just as quickly drew her hand back. She was still hesitant about calling the townhouse in York, especially after they'd all been sent away at the height of summer, with strict instructions to make no move until Genevieve gave the all-clear. That had not come, but instead, recently, had come the cautious contact. Genevieve had not invited her back to York to continue their interviews, and Aventurine had not asked—despite wondering whether returning might just be the impetus to force her out of this intense period of writer's block.

Courting a Kafka-esque insanity, that's what she was doing.

Next thing she knew, she'd be metamorphosing into a giant insect.

Gah. Aventurine settled at the desk and opened the laptop. Her document stared back at her accusingly, so she opened her browser and typed in Neil's name. The earliest pages she found mentioning him were of the discovery of the body, in the brush at the foot of the wall near the old train station cut in the York wall. Anyone with information asked to come forward. *Body of Man Identified.* She swallowed and blinked hard several times, then read the accompanying story. Then the next one that appeared: *Prize-Winning Journalist's Body Identified.*

She hadn't dared look since that night on the wall. Now she devoured every news story she could find, including some with video links to television news sources. Speculation: did he fall or was he pushed? No evidence of any connection to anyone in York, save for a mention by the owner of a dingy-looking B and B that Neil had indeed stayed at during the previous week, but had checked out before the previous weekend. No new leads, and the story, as stories do, died away, to be replaced by other, newer news. There was the discovery of the rental car in a side street, but that only raised interest again for a few days. With each new article, Aventurine felt her heart rate rise and her mouth grow drier. Had she left any fingerprints in the rental car, that terrible night in Southampton? Only Genevieve had touched the car when they'd recovered the bag of Avi's electronics and notes, and she'd been wearing gloves. But so far, there had been nothing linking her—linking *any of them*–to Neil. If they'd investigated his history, as any thorough police officers would, they would have found her in his past twenty-five years ago. But that was all, she told herself, slapping the computer shut again. *That was all.*

Aventurine felt dirty, her skin painful and foreign. She stripped off on the way to the shower. It was still only mid-afternoon, but this scouring the internet, on top of the futile search of Nicola's cottage, had made her feel uncomfortable and muddled and a bit frightened. She adjusted the water temperature and stood with her head under the stream, trying to wash her way clear. She had to think like Genevieve. She had to order her thoughts: everything she knew, and everything she didn't know and would have to try to find out. What were the questions she needed answered?

When at last she dried off, she wrapped herself in the towel and pulled out her notebook. *WHERE IS NICOLA HALLSEY?* she wrote across the top of the page. On the facing page, she wrote *WHO IS NICOLA HALLSEY?* Then she sat for a moment, staring at the two questions, before beginning to jot down ideas and information under one or the other.

She could figure this out. She didn't need Genevieve to do it for her. She had sat at the woman's feet for long enough, learning, always learning. Now it was time to put that crash course into practice.

Ten

In the night Aventurine dreamed of sirens. She was running from them, panting, desperate, through a dark and thorny thicket beneath the bare limbs of towering trees. The ground, wet underfoot, sucked at her shoes with every fleeing step. Just sirens, she finally realized, leaning against the damp trunk of an oak, the bark rough beneath her palms; she leaned forward, trying to draw a breath into her protesting lungs. Not lights, strobing red or blue or yellow. Just sirens, insistent, blaring.

She dragged herself up and out of that dream with difficulty, her heart pounding erratically in her chest. She opened her eyes and stared upwards in the darkness.

The sirens continued.

Aventurine sat up, and the notebook fell from the bed with a clatter. Not a hotel emergency—the sound of the sirens was distant. She tried to gauge the direction. The maze of hallways in the upstairs of the hotel didn't help: which way was north? West?

The clothes she had abandoned earlier still lay where she'd left them. With a weird sense of panic rising from her gullet, she gathered them up and dragged them back on. She grabbed her key and purse, threw on her jacket, plucked the phone from the charger, and slipped out of the room. There were low-level emergency lights that guided her to the stairs; on the ground floor, she slipped out into the rear parking lot.

It was easier here. She left the car park, turned left, and then left again at the water tower. In only a few moments she was out on the Bailgate. The sirens, she could make out now, were coming from the direction of the Cathedral. Avi broke into a run.

She followed the sound, scanning rooftops for the reflective glare of emergency lights that would help her find the source. She turned along the Exchequergate, still at a run, clutching at her side where a sharp pain stabbed. Overhead the Cathedral towered, lit up against the night. At the end where Exchequergate debauched onto Minster Yard, she was finally able to see the strobing red and blue off to the right, where the road curved around the scaffolded west front toward the Medieval Bishop's Palace.

A police officer stood guard over that way, his face an impassive moon in the weird lighting. A few late carousers were milling about, attempting to peer past him. Aventurine leaned into the cold stone wall of the gate, in the shadows, trying to see, trying not to be seen. An ambulance? Fire brigade? Several police cars? Lots of noise. She strained her eyes, smelled the air. No fire.

Aventurine felt her knees go weak. She leaned heavily against the wall, tipping her head back and closing her eyes. Her heart was still pounding.

"What's going on?" she heard someone ask the officer at the curve of the yard. The answer was unintelligible, but the tone was somehow both bored and impatient. Aventurine steadied herself and slid sideways in the shadows, drawing nearer. But it was no use; whatever was happening further along Minster Yard, it was impossible to see from this vantage point, and the policeman obviously was stationed to keep gawkers away. The uneasiness which had hung about her since waking from the dream had grown monumentally, and she couldn't turn away. She put out a hand and felt only cold stone.

No use. She turned to the left and hurried again, this time around the far side of the Cathedral to Eastgate, then down Priory Gate.

The noise grew louder. Minster Yard was blocked at this end as well, but she could see along the way to the ambulance. As she watched from the shadows, trying to catch her breath, several uniformed attendants muscled the gurney up and inside. It was, Avi saw with a clarity that surprised her, empty. The ambulance pulled away and turned down Pottergate. Parked behind it was the van from the coroner's office. Not a rescue, then. A death.

Oh, please God, she muttered to herself. *Not Nicola.* Followed quickly by *not the woman from the hotel beer garden.* It would kill Henry, she knew it would. And in some small place inside herself, she knew it would kill something of her, the death of her doppelganger, a woman she had never met.

Then suddenly he was there, Henry Hallsey, in an overcoat over what looked like his pajamas, running toward the policeman standing guard.

"Who is it?" he demanded, his voice high and quavering. "What's happened? Is it my daughter?"

"Henry!" she cried, pushing herself away from the wall and rushing toward him. "Henry!"

"Keep back, sir," the policeman ordered, grasping Henry by the upper arms as he tried to charge forward. "There's been a serious incident. You need to stay clear of the scene."

"But my daughter—"

Henry's hair was mussed, as though he'd come directly from bed, from his house. *Wherever did he live?* Avi thought inanely. How had he known to rush down here? He attempted to wrench his way free of the officer, but to no avail.

"Please, what kind of incident?" Henry's voice was still rising, to the edge, perhaps, of hysteria. "Please tell me. My daughter—she's been missing for days—I filed a report—"

Aventurine reached him, and put a quick hand on his shoulder. "Henry," she repeated, trying to get through to him.

He turned. The weird lighting carved out the skull beneath his skin, his eyes dark hollows, his cheekbones stark and sharp.

"Nicola—" He caught himself. "No. Aventurine. It's Aventurine."

"Yes." The policeman had let him go, and now Aventurine took both arms in her grip. "Henry. Pull yourself together. Take a breath. *Take a breath.*"

He blinked several times, as though trying to force back tears. "Do you know what's happened, Aventurine? Is it Nicola? Have they found Nicola?"

"I don't know what's happening. The sirens woke me." She turned to the constable, who was watching them both with some interest. "Please. Officer. Mr. Hallsey made a report yesterday at the station about his missing daughter. Can you give us any information?" She swallowed, blinked. "Could this be her?"

Instead of answering, he turned away slightly and spoke into the com on his shoulder. Aventurine couldn't make out the words; the strobing lights were beginning to give her a headache, and everything had a brilliant nimbus around it. The officer turned back and indicated a spot at the verge. "Wait here, please, sir, and ma'am. The sergeant will be over to speak to you in a moment."

The late night—or early morning—cold was beginning to seep into Avi's bones. She moved to the side of the roadway, still holding onto Henry's arm, shivering.

"Aventurine," he said, his voice still unsteady. "You're cold. Take my coat." He began to peel it off; he was indeed still wearing his pajamas underneath, yet another sign of his distress.

"No." She didn't know whether to step away from him, or to grasp his arms more tightly, to prevent him shedding his overcoat. "No, Henry. Keep it on. I'm fine."

"You're shivering."

"I'm fine."

A second uniformed officer was approaching, the lights reflecting off her jacket, and with her a man in a regular coat. All he needed was a fedora to be a stereotypical police detective from a low-budget film. The sergeant, obviously. The pair conferred for a moment with the policeman on guard duty, before approaching.

58

"Mr. Hallsey?" he asked. His quick eyes took in both Henry, in his disheveled state, and Aventurine. "And you are?"

"Aventurine Morrow."

"American, eh? And what are you doing here?" *Here* might have been at the Cathedral in the middle of the night, or in Lincoln, or in the UK in general. The question sounded like an accusation, and Aventurine's hackles rose, though to be fair, everything out of the sergeant's mouth sounded like an accusation.

"I'm a friend of Mr. Hallsey's."

He threw a glance over his shoulder at the uniformed officer, who immediately made a few marks in a small notebook.

"You think you know the victim?"

Henry staggered backward as though struck, his face becoming more death-like in the uncertain lighting.

Aventurine gripped his arm more tightly, and swallowed. "There is a victim, then."

The glance flickered to her at her interruption, then back to Henry. "Mr. Hallsey?"

"My daughter," Henry managed, his voice thin. "I filed a report yesterday—"

The sergeant waited, his hands holding back his jacket at his waist.

"Is it my daughter, then?" Now Henry was still, as though shoring himself up for another blow.

"There is no identification on the body. We don't know yet who the victim is."

Several blows. Each word punched at the elderly man at her side. He opened his mouth, but after a moment closed it again, falling silent.

"Come talk to the DI," the sergeant suggested, though Aventurine thought it not really a suggestion. She wondered, fleetingly, as though the detective was enjoying this.

"I'll come with you, Henry," she said, though there was no way in hell she wanted to look at a dead person ever again. Any dead person. She didn't have the fortitude of Genevieve Smithson, and she knew that all too well. She slid her hand along his arm until their fingers were entwined. His bony hand was icy.

"No, no, Aventurine," he said, though he did not look at her. "You go back to your hotel. There's no need—" but his voice broke off.

"There's every need." Irrationally, she thought of the little red suitcase, so much like Avi's little blue one. Her imagination veered away from the suitcase's owner, and her face, so like Avi's own. "I'm coming with you."

The sergeant looked on with a deceptive impassivity. Then he nodded. "Come along, then, both of you," he said. "Get me a copy of that report," he tossed over his shoulder to the officer, who jotted something in her notebook. Then back to Henry. "You filed it when, you said? Yesterday?"

Henry nodded.

"Yes," Aventurine added loudly, in case the detective had missed the nod.

He turned on his heel and led the way across Greenstone Place. They fell into step behind him, and the other officer brought up the rear.

So many police officers—and scene of the crime officers, she remembered that they were called. Lights had been set up beyond the arched gateway to the Old Palace. The four came across the pocket-handkerchief-sized green from Minster Yard, pausing at the entrance. Their footsteps were drowned out by the hum of vehicles, the power to the lighting.

"You brought them?" Another, taller detective, also wearing an overcoat, and with inscrutable eyes in a tired face, turned toward them. His voice was gravelly, as though he smoked too much. He did not offer to shake hands. "DCI Burroughs," he said.

"This is Henry Hallsey, and Aventurine Morrow. Mr. Hallsey filed a report about his missing daughter, and thinks this might be her." Again, the sergeant's words seemed to hit Henry like a series of punches; Aventurine felt him flinch with each one.

"It's not that we *think*," she broke in. "We don't know."

The chief inspector did not bother to reply.

Yet another officer appeared, and reported that the perimeter had been locked down.

"Take Billings, O'Mara, Thorpe, and Suarez for the door-to-door," Burroughs ordered. "Someone had to have seen or heard something." He turned back to the two. "What is your daughter's name again, Mr. Hallsey?"

Henry licked his lips. "Nicola. Nicola Hallsey. She's thirty-six." His grip on Aventurine's hand tightened.

The chief inspector's eyes flicked to his sergeant and back again, the meaning clear. *Could be.* "Get the pictures," he ordered. The other detective shouted over his shoulder, and someone handed him a tablet, which he in turn passed on. Burroughs flipped through the screens until he found what he wanted. "All right, then. Prepare yourself. It's not pretty."

The humming of the lights on their poles made Aventurine's head pound. She toed the sheet of poly underfoot, protecting the ground, and it made a strange crackling noise as the circle of crime-scene-suited photographers and investigators crossed and recrossed at the edge of a tall, but ruined, stone wall. Several people looked up, murmured indistinctly to one another, and returned to the job at hand.

Aventurine was holding her breath. She closed her eyes tightly for a moment, willing her courage, and then opened them again to look at the image on the tablet.

A woman, dressed entirely in black: jeans, a jacket. She wore what looked to be black soft-soled shoes, and off to the side in the grass lay a black knitted hat. Her arms and legs were splayed in the photograph, half on the pavement, half on the grass. Her hair was brown, and fell across one side of her face, while the other side was bruised. One eye was open. A trickle of blood ran out of the corner of her mouth. But it was her neck, bent at an impossible angle—obviously broken.

Aventurine raised her eyes to the top of the stone wall. *Did she fall or was she pushed?* she thought for the second time that day, the words a sing-song inside her head. She turned away quickly, burying her face in Henry's shoulder for a moment.

"It's not—her," he said. When he spoke again, his voice had gained strength. "It's not Nicola."

Aventurine was surprised at how much she felt like sobbing, from absolute relief.

It wasn't Nicola.

Part II:

Gates

Eleven

Aventurine saw Henry back to his car, parked on Eastgate. When he attempted to unlock the door to the Renault, he dropped the keys, then dropped them a second time. His hands were still shaking.

"Let me drive you," she suggested, though she wasn't sure how much more steady she was. Henry shook his head, but when he dropped the keys yet again, she retrieved them before he had a chance.

"It's fine, Aventurine," he said. "I'm fine. And besides—how would you get home?"

She waved his protests away, and raised her eyebrows at him until he finally dropped his shoulders in resignation, and opened the passenger side door.

He directed her through the streets as it began to rain. In the darkness she had to concentrate on staying to the left: she hadn't driven in this country since the day she'd turned the rental car in, in Norfolk. The rain picked up as they drove east, out of the city proper, and into a series of villages that hugged the shoulders of the road. At last Henry indicated a left turn that dropped into a glade, the road narrowing to little more than a lane. Another turn, and they were in the short way leading through a stone wall and to a pocket-sized parking spot before a small semi-detached house. A light shone over the front door, and another just inside the curtained front window.

She checked the clock on the dashboard before she turned off the car. 4:42. It would be light in a couple of hours.

"Come in," he invited, yawning. "You might as well join me in a cup of tea. I don't think I'll be falling asleep again."

They climbed out. Aventurine handed Henry his keys, and he unlocked the door of the trim little house and led the way in. A single lamp burned on the end table at the sofa. The television was on, the sound turned low. Henry cast it a glance, but left it on and beckoned her to follow him through to the narrow kitchen, off of which a greenhouse room opened into the rear garden, still in darkness. He flicked on the overhead light, and brought the electric kettle to the sink to fill it.

Aventurine leaned against the end of the counter, her arms crossed over her chest. Henry was not looking at her, and she had the prickling sensation that it was intentional, that he was somehow afraid to meet her eyes.

"Henry," she said, watching him depress the switch on the kettle, which then glowed an unearthly blue. He didn't turn, but drew a teapot from the cupboard, along with two mugs, and a canister of loose tea. "Henry, how did you know?"

"Know what?"

She knew he was being deliberately obtuse.

"About the emergency call at the Bishop's Palace? You got there from here pretty damned quick."

Henry was concentrating on his tea preparation. He spooned some loose tea into the pot, then rooted in a side drawer until he pulled out a strainer, which he set across the rim of one of the mugs.

"I—" The water was boiling, and he turned away again to pour it into the pot. He didn't even rinse with the hot water first, she noted. He had to be really distracted. "I'm sorry. We'll just let that steep a minute or two, shall we?"

Aventurine made an impatient movement. Henry flinched, and for the merest moment she felt guilty about startling an old man. Then she forced the feeling down.

"How did you know?"

There was a scratching at the glasshouse door. Henry opened it, to admit an orange tiger cat, who twined about his legs in greeting before approaching his half-full dish of dry cat food.

"Percival," Henry said, by way of introduction. "My wife's cat."

Dodging. Again. He poured a mug of tea and set it on the counter before her. Then he poured a second.

"I'm waiting, Henry."

His blue eyes shifted to her and then away. "I have an alarm."

"An alarm."

"On my phone. For the Cathedral." He cleared his throat. "I'm not supposed to. Nicola set it."

Nicola, who worked for the security company.

He led the way to the table in the glassed room, and drew out a chair. "You won't let on, will you? I wouldn't want Nicola to be in trouble. She swore me to secrecy."

"Who would I tell?" Aventurine sank into the chair opposite his. "Even if I wanted to, which I don't."

"I didn't realize the entire complex was covered in the alarm. And when it woke me—I was only dozing in front of the television—I haven't slept much these past few nights—"

The tea was too hot to drink. When Avi set the mug down, she splashed some onto the table. Absently Henry handed her a serviette from the holder. She could imagine him in the front room, in the dark, the television still on, waiting for Nicola to call, to text. The image in her mind's eye was stark in its sadness.

"I just thought I'd like to know if there was trouble in the Cathedral when I wasn't there. And tonight, when I heard the alarm go off, my first thought was of Nicola. Irrational, I know. Maybe something had happened to her, maybe there." He hung his head. "I know how it sounds. But you don't know what it's like, Aventurine: waiting. Not knowing where she is. *Not knowing.* I was half asleep. I just jumped up and ran, because I didn't know. *And I needed to know.*"

Just as the dream of the sirens had urged her forward. She understood more than he realized. This recently had been Mick's life: waiting. But Shep had not returned.

The orange cat was winding its way between her ankles, and when she looked down, Percival leapt up into her lap. She ran her hand along his smooth coat, along his backbone and out the length of his tail. After a moment he began to purr, loudly.

"Just push him down if he bothers you." Henry wiped a hand across his tired eyes. "He misses Bethany." That *he* missed Bethany went without saying. That somewhere on the edge of what he was prepared to accept, prowled the possibility of missing Nicola.

"He's not bothering me. I like cats." Percival had begun to knead her leg. She hoped he didn't decide to use claws. She petted him some more. His purr remained steady.

"But now, at least, I know that woman wasn't my daughter." Henry's laugh was short. "It's like Schrodinger's cat, isn't it? As long as I don't have any information, Nicola is both—fine—and not fine, at the same time." For a long moment he stared into his tea mug as though unable to recognize its purpose. Then he frowned, lifted it to his mouth, and took a drink. He grimaced.

Aventurine reached for his arm across the table. "She's fine. She's fine. Keep thinking that. We'll figure this out."

Henry cleared his throat. "Aventurine. It's Sunday morning. She's been gone since Thursday morning—*at least* since Thursday morning. And we all know that the longer someone is missing, the less likely—"

"Stop. We'll find her."

But Aventurine knew exactly what he meant. And she hoped desperately that she wasn't lying to him.

Twelve

Aventurine got a taxi back, and it was nearly breakfast time when she arrived at the hotel. She'd never felt less hungry in her life.

She dragged herself upstairs and into the shower. Then she dressed, choosing her warmest sweater, but still found herself shivering. The hot water machine on the desk couldn't make tea hot enough to help; she found herself cradling the mug in both hands. She looked longingly at her unmade bed, but knew she wouldn't sleep if she tried. Every time she would close her eyes, the ruins of the Medieval Bishop's Palace would probably rise in her dreams, truncated stone walls leaning drunkenly toward her. No, better to give sleep a pass for now, knowing that she would dream of walls falling, of the danger of being crushed.

Walls, she thought, staring into her black tea, too unappetizing to drink. *Death.* She squeezed her eyes shut. She opened them again to the buzzing of her phone. She looked around, confused, trying to remember where she had set it down. Finally she found it and answered the call. Genevieve. At whatever this hour was of the morning.

"How—what—"

She set the mug aside too quickly, and tea slopped onto the desk. Quickly she dodged to the bathroom for a towel to mop up the mess.

"You were at the Bishop's Palace last night." Genevieve's words were not a question.

Big Brother is watching you. How in God's name did she know that?

"Where are you? Are you spying on me?"

"Immaterial at this point. But you were there with Henry Hallsey."

It felt like an interrogation. *We ask the questions here.* Aventurine realized she was holding up a defensive hand, one no one else could see. She busied herself by pouring more hot water into her mug. "I found him there, yes."

"The body, then. The *incident.* Was it his daughter?"

The water still wasn't as hot as she wanted it to be. She took a desperate sip of her tea anyway. "No. It wasn't."

A prolonged sigh.

"You shouldn't have gotten involved."

"I didn't have a choice. It was Henry. He was terrified." Aventurine didn't know why the old spy should make her feel like she needed to justify herself. She had no idea how much Genevieve knew, let alone *how* she knew it.

"You had a choice. You made the wrong one."

"Genevieve, you're a cold-hearted bitch."

A noise which might have been a sardonic laugh. "I am a very much alive cold-hearted bitch. There are benefits. You of all people should know that."

"Tell me, then, how trying to help an elderly person is the wrong choice." Avi hoped Genevieve had registered the emphasis on *elderly person.* Especially since, no matter how old Henry Hallsey actually was, Genevieve still had about twenty years' head start on him. "And know even before you start in that I'd much rather err on the side of compassion, *if,* in fact, I've made a mistake."

"You need to stay out of the path of the police. You don't want them to notice you for *any* reason. You don't even want a traffic citation." Her voice was hard, as though she were correcting a particularly recalcitrant child. "I've told you that."

Again with that sense of Schrodinger's cat: as long as Aventurine stayed under the radar, there was no real way to connect her to Neil's death. But there was also no way to find out whether anyone had made that connection without lifting her proverbial head to have a look around. She bit her lip. Genevieve was right. Of course Genevieve was right. Hadn't Avi spent yesterday afternoon reading everything she could find online about the ongoing investigation into Neil's death? If she could have hung her head in shame before the old woman, she would have done it. She felt suitably chastised. But damned if she was going to grovel on the phone, so she remained silent.

"Now. Tell me what happened."

Aventurine did, going through her story slowly. She reached to the side table and dragged over her notebook, with her attempts at organizing her thoughts about Nicola. Genevieve did not interrupt, but let her lay out the facts as she knew them, and her suppositions as well. Avi wondered whether, at the other end, Genevieve would be taking notes, or simply committing things to her prodigious memory, to avoid a paper trail.

"There was no sign at the cottage that she'd been taken by force," Genevieve repeated after a moment. "This is interesting, but not necessarily something that rules out the possibility."

"What do you mean?"

A clicking of the tongue. "Don't be obtuse, Aventurine. Just because Nicola Hallsey was not taken by force from her home does not mean that she wasn't taken by force from *somewhere.*"

Aventurine squeezed her eyes shut.

"Further, if we accept that the argument you witnessed on the hotel terrace wasn't just a coincidence, and that was in fact Nicola, it's also indicative that she was indeed taken by force, perhaps on the way home, or on the way to work."

"But what about that woman getting into the car the next day? On Union Road, beyond the Castle?" It felt as though Aventurine were trying to get a foothold on a slippery slope. "That didn't look like force. It looked like—rescue."

"Then why hasn't she contacted her father?" Genevieve demanded. After a moment she sighed. "Aventurine, all we really know is that she's missing. The possibilities are endless. She could be on an assignation that she simply doesn't want her father to know about—which sounds like the scenario the police are plumping for—and if that's indeed the case, I hope she's having a hell of a time."

"I don't think Henry's and her relationship is like that—"

"And you don't know. Another possibility: she's lying dead in a ditch somewhere."

"Oh, my God, Genevieve."

"I know you don't want that. And God knows her father probably doesn't, unless he's responsible for it—and possibly not even then."

"Oh, my *God!*"

"Just pointing out how little we—*you*—really know. But putting yourself out there with this Henry Hallsey and the police last night was not really in your best interest."

Aventurine considered hanging up the call. She considered never answering a call from Genevieve again. Neither of which, she knew, at the same time, were plans that she would ever carry through with.

"So what are you going to do now?"

The room phone rang, an annoyingly cheerful sound. Aventurine glanced over to see the blinking light from the front desk.

"I'm going to answer this other telephone call. Hang on."

She picked up the receiver.

"Ms. Morrow? Registration here. You have a visitor. A Chief Inspector Burroughs? He wonders if you'd spare him a few minutes."

Aventurine's heart sank. *Why did Genevieve have to be so Goddamned right all the time?* "Tell him I'll be down shortly. Thanks."

Then she returned her attention to the cell phone in her hand. "Listen, Genevieve. What I'm going to do is end this call and head downstairs. A police detective is here to see me."

"Damn it," Genevieve hissed. "Aventurine, say nothing. Smile vacantly and *say nothing.*"

Easier said than done, if one wasn't an SOE agent.

It wasn't until she was on her way through the labyrinthian hallways that she paused to wonder again: *how had Genevieve known about Henry Hallsey?*

Thirteen

She came down the stairs and found Pete the barman slicing fruit. Again.

"In the corner. Got him a cup of coffee." Pete raised his eyebrows and flexed his arms a bit. "Everything all right with you, then?"

"It's fine. Thank you." She took a deep breath and threaded her way through the tables to the one between the window and the cold fireplace. The chief inspector was flipping through a small notebook. On the table before him lay a manila folder. At his elbow, a cup of coffee steamed. Black. Aventurine could have guessed. He stood as she approached, and indicated the chair across from him. As she sat, Pete appeared with a cup of tea, a small creamer, and a ceramic holder of sugar packets: he hadn't learned her tea habits yet, and she was grateful to have retained some of her secrets.

"Ms. Morrow, you might remember me from last night. DCI Burroughs." He slipped his ID card from an inside pocket and held it out. She barely had time to register the photo and insignia before he tucked it away again.

She wished she *did* take her tea with milk and sugar, so she could busy her hands. *Philistine,* Genevieve had called her on their first meeting, since she drank her tea black. But she wasn't trying to fool this policeman into thinking she was British.

"I remember you," she answered. "How can I help you?" *Or not help you,* she thought, remembering her instructions. She smiled.

Her face felt as though it would crack.

He shook his head, returning her smile, an amiability she didn't quite buy. "Just routine enquiries."

Aventurine took a sip of her tea, which she was relieved and pained to discover was still boiling hot. She nearly laughed, but caught herself. "You really say that?"

His quick smile didn't reach his eyes.

She composed herself, remembering Genevieve's warning. "What can I help you with?"

His glacial eyes seemed to be measuring her, storing away her appearance, her expressions, all for later examination. She took a deep breath, and reached for her tea again.

"You were down at the Cathedral after midnight. Why?"

"I couldn't sleep. I heard sirens." *Ambulance chaser.* The sun's light shone through the window directly onto her face; he had chosen the seats intentionally, of course.

"So you walked down to look?"

"Yes."

"Any particular reason?"

She shrugged. "Not really."

"And you met up with—" he checked his notes, though Aventurine was certain he didn't really need to. He gave her the impression that he remembered everything. "Mr. Hallsey. Mr. Henry Hallsey."

"I didn't know he'd be there until I saw him."

"You're friends?"

"I met him on a tour of the Cathedral this week. He seems an interesting man."

"So you don't know him well."

"I only met him this week," she repeated. The tea was bitter. She took another sip.

"Yet you accompanied him to the station to make a report about—" again the glance at the notebook— "his missing daughter. Miss Nicola Hallsey."

"I did. When I saw him again on Steep Hill, he seemed upset. He told me why, and I encouraged him to make his report."

From his inside pocket, he drew out a pen, and scribbled a few more lines in the notebook. He glanced up at her, and then back down again. "Just making a few notes, here, Ms. Morrow. So I won't forget."

"Of course." She doubted he would.

"And the missing daughter. Nicola. You've never met her?"

Despite herself, Aventurine felt the flush crawling up into her face. "No. Never."

Damn the lighting. The detective examined her face speculatively. Yet again he reached into that bottomless pocket, this time drawing out a photograph, which he lay on the scarred table between them. A copy of the one Henry had left when filing his report with the police. The one on her phone right now, which she had forwarded in disbelief to her twin sister.

"You've never met Nicola Hallsey."

"No."

"Never met her father before you took his tour at the Cathedral."

"No."

DCI Burroughs nudged the photograph a bit closer across the table. "She looks very much like you."

Understatement of the century. "I know."

"She could be your sister."

"We do have the same coloring, yes."

He leaned back, his eyes on her face. "It's a bit more than coloring."

There was no way she could take his bait, because there was no way she could explain any of it. Distractedly, she wondered whether Micheline had received the DNA testing report yet.

"Is there something you're not telling me?"

Burroughs seemed calm, very patient, as though an expert in waiting people out. In waiting her out. Well, he'd be waiting for a long time.

"There isn't. I was as surprised as you are. I forwarded the picture to my own sister, back in the United States, and she was shocked as well."

"You're going to tell me it's some sort of genetic aberration."

"I can't tell you anything. I don't know why we should have similar appearances." Was she talking too much? *Don't say anything.* Genevieve's voice echoed in her head.

Burroughs left the photo on the table between them.

"Let's shift gears, then, shall we?" He drained his coffee, and lifted the cup in the direction of Pete behind the bar. Then he slid the manila folder closer and opened it. The top few pages were text-heavy printouts that she tried to read upside down. Burroughs glanced through each slowly, as though familiarizing himself with the contents—though of course, he already knew everything that was there. It was a stall tactic, one that was meant to put Aventurine on edge, and even though she knew exactly what he was doing, she couldn't tamp down her anxiety.

Keep your head down, Genevieve had said. *Not even a traffic citation.*

"This woman," he said. He drew forth an eight by ten photograph, and for a moment Aventurine panicked. She did not want to look at the picture of the victim again. The blood, the bruising, the neck twisted at such an odd angle. She closed her eyes for a moment.

"Are you all right, Ms. Morrow?" The question did not hold even an iota of concern.

She opened her eyes again and met his cold stare. He slid the photograph toward her, and she took a deep breath before looking down.

Not the same photograph; not the victim at the scene. Instead, this was a morgue shot, the eyes closed, the skin pale and waxy. Aside from the bruising on one side of her face, the woman could have been asleep. Aventurine let out a breath in relief.

"Thank God," she breathed.

"For what?"

She glanced up at his face again. His impassive face, beneath that unmoving dark hair, which might have been carved from the same stone as the saints and bishops in the Cathedral. "I thought it might be the photo—from last night."

Burroughs said nothing.

Aventurine dropped her eyes to the morgue photograph once again. The woman, as she remembered, had shoulder-length brown hair, but in normal lighting, she could see the red highlights in it. Natural, or enhanced, she wondered, and then chided herself for being so callous. The bruising and swelling was confined to one side of her face, along her cheekbone and up into her hair, as though she had landed there upon her fall. Both eyes were closed, and with the purpling around one, and the memory of her open eye from the other photo superimposed over this, Aventurine was grateful.

"You said you didn't know her last night," DCI Burroughs said, looking at his notes, though again, Aventurine was certain he didn't need to. "I wonder if you might change your mind, looking at her in better lighting."

Aventurine forced herself to look once again. Then she shook her head. "No. Still nothing." She sat back, and remembering her tea, took a sip. Pete chose this moment to glide over, refill Burroughs's coffee, and pour more hot water into her teapot as well. She thought she saw the counterman's eyes flicker to the photo, but then he was quickly gone again. The bell at the front door tinkled, an incongruous sound, and a couple, pink-cheeked and windblown, entered and went to the bar. "Hold on," she said slowly. "Do you mean you don't know who she is?"

"Not yet."

"No identification? In her pockets? A purse?" But of course the scene-of-crimes officers would have found those. Her questions were foolish, born of shock, and of an odd sort of sadness: to die like that, and no one knew who you were. No one knew enough to miss you. *At least they'd left Neil his wallet.* She felt the flush again, and quickly shoved that thought aside, in favor of Nicola—and this made her bite her lip. *We'll find her.* She had promised Henry. What if they didn't?

"We're following up a number of leads."

"Of which I, supposedly, am one?"

Don't bait him.

Burroughs raised his dark brows. "Or might provide one, perhaps." He closed the folder and slid it aside, but still left the photograph of Nicola between them. She smiled up at them, the dimple in her left cheek pronounced, a sparkle in her green eyes. If only she knew—any of it. All of it. Aventurine realized the detective was watching her as she studied the photo, and she steeled herself to meet his gaze.

"One last thing," he said. "Your passport. Do you have it with you?"

"Of course." Aventurine had traveled enough to never go anywhere without it on her person. She opened her purse now, then opened the inside zippered pocket to draw it out.

"May I?" Burroughs held out a hand, surprisingly long-fingered and elegant. Aventurine didn't suppose she really had a choice.

"Of course," she repeated, handing him the little blue-bound booklet.

He flipped it open to the page with her photo and details. With his other hand, he made further scribbles in his notebook. Then he paged through the passport, noting the stamps from the previous seven years. France. Iceland. He paused for a moment at a stamp, skewed on the page, then flipped a few pages back again. He seemed quite interested in the two pages. At last he looked up.

"You were here already this year. In June."

She mentally cursed the blood rushing up into her cheeks. No wonder she was terrible at poker. She was certain he'd made a mental note of her discomfort. "Yes. With my nephew."

He looked down, then up again. "You returned to the US, but came back again a week ago. Not quite four months later. Why is that?"

"Research," she said, only partially lying. "I'm a writer."

A non-writing writer, courting insanity.

Genevieve's voice, hard: *don't tell him anything.*

There was no point in telling him about the writer's block; nobody except any other writer would truly understand.

"And what are you researching, if you don't mind my asking?"

Aventurine certainly did mind him asking; she kept her writing close to her chest while it was happening, but even closer, now that it wasn't.

But his request was another probe disguised as casual interest: in truth, there was nothing casual about *anything* he wanted to know. And she had a feeling that, should she resist answering, the request would become an order, a demand. Still, she couldn't bring up Genevieve, lest that lead to *saying too much* and getting them all into trouble. Serious trouble. All of them. Including, and especially, Paul.

"Katherine Swynford," she answered quickly. Too quickly? "I've come to visit her tomb."

"And the Swynford Jewel?"

Aventurine thought of it in the locked and alarmed case in the Medieval library, the rich ruby glow of it. "I saw that the other day when I was in the Cathedral."

DCI Borroughs made some more notes, and then, instead of closing the passport, reached at last for the photo of Nicola Hallsey. He held both pictures side by side, frowning slightly. Then he snapped the passport cover shut and handed the little book back to her. "Uncanny," he murmured.

Aventurine said nothing.

"Thank you for your time," he said, leaving some coins on the table next to his half-empty coffee cup. He stood. She had not really thought about how tall he really was. "If you'd keep yourself available—we might need to ask you some more questions."

With that he was gone, and Aventurine realized she had never asked the question that had plagued her: *did she fall, or was she pushed?*

The headache which had also plagued her since the early hours was back in full force. She added some coins to those on the table, and returned to her room in search of paracetamol.

Fourteen

Aventurine slept most of the day and night. The next morning she woke early enough to stumble groggily down to the breakfast room. She ordered tea and toast and scrambled eggs and Lincolnshire sausage, but skipped the rest of the full English. Blood pudding? The thought dizzied her. She still felt headachy and tired, and was certain the other guests at breakfast must surely be able to hear the creaking of her bones as she shifted stiffly at the table. It was not yet eight when she wiped her lips with the napkin, and headed back to collect her things, checking in her bag to be sure she still had Nicola's house key.

The morning was quiet. More rain overnight, but it had stopped now; the wind was from the northeast, and cold. Leaves and trash skittered under the Newport Arch, and she was glad to get through the urine-smelling tunnel to the other side. When she turned the corner at the hospital, the wind hit her full-force, and she found herself blinking and hunching her shoulders. The Nettleham Road was nearly deserted as well; as she approached the cottage, someone was walking along the opposite pavement, so she went on by, not wanting anyone to notice her letting herself in at the front door. But then again—from a distance, she might only look like Nicola returned, if the neighbors noticed her presence at all.

Even so, the turning of the key in the lock was surprisingly loud. Aventurine glanced over her shoulder, pushed the door open, and slipped inside.

To find an absolute mess.

The cottage had been tossed.

Aventurine stopped, listening, for the slightest movement, the slightest shift of air. But the front room felt empty, the silence cold and unyielding. Whoever had done this was long gone. She pressed the door closed in its frame and locked it, then leaned back against it, surveying the damage.

Books were torn from their shelves, and tossed into a pile in the middle of the floor. The cushions of the sofa and chairs had been pulled out, and then pulled apart, stuffing cascading in yellow waterfalls. The photograph on the wall over the wood burner had been pulled down, and then pulled from its frame: Henry and Bethany Hallsey stared up at her from the carpet, and there was a rough dirty footprint across Henry's face. Aventurine stooped to pick the photo up, and attempted to brush the dirt away—it just seemed a sign of contempt she couldn't bear. The footprint didn't budge; the photo was ruined. She set it gently on one of the chairs, where the upholstery had been half-ripped away.

Dazed, she moved into the kitchen and found the same carnage. Dry goods and cans were tossed every which way on the floor; the cupboard doors swung open drunkenly. A bag of flour had been poured out into the sink. The rubbish bin had been upended. In the glassed-in dining room, the chairs and table had been overturned.

Aventurine felt the bile rise from her stomach into her throat. If this is what had been done to the downstairs, she was hesitant to see the destruction she knew would await in the bedroom, in the office. She took a deep breath and forced herself up the stairs. Sure enough, the bedroom had fared no better, the duvet and sheets torn away, the mattress cut open and dragged halfway off the box spring. Makeup and pill bottles filled the bathroom sink, and the towels and bathmat were mounded in the bathtub. The top of the toilet tank had been removed and lay broken on the floor. She turned slowly to the office, dreading what she would find there.

Chaos. The first thing she noticed was that the space the laptop had occupied in the center of the large work table was now empty. The wardrobe door hung open, a hinge broken, clothes hurled to the floor. The Dopp kit was emptied onto the floor, and a lipstick tube opened, the shimmery pink ground into the carpet. The desk chair lay on its side. Files from the open cabinets were scattered everywhere.

Aventurine felt sick. The sweat broke out on her forehead. She felt violated, even though this was not her home. But it was the home of her doppelganger, someone who—and even the chief inspector apparently agreed on this—could easily have been her sister. Or her, ten years ago.

Numbly she righted the desk chair, and sank into it, dropping her head into her hands.

What to make of this mess? Someone had searched the cottage thoroughly, leaving a sea of destruction behind. Who would have done such a thing, and why?

The searching had been so incredibly destructive-—it was almost as though there was malice behind it. So much broken, so much ruined. Aventurine thought of the photograph of the Hallseys, dirtied and lying on the floor, and felt the tears prickle in her throat and behind her eyes. She pressed the balls of her hands into her eye sockets, willing herself not to cry, not to be sick.

Who would hate Nicola so much?

The man from the pub terrace.

Slowly she sat up and leaned her head against the back of the chair. She let out a long breath, trying to regain her equilibrium.

What were they looking for? And had they found it? She shook her head. If Nicola had hidden anything, it would have been found. Her glance fell on the empty space on the desk. They'd taken the laptop, so perhaps there was something on it they thought they needed. *Good luck breaking into it,* she thought dryly. *Good luck figuring out that password.* She knew there were ways to do it, programs that could help, but she didn't know very much about them, or whether someone breaking in and rifling a house would have the wherewithal to break into a computer and rifle the files.

When she looked through the window and across the road at the opposite house, she saw that the upstairs window remained curtained. It seemed unlikely that anyone over there had noticed anything, especially if it had happened in the middle of the night.

Aventurine groped in the front pocket of her bag for her phone, poised to call Henry. Then she stopped, overwhelmed by the enormity of the mess. Call him, and tell him what? That while they were busy trying to find out what had happened to Nicola, someone had broken into her house and searched it for—who knows what? She dropped the hands holding the phone into her lap, and leaned her head back again, fighting back the tears that continued to surprise her. She couldn't call Henry. Not right now. Not until she had figured out what to tell him.

And the police. They should be called, but the last thing she wanted to do was have another interview with DCI Burroughs. She could just imagine it: *you barely know her father, and he entrusted you with a key to her house. The house of a woman you've never met. Who conveniently looks just like you.* She could just hear the sound of his voice when he spoke the words that no rational investigator would believe.

Shit.

Her neck prickled, and her eyes flashed open.

Aventurine heard it again: the whisper of movement from downstairs—a sound that was not quite a sound, but a rearrangement of air.

She glanced around hurriedly. She must have, incredibly, dozed off in the office chair, surrounded by the mess that was the ransacked house. Now she sat perfectly still, hardly daring to breathe. Trying to still her heartbeat, which was so loud surely anyone could hear it.

Someone was in Nicola's cottage with her.

Again she glanced around the room, looking for something to use as a weapon, and at the same time chiding herself. She had been dozing, and something had awakened her. A dream, perhaps. A noise from the street below the window. There was no one else—nothing else—here.

Then, the slightest of clicks. The snick of a lock? The tap of a fingernail on a table, the flick of a light switch?

Whoever it was moved stealthily. Like a cat.

Nicola didn't have a cat. *Henry* had a cat.

For a moment Aventurine straightened. Perhaps Nicola had returned.

Surely, though, if it were Nicola, she would not be stealthy: it was her house. Surely, if it were Nicola, she would be making horrified exclamations about the state of her downstairs. It couldn't be Nicola. Avi bit her lip.

She had heard no footsteps, but her hackles were raised. She was an animal in danger, trapped up here on the upper floor, with no way to get out, no good place to hide. Even had she wanted to hide under the bed, it had been destroyed. Had she wanted to hide in the wardrobe, the door had been broken. Slowly she levered herself out of the chair, praying it would not creak or squeal, then took the two steps to hide herself behind the door to the tiny hallway. Not that it would matter—her hiding would only delay her inevitable discovery.

Another slight snick.

Aventurine held her breath.

"No need to cower up there, Aventurine. Just come down."

Genevieve.

What the hell?

The old woman was standing near the wood burner, gazing around slowly as though memorizing the room. She wore a beige coat, a beige watch cap pulled down over her grey hair, and her hands were gloved. Aventurine descended the stairs slowly, feeling as though she were a schoolchild, caught red-handed in some petty mischief.

Gloves.

Damn it. When the police got involved in this mess, they would find Aventurine's fingerprints everywhere. She had been such an idiot about the cottage. But, she thought defensively, there was no way to imagine, when she had come in at Henry's behest two days ago, that things would progress as they had.

"How did you get in?" she demanded. Then she shook her head, ran a hand over her eyes. "Wait. No. Don't tell me. I don't want to know."

Genevieve did not deign to answer. Wordlessly she passed into the kitchen, then past Aventurine and up the stairs. Avi could sense her moving about for a few minutes before she returned to the ground floor.

"They've taken the computer," Genevieve said. "Did you notice anything else?"

Aventurine threw up her hands peevishly. She was spiraling down from her fright into frustration and annoyance at Genevieve's high-handedness. "I don't even know what I'm looking *at*, let alone what someone could be looking *for*." Her voice was climbing, and noticing the other woman's calculating eye, she fought to bring it under control. "But you know what? I would guess they didn't know either, because otherwise this place wouldn't be so thoroughly trashed. Once whoever did this found what they wanted, they'd have left the rest alone and just—gone."

Genevieve nodded. "I expect you're right. Unless it was a personal, angry, vicious attack. You know the kind. *I can destroy your life, and you can't stop me.*"

Except that she didn't say the rest: *unless you kill me.* As Neil had been killed.

They stared at one another. Calculatingly.

"All right, Aventurine," Genevieve said at last. "We have to get out of here, and we can't go together." She had shifted into command mode, and Avi, as always, had neither the strength nor the inclination to disobey. "I'll go first, as though I were just visiting and am now leaving." Her gaze remained steady. "I want you to give me twenty minutes. Then you leave, making a show of locking up behind you in case any of the neighbors are watching. Swing that blonde hair around. Do your best Nicola Hallsey impression."

Aventurine gulped and nodded. She could see the logic.

"Meet me at 6:15 at the Treaty of Commerce, down on the High Street. Close to the station." Stepping over the pile of books, Genevieve unlocked the door and let herself out. Then she half-turned. "Thanks," she called over her shoulder. "I'll be sure to look into that." With a wave, she closed the door behind her.

Aventurine locked it again and sat down in one of the ruined armchairs to wait.

Fifteen

Aventurine wandered down Steep Hill and into town, stopping in Boots for more contact lens solution and a packet of Thornton's Pearls for later: so far this day seemed to demand an infusion of chocolate, and, the way things were going, it was just going to get worse. She did a bit of window shopping until she heard a clock somewhere chiming six—the streetlights had come on, and it was getting a bit chilly—then she pulled her jacket more closely about her and passed the train station, continuing slowly down the High Street. She found the pub easily enough, in a timbered building squeezed between a mobile phone shop, and a place painted with garish advertising, promising that she could win £50. The street was surprisingly empty—though when she'd looked up the pub online, the listing had said that their busiest hours were around noontime, when the shoppers were out in force, and when they served lunch.

Inside it was dim and heavy-timbered, with the bar along the right-hand side. The woman wiping down the taps looked up and smiled crookedly when she approached. Aventurine ordered a pint of the Exmoor Fox, mostly because she liked the name, and hoped it wasn't too pale an ale; but she didn't want to engage in too much conversation with the bartender—didn't want to give her any reason to remember her. She pocketed her change, then stepped aside to let three men in football jerseys get to the bar: they seemed well-acquainted with their server.

Only a few people were at their early evening pints; at a big table in the front window, two couples were deep in conversation. Aventurine turned and made her way toward the back past the archway, where she found Genevieve seated back to the wall, a shandy and a bag of crisps before her on the table.

"Oh, hello," Genevieve greeted her cheerfully. "Come join me." A slight note of surprise, as though they had not seen each other only a few hours previous, as though she had not ordered Aventurine to this appointment.

She had changed her appearance subtly. The hat was gone, and her iron-grey hair was brushed to the side, with a small flip. She wore lipstick, some of which had rubbed off in a kiss on the rim of her glass. For a moment Avi started: she had never seen Genevieve wearing lipstick, and it was jarring. She might have been someone else entirely.

"How have you been keeping? And your family?"

The footballers, despite the darkness and the falling temperatures, had taken their pints out to the rear garden. The door banged behind them ushering in a wave of cool air. Genevieve still wore her coat.

Vaguely disoriented, Aventurine slid out a chair and settled into it. She set her pint down: the Fox, she had been happy to see, was not pale at all. A rather amber, foxy color.

"I'm well," she said cautiously. "They're well."

"And have you heard from your younger sister's father today?"

It took her a moment.

"No. I'm wondering whether to call him later."

Genevieve's eyes narrowed slightly. Her smile remained friendly, curious. "Perhaps you should just drop by. What do you think? I'm sure you have a lot to tell him, much more than you could get through in just a phone call."

Aventurine wondered whether she could remember how to get back to his little semi-detached house in the village, the name of which escaped her. She nodded, took a drink of the pint.

"Would you like a crisp?" Genevieve pushed the packet toward her with a finger. "I thought I was feeling a bit peckish, but now I find I don't really like the taste."

This woman, who could cook better than anyone Aventurine had ever met—having learned from her French mother as a child—didn't like the taste of crisps. She looked at the packet. Cheese and onion. Not Aventurine's favorite, either.

Genevieve shrugged in a way that seemed startlingly French. "This was the kind that seemed most popular on the rack."

Avi nodded. Of course. Choose the most popular thing. It was all part of the game of looking like everyone else, acting like everyone else. She was learning, and there was no one better to learn from.

"I'm surprised this pub isn't more crowded," Genevieve continued conversationally, looking around. More people were coming in from the street. They were standing a couple thick at parts of the bar. Someone got out darts. "More noisy."

More noise meant less chance of being overheard. Gratifyingly, at that moment someone laughed loudly from the bar. More people piled in from the street, and there were loud greetings all around.

"Can we stop talking in code now?"

Genevieve glared over the rim of her glass. Despite the lipstick stain, very little of the shandy appeared to have been drunk.

"You'd never make it in the service."

"We're not in the service."

Another bark of laughter from the bar, answered by high peals from a woman.

Genevieve waited until two more men banged out through the rear door, then leaned slightly closer, smiling as though having to be heard over the noise was just something to be put up with, rather than something to be desired.

"This is a long game, Aventurine."

Aventurine looked down, chastened. She wasn't sure what game Genevieve referred to, but obviously she was supposed to know.

"It took a couple of days for Neil to be found. It took a while longer for him to be properly identified. No one has made a connection between him and you, but that doesn't mean they won't. So you need to be more careful."

"Forever?"

Genevieve picked up the crisp packet and made a moue of distaste, examining the ingredient label on the back. "If need be." She let out a barely audible sigh, still frowning at the packet. "You made a grave error in coming back here, Aventurine."

To Lincoln?

Avi swore the old woman could read minds. *Her* mind.

"Don't be obtuse, Aventurine. It's not attractive. You shouldn't have come back to England at all, at least until more time had passed. A year, minimum."

How to explain? "I couldn't write at home—"

"And have you written here?"

The words were knives, stabbing, stabbing. Aventurine closed her eyes tightly.

After a moment, the slightest of touches on her sleeve.

"I'm sorry. I shouldn't have said that."

Shaken, Aventurine opened her eyes again and picked up her pint. It suddenly tasted sour and unpleasant, and she was irrationally furious with Genevieve for ruining a perfectly good beer. She took another long drink anyway, out of spite.

The proprietor appeared, looked outside into the darkness, and seemed satisfied with what he saw. Genevieve gave him a resplendent smile.

"How are you ladies this evening?" he asked, dusting off his hands.

"Never better," Genevieve said. "Just catching up, thank you."

He greeted some other guests on his way back to the bar. Another couple came to take the table across from them. They set their drinks down, and promptly laced their fingers together, leaning in close.

"You're still in danger, Aventurine," Genevieve said at last, her voice low. "And as long as you are, so are your sister and your nephew. You need to remember that."

Still Genevieve's hooded eyes took in the room, much as though she were trying to find someone. It was growing more crowded as the evening drew on,

"Where is your nephew?" Did she hesitate slightly over that last word, or had Aventurine just imagined it? "Or perhaps the question should be—*how* is he?"

There was always the question of how much Genevieve knew. More than she let on, of course—or perhaps less, but giving the impression of more. Aventurine shook her head. "He's still—remote." It was difficult to think of any other word for Paul. She picked up the menu, but the words made no sense to her. "Hurting. He's in Italy right now. Milan."

"With Lance?"

"With Lance."

The old woman's gaze softened, but only for a moment. "Perhaps that's what he needs. The company of someone who isn't connected to his father and—his mother."

This time Aventurine was certain she had not imagined the hesitation. Genevieve wasn't looking at her, but rather inspecting the tiny menu. Avi was surprised at her reaction, and was grateful for Genevieve's downcast eyes. A sharp wince, a slight intake of breath: she had never told the old woman about them, about their tangled relationship, but of course Genevieve knew. Somehow she knew. Micheline would never have told her without telling Aventurine, but Paul was the wildcard. Perhaps he had, in the depths of his anger and sense of betrayal, told her—those two did have that peculiar bond.

"Perhaps." With some effort, Avi kept her voice non-committal.

"And your sister—where is she?"

"Back at home in Connecticut. She's still floundering, too." Aventurine set the menu aside and lifted her glass. The knot in her chest tightened painfully, as it always did, when she thought of her twin and her impossible grief.

They left the pub once Aventurine's glass was drained; it was beginning to warm in there, what with the number of people who had appeared seemingly out of nowhere on a weeknight. Avi's head was spinning.

"Walk," Genevieve ordered. "Concentrate. No public drunkenness."

"I'm not drunk."

"You're a lightweight, and you always have been." The old woman sighed, pulling the door closed behind them, muffling the noise of the drinkers. "Let's go round to the Pool for a bit. Slowly, as though we have no worries in the world. Look interested in the docks."

"It's dark."

"That's why they invented street lights."

Aventurine paused to button up her jacket. "Are you developing a sense of humor?"

"Never," Genevieve retorted. "Those are dangerous, too." But as they passed by a lighted window, there appeared to be a glint in her eye.

They turned away from the high street, then turned again. There indeed was Brayford Pool, and snugged up to the docks were a few hardy boats not yet tucked away for overwintering. Power boats, not sailboats, Avi was glad to see: she could probably make it through the rest of her life not seeing another sailboat, and that would be fine. For a while they were silent, Aventurine following her companion's lead as they ambled up to cross the bridge. Ahead the river ran beneath a black-and-white building straddling an archway.

"They call this the Glory Hole," Genevieve said. "Though the smell suggests other names."

They took the stairs and turned, Avi realized, back onto the high street. She recognized some of the shops she had passed earlier. "What was that in aid of?" she demanded. "We could have just gone straight from the pub."

"Sightseeing," the old woman said genially. "Or practicing evasive maneuvers, should you ever need them." She had her hands tucked in her pockets. "Keep looking at things."

Nearly all the shops were buttoned up for the evening, even the enormous Boots. At a stationery shop, they paused to examine the window displays, done in autumn colors, all browns and oranges, yellows and reds. Aventurine sighed, looking at the paper she would never use, especially if she never broke through this writer's block.

"Point at something, and don't look up," Genevieve said. "We're right under a security camera."

"One that's not broken?" Avi pointed to a display of fountain pens, surrounded by bottles of inks in autumnal colors.

"If it is, another one is certain to pick us up along here. So look interested in things."

"You keep saying that."

"I'm a professional."

"Isn't this all overkill?"

Genevieve leaned closer to the window, examining the pens. "Aventurine, *someone* is responsible for all of this: the murder. The disappearance. The ransacking of Nicola's house. We don't yet know what we're dealing with. Trust me."

Trust her?

Aventurine swallowed. "So… what are we going to do about Nicola's cottage?"

Genevieve, apparently having examined the stationery enough, turned and led the way along the pavement. She passed the next shop, then the second, but then turned back to the display—gloves and hats, this time, before answering. "We're not going to do anything."

"What do you mean?"

"We report nothing. We tell no one."

Something about this seemed inherently wrong to Aventurine, though she couldn't quite formulate her objections. She stared at the old woman, until nudged to examine a basket full of hats.

"But—Henry—"

"Can he keep a secret?"

"Genevieve, he's terrified. He's trying not to let on right now, but this is his daughter, and she's been missing for at least four days."

"But can he keep a secret?" She turned and walked on slowly, the perfect picture of a casual Sunday evening stroll.

"What if he goes over there? What if he finds that mess?" Aventurine turned away from the gloves, but Genevieve had already moved on. She hurried to catch up. "It will wreck him. And you know he'll just call the police again, to report *this*. I mean, it's Henry. He's probably never done a thing wrong in his life. He seems to be a morally upright citizen. I bet he's never even crossed the street against the light." She looked up at the sky beyond the streetlights, and could see nothing. "He doesn't have the cause to be wary of the police that we have. That *I* have."

Genevieve nodded in approval. "You're learning." She tucked her hands into the pockets of her coat once again. The heels of her boots—she was wearing boots with heels?—clicked on the pavement.

"We've got to warn him. We've got to tell him to say nothing."

"No snap decisions. We'll have to feel him out." Again the nod, but smaller this time. There was the crease of a frown between her brows. "Call him. Tell him we'll be to his house in the morning."

"But—how?"

The look Genevieve cast was scathing. "You've rented cars before. Do it again. First thing in the morning. Thanks to your thoughtless blunders, the police already know you're here, and you told the chief inspector that you're researching. So rent a car to do research."

She stopped, turned, and lifted a hand as though bidding Aventurine goodbye, no doubt for the benefit of the cameras. "Katherine Swynford, is it? We can take a day trip to Kettlethorpe, then."

Aventurine also raised a hand, and half-wondered peevishly what Genevieve would do if she leaned in to kiss the old woman, for the surveillance tapes. But she didn't quite dare. "Where will I meet you?"

But the old woman was gone, clicking back down the street, without answering.

Sixteen

The car rental place opened at nine in the morning, and Aventurine called first thing. She was able to hire a Renault—someone had just that moment canceled—and the representative, when she asked for directions, told her they'd drop the car off for her, in the lot behind the hotel. Thus she was waiting in the doorway when the car arrived, and the agent proffered the remainder of the registration paperwork. Then the woman handed off the key, popped open her umbrella, and disappeared into the gloomy day.

Service. Avi was impressed.

I have the car, she texted. *At the hotel.*

Tesco. Wragby Road. Delete this conversation. And all the others.

Aventurine did as she was told. She wondered as she climbed into the car and slung her bag onto the passenger seat just how much Genevieve really knew about cell phones. Surely there were ways for electronics experts to trace texts, even those that were deleted. Then again, if someone not an expert—someone like DCI Burroughs, for example—were to merely open the phone and look at it, they'd see nothing. Perhaps it was only a time-buying exercise, as so many of Genevieve's exercises were.

It wasn't until she pulled out into traffic, after having found the Tesco on the Sat-Nav, that she realized how far she had been subsumed into the paranoiac world of the old spy. There was probably nothing to worry about. DCI Burroughs would not be even vaguely interested in her phone. No one would care that she was meeting Genevieve in little pubs in Lincoln—or in food markets, for that matter. His interview had been merely routine, eliminating extraneous information. That was all. She had to get a grip, or pretty soon she'd be wanting fifteen dead bolt locks on her hotel room door.

Still, Aventurine couldn't shake the anxiety. She slowed at an intersection, scanned for and found the traffic camera, and moved forward only after all the other cars had passed.

She found Genevieve waiting at the bus stop before the Tesco, holding a couple of carrier bags. She had barely braked to a stop before the other woman was in the car, the bags in the rear seat.

"Straight to Henry Hallsey's," she ordered. "Did you get his address last night?"

Avi had, and had already programmed it into the Sat-Nav. She pulled away from the curb. "What did you buy?"

"Enough to make it look as though it were a legitimate trip to the market," Genevieve countered.

They left the car park and headed northeast. At first Aventurine recognized nothing of the route, but then a couple of shop fronts and a petrol station stirred something in her memory. Of course, it had been the middle of the night when she'd driven in this direction last, and then had taken the cab back into Lincoln the next morning. She bit her lip, wishing the Sat-Nav voice wasn't such a cross between mechanical and smarmy.

She cast a glance over at her companion every once in a while, but Genevieve was by turns looking out the window, and leaning back with her eyes closed.

"Where did you stay last night?"

She half-smiled, her eyes still closed. "The flat. A sweet little nondescript flat in the middle of the city. Mary Wentworth's flat."

Genevieve spoke as though Aventurine should know the name.

"Who is Mary Wentworth?"

"*I* am Mary Wentworth."

Something rang a bell in Avi's memory. "Mary was your sister's name."

"But Wentworth wasn't."

She was being deliberately frustrating. Not for the first time did Aventurine wonder whether it was simply a lifetime of working for the government that made this behavior second nature—hell, first nature by now—or whether Genevieve simply enjoyed it. Most likely, a combination of both. One of those vicious cycles, as it were. Avi sighed, a pronounced, annoyed sound. If anything, Genevieve's little smile deepened in her lined face.

"So how do I introduce you to Henry?"

"Oh, play it by ear. Or look for my signal. You'll know. But should you need to introduce me to your policeman, or even if you only have to mention my name, it's Mary. Easy enough, don't you think? A nice, old-fashioned, unassuming name."

At last they pulled up in front of Henry's house, bumping up on the grass verge before the low stone wall. The door opened as they approached. Henry was in his shirtsleeves, his face grave and grey.

"Still no word?"

It had become their accustomed greeting. Today made how many days? Aventurine was beginning to lose count.

"Nothing," he said. He held the door for them both, then closed it behind them before turning. He seemed unconcerned that Aventurine was not alone.

"Henry, this is my friend—" Aventurine stumbled.

"Mary," Genevieve supplied. She held out the hand not holding the carrier bags. "Mary Wentworth. And you're Henry—I'm glad to meet you at last. Aventurine has told me so much about you."

His blue eyes slid between them, a slight frown between his brows. "I—don't know how. I've only known Aventurine for a few days." He sighed. "Though it feels like longer."

It did feel like longer, to Aventurine, too; but she could imagine that the past several days had been several lifetimes for Henry.

"We have something to tell you, and I didn't want to go into it on the phone last night."

Again the glance, and Avi was sorry she'd brought up the topic in just that way. "Nicola. Have you heard from her?" He paused, a veined hand on his chest. "No, that doesn't make sense. You've never met her. There'd be no reason for her to contact you." Another pause, his throat working painfully. "The police–have they—"

Aventurine moved quickly to Henry's side, laying a hand on his arm. He held himself stiffly, and she could feel the tension running through him, almost hear it. "No. Nothing like that. Nothing at all like that."

"We'd better sit down and talk this through," Genevieve said. "But first—is your kitchen through here, Mr. Hallsey?" She motioned with the bags. "I'll just take these through, shall I? And make some tea."

Henry barely paid her any heed as she disappeared through the doorway. He allowed Aventurine to lead him to the sofa, on which he sat awkwardly, like an automaton of sorts. "I keep checking for messages from her," he said, his voice barely above a whisper. "At the same time I don't quite dare look at the phone—what if the police call? And when I dialed her number, all I kept getting was the voice mailbox—but now I get a recording saying the mailbox is full."

Aventurine wondered how many times he had dialed the number. Too many. He was looking worse every time she saw him.

"Are you on the rota for the Cathedral today?" she asked.

He held up his shaking hands. "I am, but I keep thinking I should call out. I don't know how I can walk around pointing out Bishop Grosseteste and the Imp and Katherine Swynford as though nothing is happening. As though I'm not living in this nightmare."

"You can do the tours by rote, I imagine," she said encouragingly.

"But I can't think," he protested helplessly. "I can't answer questions from visitors, because it's like I don't hear them, like I don't understand the words." He lifted his blue eyes, which were filmy, to meet her gaze. "I feel like I'm going crazy, Aventurine."

Genevieve returned, carrying three steaming mugs by their

handles. "Let me just set these down. I couldn't find a tray. I'll have to go back for milk and sugar." She cast a quick glare at Aventurine and disappeared again.

Henry looked down into his black tea and grimaced. "Who is that woman?"

What to say? *Play it by ear,* Genevieve had said, and had chosen the pseudonym. Obviously, the story had to be a bit sparse in details.

"A friend," Aventurine said carefully. "I hadn't seen her in a long time before I ran into her in Lincoln yesterday." She shifted uncomfortably on the sofa. "I'm sorry, Henry. I should have asked you first, but I told her about Nicola. I told her how worried you are."

Genevieve bustled back in, and set the milk and sugar on the coffee table before them, pushing aside a book. Henry automatically took the proffered spoon and stirred in a lump of demerara sugar, a dash of milk. His hands were still shaking; the spoon clinked loudly against the side of the mug. Genevieve sat across from them in the easy chair, and slewed another warning look at Avi.

"Tell him, Aventurine," she ordered. "Tell Mr. Hallsey about what you saw on the hotel terrace."

Her meaning was clear.

But Aventurine's eye had caught on the book, a kind usually referred to as a bodice-ripper. The lurid illustration, the author name at the bottom of the cover: *N. B. Hallsey.* She felt her jaw drop, and reached for the book. *A writer courting insanity.* Of course.

"This book—"

Henry barely glanced at it. "One of Nicola's. Women's literature, I guess people call it. She's published a handful, even though they don't make her much money in royalties."

Aventurine's breath came out in a whoosh. "Of course. She writes books. Nicola writes books." Holding this one in her hand, she couldn't help but think that the whole situation was becoming more and more weird by the moment with every scrap of information she gleaned about Nicola.

Henry nodded, momentarily distracted. He levered himself from the sofa and moved to a small bookshelf in the corner. When he returned, he fanned out a selection of books on the table, all with similar covers.

"You mentioned to me that Nicola wrote books when she's not working," Avi said slowly. "But you never went into detail."

"I've been worried about other things, Aventurine," Henry pointed out stiffly.

Flushing, Aventurine leaned forward and took the top book into her hand. This one a paperback: she scanned the cover quickly, then opened to the front matter. Finally she flipped to the back cover, where she found a photograph of the author. Definitely Nicola. And wearing the same hat Avi had seen on the mystery woman nearly a week ago.

Silently she handed the book to Genevieve, who leaned forward. "Yes. She definitely resembles you. And your sister."

"I just don't understand it," Henry cut in. He could have been referring to the photograph, their resemblance, the disappearance. "But you haven't told me what you saw on the terrace."

Aventurine nodded and cleared her throat. "I think I might have seen Nicola. Before she disappeared."

Henry turned to face her, his face tightening. "What? Why haven't you said something? *Before* she disappeared?"

"I *thought* I might have." Aventurine repeated. She held up a helpless hand. "But I didn't really know. I saw a woman—wearing a hat and sunglasses, having an argument in the beer garden behind the hotel pub with a man." She shivered again, reliving her impression. "She ran off, and I tried to slow him down when he followed."

"A man?"

Again she held up the hand. "I never saw her full face, only his. But—the next day, Henry, I saw the same woman getting into a car. Wearing the hat." Then again, stronger, "The *hat.*"

Both Henry and Genevieve looked up at her tone.

"She was wearing it. The woman in the beer garden at the hotel. *I recognize the hat.*"

"But not the face," Genevieve probed.

"She rushed by so quickly. She was wearing oversized sunglasses—it was the last really nice afternoon. I didn't see her eyes, or her hair, for the most part. But I saw the hat, first from above, from the window of my room, and then when I went downstairs for dinner. And I saw it again, when she got into that car below the castle wall."

"It could be coincidence."

Aventurine picked up a second book and turned it over to the picture. "But that's unlikely. Very unlikely."

"You saw her," Henry interrupted.

"Yes." Aventurine met Genevieve's speculative glance with defiance. "I'm certain now that I did. On Wednesday afternoon, after I got back from the Cathedral."

"The afternoon we met. You saw my daughter."

"But I didn't know she was your daughter." Again Aventurine went through the story of the woman, the man, and her feeble attempt to foil the pursuit. "I just knew the situation made me uncomfortable, that the man was trying to force something onto the woman, and I had to help her resist, or escape, if I could." She pressed her hands to her hot cheeks. "I thought it might have been something personal, a relationship issue—and I've had a relationship like that before, so I felt I had to intervene somehow."

"Mr. Hallsey," Genevieve broke in. "Please think for a moment. Is there anyone you know of that Nicola is involved with who matches Aventurine's description? Anyone she might have had a contentious relationship with?"

Henry looked from one to the other, and then abruptly stood and crossed to the front window, where he looked out into the grey and damp morning. He kept his back to them, and when Aventurine made a move to go to him, Genevieve put out a hand to stop her.

"I just don't know," he said at last, not turning around. His voice was low, almost muffled. "She was engaged once, not long after she left university. Justin, I think his name was. And then they broke it off. I don't know the ins and outs of it, because Nicola was very private about the whole thing. Last I knew he had married someone else and emigrated to Canada."

"Justin. What was his last name, can you remember?" Genevieve was frowning. No doubt she would be able to pull a few strings and find out whether this Justin was still in Canada. "And do you remember what he looked like?"

"Fisher. Justin Fisher." Quickly Henry crossed to the side table and pulled out a drawer. He extracted a photo and set it in front of them, before returning to the window, his shoulders slumped.

A photograph of a much-younger Nicola, in her university gown. Behind her, but with a light hand on her shoulder, stood a tall young blond man.

"This is definitely not the person I saw with her," Aventurine said. It would have been far too much of a coincidence had it been, and she really didn't believe in coincidences. Did she? She looked into Nicola's younger face. Though it would have made things much easier to have a name, at least.

"And boyfriends? Girlfriends?" Genevieve asked. "Has she had anyone in particular since?"

Henry leaned his forehead into his hand. "She's had dates."

A memory struck Aventurine. "You said something to me when we first spoke of her not keeping the breakfast date. At the tea shop. You said you were wary of going over to her place after she didn't appear on Thursday, in case she'd had a date, and he was still there."

He did not lift his head from his hand. Outside, a single ray of sunlight broke through the clouds, making obvious the need to wash the window.

"She had mentioned a—new person," he said slowly. "Someone she'd met through work." Slowly he turned to look back at them, his expression agonized. "I didn't want to pry. After all, I know she must have been lonely, what with only her old father to go out to breakfast with every week. I know she wanted a—family. A husband, some kids." He came back to the sofa and sank into it, his hands twisting. "I want her to be happy."

"But you don't know who this new person could be?" Genevieve pressed.

"No. I don't think it had progressed far. A couple of dates." He lifted his filmy eyes to look into Avi's face. "You don't think that man you saw—that he was her new person?"

"It could have been." Aventurine closed her eyes and tried to recall the source of her discomfort with the scene that had played out before her. The familiarity of the hand on the arm, the reaching for the hat. The way the woman—Nicola—had repeated her *no*, and the man had still persisted. Avi shuddered now, just thinking of it. "But she—Nicola, if it was Nicola—"

"—And you think it was," Henry interjected.

"She just didn't seem comfortable with their interaction. Whatever he was demanding of her, she felt distinctly uncomfortable about. And he just kept pushing, like he could *make* her do what he wanted."

"How do you know that?" Genevieve asked. "You speak in certainties."

"She pulled away from him and said no and tried to leave," Avi said, her voice rising slightly. "He tried to stop her."

"Did he hurt her?" Henry demanded.

"He didn't have the chance."

"And you saw her the next day."

"I saw her hat," Aventurine corrected. "But it was the same hat." She flipped the book to the back cover once again and jabbed at the author photograph with a finger. "It was *this* hat."

"Tell me again," Henry said, his voice raw. "She got into a car."

"Willingly. A silver car. It was the car of someone she knew, someone she expected to be there. She got out of a taxi, then got into this car, and they drove away."

"She expected the driver," Genevieve said. "They obviously planned to meet."

"She was wearing the same clothes." The memory hit Aventurine hard. "The same dress and the same jacket as the previous day. She never changed her clothes."

"So she probably never went home."

They fell silent. Aventurine rubbed her eyes, trying to make sense of everything, but the puzzle pieces simply wouldn't fit together. There were too many holes. Too many missing pieces of information. She bit her lower lip.

Nicola, she thought. *What had happened? Where had she gone?*

Seventeen

"Drive to Kettlethorpe," Genevieve ordered when they left Henry, preparing as he was to go in to the Cathedral for the afternoon. "We need to make your renting this car seem as normal as can be. And you said to your chief inspector that you were researching Katherine Swynford."

"He's not my chief inspector. And how do you know what I said to him?"

She glanced over at Avi without answering.

Aventurine programmed the address of the church in Kettlethorpe into the Sat-Nav, and they drove on in silence. Avi was feeling headachy, and couldn't decide whether it was the weather, or the anxiety. The mystery of Nicola Hallsey—the title of a Nancy Drew book if ever there was one—twisted over and over in her tangled thoughts, each bit of information getting caught on yet another. None of it made any sense. And—a new thought—what did any of this have to do with the dead woman from the Old Bishop's Palace?

"Concentrate on your driving," Genevieve commanded. "You're drifting over the centerline. Don't draw attention to yourself."

The proverbial last straw. "Look," Aventurine said shortly. "We're fine. Everything is fine, *Mary Wentworth*. There's no way DCI Burroughs knows anything about what happened on the York walls. There's no way for him to connect me to that night. There's no reason for you to be so God-damned paranoid."

105

"Do you remember my telling you about Commander Smith?" Genevieve asked mildly. It sounded like a change of topic, but Aventurine knew better. She shot a glare at the old woman.

"Watch the road," Genevieve reminded her. More sternly. "I am an old woman, Aventurine, but I have no wish to die at this point in a car wreck."

The rental car was small, the power steering responsive—so much so that it felt like driving a go-kart. Of course, Avi had only driven a go-kart once before, at a fair with Paul, when he was nine or ten; he'd beaten her handily in their race. Now, smarting from Genevieve's criticism of her driving, she glanced at the speedometer and lifted her foot from the gas.

"What about Commander Smith?"

Genevieve was watching traffic out the window. She occasionally shifted her glance to the wide mirror. "You need to be aware, Aventurine," she said. "Everything you do and everything you say has the capacity, in the world, to affect something else. Frequently not in a good way. Commander Smith taught me that when I was sixteen."

"And you still live by it." Avi's voice was rife with sarcasm.

"Of course I do."

"Even though the war has been over for decades."

The silver brows lifted. "Which war, Aventurine?"

The question left Avi speechless, which no doubt Genevieve knew it would.

"Meanwhile, you're following too close to that car."

Aventurine resisted the urge to slam on the brakes. "Do you want to drive?"

"Of course not. I'm too old for that idiocy." Genevieve sighed. "And I'm too old to go without my luncheon, either. There's a nice little inn not too far from the church in Kettlethorpe. Let's stop there for a bite, shall we?"

Despite complaining of hunger, Genevieve only ordered a scone and tea. Aventurine plumped for the steak and ale pie—she could never resist steak and ale pie.

"What did you do with the groceries?" she asked after the first few bites. "Whatever did you buy, anyway?"

"A few staples for your friend," Genevieve replied. "Some milk, more tea, a few prepared meals. I left them in his refrigerator. I rather suspected that he hadn't been to the shops for a bit, in his preoccupation, and I was right."

Aventurine let out an enormous sigh. The queen of the passive-aggressive barb, Genevieve was, when she wanted to be. *Your friend.* Aventurine hadn't been the one to think of Henry's well-being, although she'd been with him, more or less, since they'd met on Wednesday.

"I put out his rubbish for the bin man, too," Genevieve continued, smirking pointedly. She knew she was being passive-aggressive, and she knew Avi knew. "I noticed all his neighbors had left theirs out for collection this morning."

"I'm sorry," Avi said sharply. "I'm sorry I'm such a bad friend. I'm sorry I'm not a God-damned spy. Commander Smith would have thrown me out on my ear ages ago."

The old woman laughed and patted her hand. "I'm sorry you're so easy to annoy this afternoon."

"Go to hell."

They ate in silence for a while, Genevieve smiling to herself, Avi feeling peeved and resentful. The headache was returning. She rather hoped the cup of coffee, swirling with cream, would push it back.

"You seem to be having no end of fun needling me today," Aventurine said at last. "And the worst part is that I'm putting up with it only because, as you keep pointing out to me, you're an old woman."

The old woman sipped her tea.

"And I'm supposed to be writing an article about you. And writing your biography."

The teacup empty, Genevieve peered at the leaves before setting it in its saucer delicately. "You could, you know, spend this time interviewing me. Asking me questions? Surely you haven't forgotten how to do that." Her finely arched brows lifted in a challenge.

"All right." Avi looked down into her own coffee cup with distaste. Good thing it wasn't tea, because the leaves, for her, would probably spell disaster. What she really wanted was to knock back a pint. Or two. But she knew not to order one while responsible for the driving, especially on the wrong side of the road. "First question, then. What the hell are you doing in Lincoln?"

"A lovely Cathedral city, isn't it?"

Aventurine cocked her head and narrowed her eyes. "Been to the Cathedral lately, have you?" She raised her own eyebrows. "No. I didn't think so. You came to Nicola Hallsey's cottage. That's where you came. So tell me: what interests you about Nicola?"

Genevieve poured the last of the tea from the blue pot, then held it aloft to catch the eye of the proprietress. The woman came to collect it, then a few moments later, returned with it refilled. Once she had regained her position behind the bar, Genevieve turned back to Aventurine. "I think the real question is: what interests *you* about her?"

"I know her father. She's missing. He's worried. She looks like me. I might have been the last person to see her before she disappeared. Something like that?" Aventurine took up a forkful of mash, slid it through the pool of gravy, and ate it. "But you forget. I'm asking the questions here."

Genevieve held up her hands. Today she was dressed in a houndstooth jacket over a butter-yellow jumper, with grey slacks. The clothing lent her a slightly different air. Slightly *Mary*, Aventurine thought wryly. The woman was a chameleon, had in fact been a professional chameleon all her life. Since the age of sixteen, if not before. "Ask away."

"I've already asked. Why are you here?"

Another long pause.

"I really am not supposed to tell you this," she said at last.

Even that admission, Avi thought, was suspect. Designed, perhaps, to give her a false sense of being trusted with secret information. After all this time, she knew that Genevieve, if she truly wasn't supposed to tell her something, *wouldn't tell her.*

"Go on," Aventurine urged.

"I'm working."

"You're retired."

Genevieve groaned. "I can go where other people can't."

"Other agents."

"Don't use that terminology. I'm not on any official payroll. I'm simply an old woman, doddering, perhaps, who has come to have a look around Lincoln and the surrounds."

"As Mary Wentworth."

Again with the sardonic expression: but this time, Genevieve opened her purse—she was carrying a purse?—and brought out her wallet. She flipped that open, to her NHS card. Her bank card.

Mary Wentworth's NHS card. Mary Wentworth's bank card.

"I *am* Mary Wentworth."

"Fine." Aventurine slumped back. The caffeine wasn't doing a damned thing for her headache. "What's *Mary Wentworth* doing in Lincoln? And what's Mary Wentworth's interest in Nicola Hallsey?"

"It's rather complicated," Genevieve said demurely.

"Try me."

More tea. "We've had word that there would be an action against the Swynford Jewel," Genevieve announced with as much concern as she might have had announcing the inn was out of mushy peas to go with the pie.

The Swynford Jewel.

Aventurine remembered how the light had struck it, in its velvet-lined case in the Medieval Library, causing the red stone to glow in its gold setting like something otherworldly. How she had talked to the hovering librarian, noted the cameras. The librarian had said there were alarms as well.

Cameras.

Alarms.

"Nicola Hallsey works for a security company," she said slowly.

Genevieve smiled, a proud teacher of a slow student.

"But she's missing. And the jewel is still there." The headache was getting worse. "I don't understand." Avi looked up. "And this isn't your line, anyway. This isn't the kind of business you've been in—for the government."

Genevieve looked away delicately, lifting her teacup to her lips. "Let's just say I'm doing a favor for someone."

"Someone calling in markers?"

"Don't be crass, Aventurine. It doesn't suit you." Another sip. That meant yes. Unless it didn't.

"But Nicola?"

Genevieve set aside her tea and lifted the last bite of scone to her mouth. She wiped her lips daintily with the napkin. "Don't you think it odd that information received says that there might be a move against the jewel, and suddenly someone from the security company hired to keep it safe should go missing at the same time?"

"But what's the connection? And what about the woman at the Old Bishop's Palace? Where does she fit in?"

"Perhaps that's what I'm supposed to find out." She lifted a hand, and the proprietress appeared promptly with the bill and the reader.

"I'll get this," Aventurine said, reaching for her bag.

"I've already got the card out," said Mary. "It's my treat, dear."

"It's going to be distressing for them when the charges are refused."

Genevieve waved that away. "Oh, the charge went through well enough. Weren't you paying attention?"

They walked along the road toward the church of St. Peter and St. Paul, which the innkeeper had insisted was only a short distance away. No doubt Genevieve was missing her daily constitutional around the York city walls.

"I'll never understand how any of this works," Avi moaned.

"I spent the entire journey here explaining how you need to be aware, to not draw attention to yourself. Do you think I'd contravene all that and attempt to pay with a fraudulent card? I don't want the police to take notice of me, either."

"But—you're working with the police."

"Did I say that?"

Even in the brisk wind, Aventurine could feel her face warm at the rebuke. "No, but I assumed—"

"Don't assume, Aventurine. There are wheels within wheels, as they say, especially within sometimes-competing agencies."

"You told me not to use that language."

"I'm not you. And I know for whom I'm working—or *not* working, as the case may be—and for whom I most definitely am not. Your DCI Burroughs is someone I am best off steering well clear of."

Aventurine looked down along the road, blinking against the wind. Trees grew up on the verge to her left, while on the right, autumn-barren fields stretched away. Again she sighed. Such an awkward relationship she'd developed with the old witch over time. She touched the aventurine bracelet on her left wrist with the fingers of her other hand. She supposed she loved Genevieve, but she had long ago given up believing that the feeling might be reciprocated. Genevieve might bear her a certain fondness—and probably did— and might even, sometimes, enjoy her company. But to the old spy, everyone was a pawn in the game, to move and to use to further her own ends. Avi might have believed—might have even hoped— that Genevieve had come from York to help her with the puzzle of the missing doppelganger, but once again, it had been made fairly obvious that the old woman had her own agenda. She *always* had her own agenda.

"Why are we even here?" she asked at last, aware of the vague petulance in her own voice.

"In Kettlethorpe?" Genevieve's hands, without her usual blackthorn stick, hung at her sides as she walked, but her steady cadence had not changed. She still marched along briskly enough to make Avi's thighs burn, trying to keep up. "Because you're researching. And you needed to hire a car to research." She winked. "That makes it tax deductible, you know."

"*You* needed me to hire a car to get to Henry. I assume it was because you didn't want to have taxi drivers remember us, and the bus service is a bit sparse to plan your day around."

"But now you have logged the mileage to Kettlethorpe, you've eaten in an inn there, and should your friend the chief inspector ask around, you have been here."

"So cover. I'm establishing cover."

They came to the intersection with the Kettlethorpe Road, and after a moment's thought, Genevieve indicated the right turn. Fields now at either hand, but up ahead, they could see the village.

"What if," Aventurine asked slowly, "Burroughs asks about my companion?"

"Mary?" Genevieve fluttered a hand. "She's just an old friend with a soft spot for Katherine Swynford. Nice old bird. It's probably a kindness that you're taking her around with you. She probably doesn't get out much."

It was enough to make her head spin. "What if he wants to interview you?"

Now Genevieve leaned in, frowning. "I'm sorry—can you repeat that? I didn't catch what you said."

Her voice had changed. It was a bit quavery. Her eyes, though, held Avi's with a kind of gleam.

"You love this, don't you?"

"I miss it," the old woman said. "I spent most of my life pitting myself against circumstances, and figuring out ways to defeat them. There was only one circumstance I could not defeat, but I did my best with the hand I was holding."

"Honoré."

Was that a spasm of pain that crossed her features? It was gone too quickly for Aventurine to be certain.

"We won't talk about that right now, if you don't mind."

They wouldn't talk about it now even if she *did*, the tone said.

They passed the entrance to the village hall on the left, and continued on to the lychgate. *Death unto Life,* the carving over read announced, or warned. So Medievally cheerful, Aventurine supposed. An alley of shrubbery led through the graveyard to the blocky tower of St. Peter's and St. Paul's.

"I thought the church would be older," Aventurine mused.

"Victorian. Pretending to be Norman, at least in the tower." Genevieve did not sound at all impressed. "Sometimes I swear those Victorians didn't have an original bone in their bodies."

They made their way along the alley toward the great black door. It was difficult to make out the gravestones on either side of the greenery, but at least the shrubs served as a windbreak. Avi blew on her cold hands. Genevieve, of course, had drawn on supple leather gloves.

"There was an earlier church here, on the side," the old woman continued amiably.

Aventurine cast her a glance.

"Don't look at me with that goggle-eyed surprise. I looked it up online. I'm supposed to have an interest in everything Swynfordian."

"Mary is."

"*I'm Mary.* You should have an interest, too, since you expressed one to your DCI." She sighed, an exaggerated sound. "In any case, this would not have been the church the Swynfords would have attended. There's not much of that. A stone carving, and that's pretty much it." They reached the door, all decoratively and ornately carved. Genevieve sighed again. "So Victorian," she complained. "You know people actually collect Victoriana? I can't quite understand it. It's all so *stylized.* So *maudlin.*" She sounded as though she wanted to spit.

Aventurine added *Victoriana* to the endless list of things she had to further investigate. Perhaps she'd collect some of it, too, she thought meanly, the more stylized and maudlin the better. If only to piss *Mary* off.

They turned to the side, and circled back in among the graves. "What are we looking for here?" Aventurine asked. She shoved her own hands into her pockets now; they were icy, and the wind outside the shelter of the alleyway had grown stronger. Her cheeks, too, felt like ice. Other than the gloves, Genevieve seemed to have made no further allowances for the weather, and seemed calmly unaffected. Even her iron-grey hair seemed unruffled.

"The gateway to the Swynford estate," Genevieve said. "That's about the only thing left from the Medieval building, the one Katherine would have known. The grounds and new manor house are in private hands. Though the moat was cleaned out with a handful of taxpayer pence recently, it's been discovered."

"More Katherine. Are you trying to make me write about her?" *The Badass Bitches of Britain.* Was this particular one reading her mind?

"Far be it for me to tell you what to write."

"So again, what you're telling me is that this entire visit is all about performance," Aventurine said slowly, her cold hand caressing the curve of a colder stone. Under her fingers the lichen was damp and rough.

"You never know who your audience is." It was a sideways agreement, but an agreement all the same. Genevieve was also studying the worn carving of a stone, further along. "'Tell the truth, but tell it slant,' your girl Emily Dickinson wrote. Besides. You never know. You might need information about our Katherine Swynford for a project. Later."

"Later," Avi scoffed. Her fingertips now felt strangely dry and chalky. "I can't even finish the project I have now."

"You've written two sentences," Genevieve replied encouragingly, patting Aventurine on the shoulder as she brushed past. "You could write another when we get back to Lincoln."

"Thanks."

If Genevieve heard the sarcasm, she did not let on.

Eighteen

She left Genevieve at the Aldi, then circled around back into town and to the lot behind the hotel. The rain that had been threatening all afternoon was now falling with an impotent fury, echoing Avi's own state of mind. Instead of heading straight upstairs to her room, she cut around into the bar.

Pete took one look at her face and shook his head. "Tea?"

"No. Thank you. Pint."

He drew off a pint of the 42, and slid it across the bar. "Tab?"

"Sure." She carried her glass to the far corner of the room, away from the window, hoping the dimness would allay her headache, or at least her bad temper. And if she managed to get herself a little drunk? So be it. Her room was just upstairs. She'd find her way.

From her bag, she drew her notebook and a pen. For a long time she just stared at the blank page, until, despite herself, she began to write down her impressions of the afternoon, of Kettlethorpe, and the defiant archway leading to the private home which had replaced the Swynford estate. Words. Descriptions. Perhaps they would go nowhere. Perhaps she would not need them for anything. But Genevieve's words hung with her. Perhaps she *would* need them later.

She had lost track of time, and, despite her best—worst?—intentions, was into the refill Pete had carried across, when a shadow fell across her notebook.

"Well. Look who I found."

Aventurine looked up into Gio Constantine's face. He looked as surprised as she felt.

"Gio? What the hell are you doing here?" When she pushed away from the table, she felt her head spin. That second pint had not been a good idea.

He pulled out the chair opposite and settled into it. "I can ask the same of you," he countered. "What the hell are you doing here? In this pub? In Lincoln? In the UK at all?" He glanced over his shoulder, caught Pete's eye, and pointed to Aventurine's pint, then made a circle.

"I'm writing," she lied.

He laughed, the skin around his eyes crinkling attractively. No doubt he knew it; no doubt he practiced in front of a mirror in the morning. Damn him. "You're drinking." He reached across and snagged her notebook with a finger, dragging it closer so that he could read what she had written. She didn't feel the strength to put up a fight.

Pete set a pint before Gio, and glanced at Avi's half-full glass.

"Just water, Pete, if you would?"

He nodded understandingly and disappeared.

Gio lifted his glass. "Here's to a chance meeting between good friends."

Grudgingly, Aventurine lifted her pint as well, and clinked. Her sip was tiny. Her stomach was already protesting. "I'm researching," she amended.

"Another book?" How had he downed half of his 42 in that one drink?

"Maybe. You?"

"Gig. At the Blue Pearl, around the corner."

"Tonight?" Avi looked at the time on her Fitbit. It wasn't yet four.

Gio nodded, running a hand through his greying hair, yet another thing that made him look distinguished, rather than aging. He'd never bothered to cover it, despite the cracks he was always making about his colorist; he'd been in the gradual process of turning into a salt-and-pepper fox in the decade that she'd known him. "At nine. You want to come? Be my road crew? It'd be just like old times."

She made a face.

"Come on. You need to keep in practice, in case the writing gig doesn't work out for you."

It was a joke, but Aventurine winced anyway.

Gio was quick to notice. He reached out a hand, wrapping his warm fingers around her wrist. "What is it?"

Avi looked away, toward the window, streaked with rain. Three women came in through the door before the wind. Pete appeared, set down a glass of water, and disappeared again.

"I think I've lost it, Gio."

"Explain, love."

"Writing. I've written—" she half-laughed, and found tears in her eyes—"two sentences in four months." Aventurine gulped. "I sit before the keyboard, and put my fingers on the home keys, and for the first time in as long as I can remember, nothing comes out." She took the notebook back and slapped the cover closed. "Even this—this—is just notes, not going anywhere, not making any sense." She looked up to find his expression so concerned that she thought she'd break down, hurl herself against his chest for comfort. "I'm a non-writing writer."

His half-smile was more sweet than she could bear. "Courting insanity, are you?"

Avi shook her head. "I feel like it. Gio, I've never suffered from writer's block before. I can feel it in my chest, like a heavy block of granite. Nothing can get by it. I can't write anything."

The grip on her arm tightened. "Oh, sweetheart. I don't think I've ever seen you this distressed. Do you know what's causing it?" He shook his head fiercely, before she could say a thing. "Don't answer that question. It was stupid of me to ask it. If you knew, you'd be able to get rid of it."

His eyes were so kind. He had, after all, known her a long time. And he was a writer, too, albeit of lyrics and music.

She wondered whether she should tell him about York, about Paul and Lance and Genevieve and Neil, and that terrible night which had bound them all inextricably together. But then she remembered Genevieve's warning. *None of you are safe.* Until the case was closed, there was always danger.

"How is Paul?" Gio asked, almost as though—but not quite—he had read her mind.

"Let's not talk about him," she said. She looked at the time again. "Nine o'clock, you said?"

Gio narrowed his eyes. "Yes."

"Plenty of time to go upstairs."

She carried her glasses to the bar and handed Pete a twenty. Without checking to see whether Gio was following, she tacked her way back through the breakfast room and took the stairs.

He was.

She let them both into her room, then locked the door behind them. Without flipping on the light, she turned to him, put her arms around his neck, and kissed him, open-mouthed.

"Slow down, Cowboy," he laughed. He reached over to pull the chain on the tiny desk lamp. A pool of light fell on the computer, leaving them in shadow.

She pulled her shirt over her head. When she looked down, her skin glowed white in the dimness. She unbuttoned her jeans and let them slide to the floor. Then she took his hand, caressing the calluses on his fingertips, before placing it against her breast. He laughed again, slipping his hand into the cup of her bra, finding her nipple. She gasped and leaned her head back, and then his mouth was at her jawline, moving along her throat to her collarbone.

"Avi," he whispered.

"Shut up."

She had his shirt off, her hands running through his chest hair. After that it was clothes everywhere, and she tumbled back onto the bed, arching her back, feeling his weight on her, hoping against hope that this would make her forget everything else, at least for a while.

Nineteen

"Where are you staying?" she murmured as he climbed back into his clothes by the light from the bathroom, after a quick shower. She stretched languorously, feeling the muscles that hadn't been used in a while. The sheets felt cool and comforting against her skin.

"Anywhere I want," he said, buckling his belt.

"Here?" she suggested, brushing the hair out of her eyes.

He leaned down to kiss her. His eyes glittered in the darkness. Avi liked the smell of his skin. She grabbed his shirt collar with both hands and pressed her mouth to his.

"If you want."

"I want."

He slipped out the door, and she rolled over, dozing off. Sometime before she woke to head to the Blue Pearl, she dreamed the dream of sirens again, but this time decided to ignore them.

"This is a song my friend Colin Moore wrote, called 'No Ghosts,'" Gio said, adjusting his capo with both hands on the guitar which hung from his shoulders. He frowned for a moment, concentrating on tightening the narrow strap over the strings, before looking up again and grinning engagingly. "Colin lives in North Cornwall, where, I understand, most of the well-to-do specters have their summer homes." He strummed once, then made another adjustment to the capo. Another strum, another slight adjustment. At last he seemed satisfied, and played a quick few notes. "Colin, I take it, fancies himself a kind of exorcist. So here's his 'No Ghosts.'"

Did Gio just wink at her from the stage?

Probably.

He eased into the song, building upon that chord progression, until, after the instrumental intro, he leaned into the mic and began to hum. His eyes were closed, and the hum washed over and around the guitar. There was something about it, the low musical line threading its way through the strings, that was slightly eerie. Aventurine felt the hair at the back of her neck prickle and stand on end.

She hadn't heard this song before. Of course, she'd never heard of Colin Moore before. She made a mental note to look him up online... but not right now, because she was being carried along by the song itself, and it took a moment to realize that the humming had turned into a quiet verse with a building intensity that made her earlier anxiety return.

Even when he'd finished, and segued into another song, and then another—all of which she knew by heart—she found herself haunted by the Colin Moore song. It might have been written for Gio and his low voice. It might have been written for her.

Aventurine closed her eyes and shivered slightly, thinking of their afternoon together. His presence here in Lincoln: sure, he had a gig. But he didn't have to take every gig offered, on a tiny stage in a tiny venue, a fair driving distance from Oxford; those days were well past for him. Though she kept her eyes closed, letting his voice caress her skin, she still could not shake the nerves. She tried to tell herself that it was just the influence of Genevieve, but the feeling hung about her like a wreath of smoke.

Trust no one.

Gio knew nothing. Nothing of the events of the summer in York. There was no way he could harm her, no reason why he would. Save personally, of course, but she had learned that lesson twice over, and this would never be that kind of relationship.

As if to prove her point, Gio slid into that arpeggio run that always led into a song from his early years: "Twice Bitten."

Avi lifted her drink from the high top and gook a gulp. The anxiety remained, the stone in her chest.

Twenty

"I tried calling you last night," Micheline said on the phone, her tone somewhere along the line between accusing and concerned.

"I was busy."

"All night?"

"All night."

The morning had dawned clear, the sun bright. No doubt it would be cold when she went outside. Aventurine supposed, stretching her free arm above her head, that she could stay in. She could take Genevieve's advice. She could lie low. She could *write another sentence.*

All trace of Gio was gone, beyond the vague scent of him on the pillow beside hers. And her clothes, still scattered around the room. It had been good to see him. It had been grand to go to bed with him. But this was the way both of them liked it best: wild, abandoned sex, and then the parting of ways. No responsibility to entertain one another, to be on. She ran a hand along her skin, imagining his touch, and smiling to herself like the Cheshire Cat.

"Are you okay?" Suspicion.

"Better than okay."

"Oh, for heaven's sake. Gio?"

"He had a gig in Lincoln. He's got another tonight, but in Matlock. I think. I wasn't listening all that closely."

Aventurine stretched again, and stood, wrapping the duvet around her against the cool morning air.

"You're a bad woman," Micheline said, but fondly. Aventurine could imagine her twin, sitting at the kitchen counter overlooking the terrace. She would have a cigarette in one hand, and would be looking blankly out into the late fall yard.

"Get yourself a Gio," Avi advised.

"Shut up. I don't want one. Don't need one." There was a long sigh from Mick. "You sound better, anyway. You haven't sounded quite right for the past week. Month. Months. So I guess Gio Constantine is good for you."

"So. Have you heard from the DNA people yet?"

"Still waiting. Have you heard from Nicola Hallsey yet?"

"Still waiting. But I've heard from Genevieve. She's here."

"In Lincoln? You're attracting all the usual suspects."

It was true enough. And a few new ones into the bargain. Aventurine thought briefly of Paul, and of Lance, wondering what they were up to, in Milan, in the rest of their lives. She had liked Lance very much. She had rather thought that Paul had, too. But there was no accounting for the vagaries—and the idiocies, she supposed—of youth. She hoped Milan was all it was cracked up to be for them. She peered into the mirrored door of the closet, leaning in to examine the crows' feet around her eyes. "There's more weird stuff going on." She relayed the happenings since she had spoken to her sister last.

"That is weird stuff," Micheline agreed when she had finished. "And I think Genevieve is right. You need to keep out of the eye of that policeman. Keep a low profile."

"But I can't distance myself from Henry Hallsey. Not when we don't know where Nicola is. Not when we don't know *who* Nicola is."

"Just follow your instincts," Mick ordered. "Stay in today. Try to write something. Or read something. Or watch Lucy Worsely on the television. Enjoy your post-coital languor."

"Jealous?"

"Shut up."

Twenty-one

Aventurine was toweling her hair after a shower when the call came from the front desk. Not Pete this time, but perhaps the woman who had checked her in originally.

"You have a visitor," the clerk said. There was a muffled exchange of voices, as though she had covered the receiver for a moment. "A DCI Burroughs?"

Any semblance of relief her time with Gio had provided disappeared like smoke in the wind.

"If you'd let him know I'll come down to him in a minute? Is he waiting in the bar?"

"He's here at the desk, Ms. Morrow. He says he'll wait here for you."

Aventurine hung up, then gave her hair a last swipe before scraping it into place with her fingers. She scrambled in her purse for the lipstick, slapped it on somewhat haphazardly, and headed downstairs. So much for lying low. She wondered fleetingly whether she should let Genevieve know, but the thought of that lifted *I-told-you-so* brow was enough to make her shove her phone deep into the front pocket of her bag.

DCI Burroughs was indeed standing in the tiny lobby, a tour brochure to the Cathedral from the rack nearby in his hands. He leaned against the wall, using the light from the rear door to read the smaller print, a frown between his thick brows. At her approach down the stairs, he folded the guide back up and slid it into its slot on the rack.

"Ms. Morrow," he said by way of greeting. "Good afternoon."

Surprised, she glanced at the time on her Fitbit. It was indeed a bit past noon. "Good lord, I didn't realize how late it was."

The desk clerk was nowhere to be seen; perhaps she was pulling double duty at the bar as Pete frequently appeared to do.

"I just have a few questions today," he said, as though a policeman passing the time of day with her was nothing unusual. He indicated the entry to the breakfast room. "I hope you don't mind, but I ordered some coffee for us. Why don't we sit in here where we won't be disturbed?" Already there was some noise from the bar, a low hum of conversation, chairs scraping back on the wooden floor. In the corner near the fireplace, he indicated a chair at a small table. They seated themselves, the coffee arrived, and Aventurine held her breath, stirring first one packet of milk into her cup, then another. Burroughs still took his black.

"What can I help you with?" she asked at last, since the detective seemed to show no indication of opening the conversation. She glanced up, a sudden pang in her chest: she had not heard from Henry today, and she had made no move to contact him. "Have you found Nicola Hallsey?"

Burroughs took a sip from his mug. "Nothing yet."

"Are you looking?"

He held her gaze for a long moment, and Aventurine was the first to drop her eyes. She shouldn't challenge him like this. Genevieve would have read the situation much better. *He came to you,* she could almost hear the old woman say. *Let him be the one to speak. Answer his questions as truthfully as you can without providing any extra information.*

"Sorry," she said. "I'm just that upset about her. It's been nearly a week."

"That upset. About a woman you've never met." He took another sip.

Aventurine set her spoon aside carefully. "Yes. We've been through this before." It was as though he were purposely trying to antagonize her. She wondered why. But she would not ask.

Now DCI Burroughs reached into that inside pocket, to bring forth the ubiquitous notebook and pen. He flipped through several pages before finding the one he was interested in, and then took a moment to read his own notes. "Ah, yes. We have. Nothing's changed?"

The question was strange. "Why should it? Nicola Hallsey is still missing, and I am still concerned."

He nodded.

"So, if not Nicola, what have you come here for?"

He slipped back his cuff to look at his watch, a silver face on a beat-up leather band. "You were surprised it was afternoon. Stay out late, did you?"

"Not really. I was in before midnight. Went right to bed. Didn't go out again." Aventurine knew she was blushing. She could feel the heat rising into her face. "Why?"

"You didn't hear the sirens last night?"

More sirens?

She frowned. "I don't know. I think I might have, in my sleep. I thought I dreamed of sirens when I dozed before going out. Around eight? Eight-thirty?"

"I wondered if, after the other night, you might not also have come down to investigate. Out of curiosity. Or perhaps out of concern for Nicola Hallsey." He tilted his head, much as a puzzled dog might, but there was nothing cuddly about the iciness of his blue eyes as he regurgitated her words back to her. "Like you did before."

She shook her head.

"So you never came down to Minster Yard."

Aventurine shook her head a second time. "No. I—thought I dreamed it. I told you. I thought I dreamed the noise." When he didn't appear to be in a rush to say anything further, she looked up again. "What happened? Was someone else—hurt?" She still didn't know, she realized, the identity of the woman with the broken neck;

still didn't know whether she was pushed or fell, or what the story was.

"No one was hurt," he said.

"A fire, then?" She picked up her coffee cup and took a big drink from it.

"A theft."

Burroughs waited, his gaze steady, cold, deceptively impersonal. Aventurine had no doubt he was making note of her every reaction, her every word, but for the life of her, could not figure out why. And that, as Genevieve would point out, was dangerous. If you didn't know what he was looking for, you had no way to prepare for the trap. *Volunteer nothing.*

"I'm sorry I can't help you," she said at last. "I was here. Dozing. Until I went out for the evening. Like I said—I thought I was dreaming."

"Here. Sleeping. Perchance dreaming. With whom? And where did you go from nine to midnight?" The detective scribbled in his book, then leaned back in his chair.

Great. A *Hamlet* buff, too. Aventurine hated *Hamlet.* "A friend. I was invited to a gig at the Blue Pearl. It got over at around 11:30, and I came back here."

More notes. Then he looked up again, with that unreadable gaze. "And aren't you curious as to what was stolen?"

"Of course I am. I just assumed you'd tell me, if you wanted me to know." Burroughs was really starting to get on her nerves. Spoiling the lovely feeling she'd awakened with, which had carried all through imagining Gio getting dressed. He'd looked good. Very good. She felt her face warm again.

Burroughs was watching her intently. He made another note. Aventurine found herself wishing she could read what he'd written. As though aware of her thoughts, the detective snapped the little notebook closed and replaced it in his pocket.

"The Swynford Jewel," he said.

"I've seen it," she told him. "Last Wednesday, when I went to the Cathedral. I told you." She frowned. "But that's the last time. The only time. Why are you asking *me* about it?"

Burroughs shrugged noncommittally. "Elimination, that's all."

Aventurine narrowed her eyes. "If you're asking every person who has had a look at the jewel since Wednesday, that's probably going to be a lot of elimination."

"True." He cocked his head.

His coffee was gone. If he was going to ask the many hundreds of people who had been in the Medieval library over the past six days where they had been last night, he'd need a lot more coffee. And probably many trips to the gents'. She wiped the smile off her face, but it was too late.

"What is it?"

"Thinking about you and your coffee. Not much, really." If he asked for the location of the men's room, Aventurine would probably laugh outright. She, too, leaned back in her chair. Her coffee was not quite gone, but it was cooling quickly.

"I'm just uncomfortable with a number of things. Coincidences, if you will." His eyes never left her face. His tone was flat. "Nicola Hallsey is reported missing. The two people who reported her missing show up at a crime scene. Later, one of them claims to be researching Katherine Swynford, and then suddenly, a valuable artifact linked to Katherine Swynford is stolen from the library, which is part of the complex where the earlier crime was committed."

So she was pushed.

"I see the dots," Aventurine said carefully. "That doesn't mean they're connected."

The detective held out his hands, in a gesture that might have been meant to be disarming. His fingers, Aventurine noted again, distractedly, were long, the nails cut short. "You see my position, though, surely. The commonality is you. So—I have to eliminate you from suspicion."

"Eliminate me, then," Aventurine challenged. "I was visiting

Kettlethorpe yesterday, had lunch at a pub there, was back here before four—the bartender can attest to that—then went upstairs with a friend. I went out to a gig last night, was back before midnight, and didn't come back downstairs until you called me this morning. Afternoon."

"A friend." Of course he latched onto that.

"Yes. A very good friend, of long standing."

"And that friend's name?"

"Gio Constantine." It felt rather like throwing poor Gio to the dogs. At the same time, something told Aventurine that being used as an alibi would be rather titillating for Gio.

The name didn't seem to ring any bells with DCI Burroughs. Avi was glad that Gio didn't have to be present for that ego blow. He liked being recognized.

"His address? In case we have to talk to him. To verify your alibi."

Alibi, was it, now? "He lives in Oxford. I'll have to look it up for you."

The notebook was open again, and Burroughs scribbled away fiercely. "Oxford. That's a long way to come for an assignation."

The policeman made it sound dirty. But at least he didn't say *a long way to come for a quickie,* she supposed. And it wasn't a quickie, by a long shot.

"He's a musician. He's up here for a gig. A couple of gigs." Right. He was playing Matlock this evening. She supposed she could look up his website, see where else he was playing.

"So you planned to meet up?"

Avi made a face. "No. I had no idea he was here until he showed up."

"So it was a pleasant surprise, then." Burroughs' voice remained flat, but something there felt judgmental.

She lifted her chin. "A *very* pleasant surprise."

"So he'll be back tonight? I could corroborate your story."

At least he didn't say *alibi* again.

"No. He's off doing more performances."

"And you're not going with him?"

"We don't have that kind of relationship." There. Aventurine hoped *that* put his judgment right up his backside, wondering what kind of relationship they *did* have. Friends with benefits, she supposed, and almost laughed to herself.

He made a note.

"If there's anything else, Chief Inspector?" She drank down the remainder of her cold coffee and grimaced. She didn't like coffee all that much, but this was especially vile. She set her cup down and gathered her purse, in preparation for leaving.

But Burroughs held up his long-fingered hand. "One more thing. Your visit to Kettlethorpe yesterday."

"Yes?"

"Did anyone go with you?"

Avi folded her hands in her lap and smiled beatifically. "Oh, yes. A friend."

"Same friend?"

"No." Ha. She had more than one, DCI Burroughs.

"Name?"

"Mary Wentworth." She thought of Genevieve, and felt mildly guilty that she had doubted the old woman's foresight. Genevieve knew; of course Genevieve knew. Aventurine also felt a quick rush of protectiveness, perhaps more than a little unwarranted. Genevieve could protect herself better than most, and no doubt would. "Do you have to bother her, though? She's really quite elderly. I don't want to alarm her."

His expression was bland. Maybe they taught that at the detective training course or something. "I only need to eliminate you as a suspect," he repeated. "Where can I get in touch with her?"

For a moment Aventurine drew a blank. Mary Wentworth was supposed to be her friend. She should have an address for someone who was supposed to be her friend. "Hold on—let me think. She's recently moved house." Avi closed her eyes against his narrowed gaze, the one that indicated clearly that he did not believe her. But then it came to her: Genevieve at the table, opening her wallet to her NHS card and some other ID. "It's on Chelmsford Street. I don't recall the number."

"Mary Wentworth, on Chelmsford Street. I'm sure we can find her, then."

DCI Burroughs pushed away from the table, so Aventurine did, too. She imagined the interview was over, and was surprised to find her hands were shaking. She busied them with her purse, and with collecting the coffee things.

"Don't worry about those," Burroughs said. "I've paid—they'll collect them." He nodded, though his eyes still remained on her. "I'll be in touch, should I need anything more."

Twenty-two

Aventurine was starving. It occurred to her that she had not eaten since lunch the previous day. The afternoon's coffee sat uncomfortably in her empty stomach, and she felt lightheaded.

At least she hadn't passed out at DCI Burroughs's feet. That would have been quite the show. He probably wouldn't have believed that was real, either.

She needed to talk to someone. Anyone. She needed to process, to organize her thoughts, to try to figure out what the hell was going on. She discarded every possibility quickly. Not Henry—was he even at the Cathedral this afternoon? She quickly texted him: *Any news?* He didn't reply immediately, as he usually did. She was at a loss: no doubt someone was keeping an eye on her, anyway, and if she ran to Henry after an interview with the police, Burroughs would probably find that somewhat suspicious. She'd already spoken to Micheline this morning.

No, it was Genevieve she had to talk to, despite her prickliness of yesterday. Genevieve, who was here somewhere in Lincoln— on Chelmsford Street?—doing work for someone she couldn't or wouldn't name. Undercover. As Mary Wentworth. At the very least, Aventurine had to warn her that she'd set the police on her. Which, now, in hindsight, was not unexpected.

Apparently the theft of the Swynford Jewel wasn't unexpected, either. What had Genevieve said, after claiming she shouldn't? That there was information indicating that an attempt at the Jewel was in the works. Well, if the old woman had been sent to prevent it, she hadn't done a very good job, that was certain. Because the Jewel had been stolen.

Aventurine ran upstairs to get her coat, then wandered out in search of a late lunch, or an early dinner—whatever—far too restless to stay in and partake, once again, of the hotel bar's offerings.

In her pocket, her phone buzzed with a text.

Where are you?

She paused, leaning out of the wind against the wall, to text back.

Going to find food. Italian.

Then, a link to Google maps. An Italian restaurant not far from where she stood, halfway along the Bailgate.

Order me some tea.

Aventurine liked Italian restaurants. She and Paul had met Lance in an Italian restaurant. Lance and Paul, now wandering around Italy. How was Paul doing? But it wasn't her place to check in on him: she wasn't his mother.

This restaurant was a cozy sort of place, small tables, checked cloths, candles stuck into the necks of bottles. Aventurine requested a table near the rear, and ended up very close to the kitchen doors. The scent wafting out to her was predominately garlic. She ordered a gin and tonic for herself, and tea for when her companion arrived. She wondered how long it would take. She wondered who was going to show up—Genevieve, or Mary? She wondered where, and how, the old woman had spent her day.

The drink came promptly, and Aventurine fell to studying the menu, trying to calm her still-pounding heart. Aftershock, she thought. She had been nervous during the interview with DCI Burroughs, but now reaction was making itself felt. Full bore. She slowed her drinking, to make the G and T last, and to prevent herself from getting downright drunk, now that she was no longer under the policeman's eye.

Late lunch or early evening meal, the restaurant was not crowded. Only a few tables between her corner and the door were occupied.

Her phone vibrated again, and she drew it out of her pocket, expecting word from Genevieve that she had been held up by something she wasn't at liberty to disclose. Instead she found a text from Paul, and her heart, having eased in its pounding, started to race again. Paul, from whom she hadn't heard in ages. With a trembling hand, she opened it.

No message. Simply a photograph of the sunset over Milan from the roof of Milan Cathedral. Even that small, the colors were rich, the dying light gilding the domes and towers. Her hand was still shaking, and she set the phone down on the table, studying the picture for some clue to her nephew's mindset.

He had messaged her. No words, but with something he thought was beautiful. She put her face in her hands, feeling an overwhelming urge to sob.

When she looked up again, Genevieve had entered, and was wiping her feet carefully on the mat before the door, hooking a black umbrella over the arm of her raincoat. Spotting Aventurine, she lifted a gloved hand and made her way to the table.

"Good choice of seating," she said, divesting herself of her coat before settling in the chair to Aventurine's left; like Avi, she had a good view of the restaurant, and the street beyond the windows. "Never turn your back on the bastards."

"I'm learning."

The tea arrived, the server having noted Genevieve's arrival.

"How are you, Mary?" Aventurine asked pointedly.

"I'm fine, personally," the old woman said. She didn't look so much tired as angry. As though someone had put something over on her. "Professionally? Well, I've had better days."

She poured herself a bit of milk, then filled the cup with tea from the little pot provided. "You, on the other hand, look tired."

"I am. And hungry."

"Didn't have lunch?"

"Nor breakfast. Nor dinner last night, for that matter."

Genevieve tipped her head to one side, her eyes watchful. "When one is going to lead an entirely new life, one ought to have regular and wholesome meals. To paraphrase Cecily Cardew."

"You're the one leading the new life."

"I'm *always* the one leading a new life." Genevieve opened the menu and scanned it quickly. "Unlike you, I have not skipped three meals. I think a Caesar salad would probably suffice for me."

"I think pollo alla marsala for me. That ought to fill me up."

"Or give you a heart attack, but to each her own."

The server appeared, and they gave her their order. She swished away again in her long black apron. Aventurine again missed Lance, and wondered whether he was taking pictures of Milan. Maybe she should call him, since she couldn't call Paul? Or maybe that would be too awkward.

"To each her own," she repeated, once they were alone again. "I've already had a heart attack today, so why not layer it on?" Aventurine took another sip of her gin and tonic. "The police were back around."

"When?"

"I had them for lunch. The delightful DCI Burroughs. He wants to make your acquaintance, so that you can provide me with an alibi for yesterday. I gave him the address from Mary's ID. I hope I did the right thing."

"You did. What about yesterday?"

"Don't play dumb with me, sister," Aventurine growled. "He apparently has to eliminate me from suspicion of stealing the Swynford Jewel."

Genevieve didn't look at all surprised.

"You knew about the coming theft yesterday?"

"I told you I had information. Besides: it's all over today's news. Police keeping mum, of course. No comment from the lead investigator." She made an expression—of—distaste? Annoyance? "I was afraid of this."

"That I'd be suspected of the heist? That's the suspicion Burroughs wants to eliminate me from. Oh, that, and the death in the yard of the Bishop's Palace. Which, now, apparently, is considered a *crime*." Aventurine pursed her lips. "You're the one who told me I had to research Katherine Swynford. I wasn't even thinking about the old girl until you suggested it."

"Oh, no. Don't put that one down to me. You were the one who told the detective that you were researching her, the first time you spoke to him." Genevieve shook her grey head sadly. "How many times, Aventurine, have I told you not to say anything? Don't lie, and don't volunteer anything. It's the only way to protect yourself. I simply cannot get you to understand that."

Aventurine felt suitably chastised, but at the same time, defensive and rebellious, as though being scolded by a hugely disappointed parent. Next thing she knew, she'd be grounded. "I'm trying. But I wasn't trained for this, by your Commander Smith. I'm not much good. I told you that."

Genevieve's demeanor didn't soften. "It's learned behavior. *Learn it.* I know you thought I was being paranoid when I took all these precautions yesterday. But—" and she cast one of her shadowed glances across the table—"I'm alive, and I'm an old woman, and when I was sixteen years old, no one thought I'd be either."

The food arrived, and Genevieve smiled brightly at the server, the pink and white old granny being taken to lunch by a much younger granddaughter. Or something.

"Remember, Aventurine," she said when the server had retreated again. "Had you never told that detective that you were researching Katherine Swynford, he would never have made the connection between your interest and a stolen jewel. If you were going to go around looking at touristy things to keep your mind off your work, you should have expressed only superficial interest in those touristy things. Play the game, Aventurine. Learn to *play the game.*"

Chastened, Aventurine turned her attention to the chicken Marsala. It was creamy, mushroomy, bite-sized pieces of chicken lying on a bed of pasta. There was crusty bread in a basket on the table, and she used a slice to mop up some sauce. To her left, Genevieve was setting her slivers of anchovy to the side.

"Too salty for an old woman," she said.

"You're too salty for an old woman," Avi countered.

"Ah. The language of young people like our Paul. I recognize it. I'm not sure if it's at all complimentary."

"Check your TikTok. You'll figure it out."

"Oh, Aventurine. My dear girl. I'm only trying to keep you safe."

For a fraction of a second there was a softness—or had she imagined it?—to Genevieve's voice. Aventurine looked up quickly, feeling that unwelcome prickling of tears once again, but the old woman was glaring into her salad, picking out choice bits with her fork. Yes, Avi had probably imagined it. And that made her feel even more like crying.

"You've got the name," Genevieve said. "We might as well adjust our actions to the situation."

They paid their entrance fee at the desk inside the Cathedral entrance.

"Is Mr. Hallsey leading tours today, by any chance?" Avi asked.

The older of the two women shook her head. "Not today, I'm afraid. You're too late, anyway, for our last one." She scribbled something on Aventurine's receipt. "Bring this in with you tomorrow, and we'll waive the entrance fee."

Aventurine caught up to Genevieve, who was marching resolutely down the south aisle. The old woman paused at the tomb of Katherine Swynford and stood with her hands folded over her umbrella handle. The rain outside had been fitful and peevish, and water dripped from the black cloth to the stone floor.

"It's a pity," she murmured against the echoing quiet of the stone vaults, "that the brass decoration is gone. She was a woman who liked a bit of decoration, was our Katherine. That Jewel demonstrates that, well enough."

"Why would anyone steal it, though?" Avi leaned back, first looking at the wrought iron of the fencing, then turning to take in the reds and blues of the stained glass windows. Jewel colors, not unlike that of the Swynford trinket which had been, until sometime yesterday, in the case in the library, glowed softly, but because of the rain, did not scatter over them, and over the stones on which they stood. Aventurine missed that. "It's worth what, tops? Two hundred thousand pounds? Five hundred? Surely if you were going to go to all the trouble to stage a heist, you'd aim higher—into the millions."

The look Genevieve cast upon her was deeply reproachful. "It's more than money for some people. Surely you know that, Aventurine."

"Then what?"

Genevieve turned on her heel and headed further along the aisle. They passed through the black and gold screen. The air inside today was decidedly cold. Only a few other people milled around. At last Genevieve lifted a hand to indicate the entrance to a side chapel. Aventurine waited a moment for a blonde woman with a pinched expression to brush past, then stepped through the narrow doorway. When she turned to face the tympanum, the full sunny utopian vision of Duncan Grant's beefcake Jesus struck her, and she gasped.

Genevieve laughed.

Aventurine sank into one of the chairs against the rear wall, her hands pressed together between her knees. The beatific sheep. The farmer—or maybe it was a disciple?—in the background. The sunshine and the flowing locks of the Savior, as played by Fabio. Suddenly she found herself laughing, too; it felt much better than being on the verge of tears.

"How much is this painting worth, do you think, Aventurine?"

Avi knew it was a test, knew she was bound to fail. "This is absolutely priceless," she giggled. She imagined Beefcake Jesus on the cover of a bodice-ripper, perhaps one by Nicola Hallsey. He'd be right at home.

"And yet it was closed off for years, inaccessible, because some people felt it was—how shall we say—inappropriate?"

Slowly Genevieve lowered himself into the seat beside her. Instead of joining her in gazing up at the painting, the old woman kept her eyes on her face.

"It's not what those people wanted for their Jesus, I guess?" Aventurine shook her head, not quite understanding where this was going. "But it's marvelous. It's like something out of this world. You can't put a price on this."

"Like you really can't put a price on the Swynford Jewel, either, can you? If you think about it being held in John of Gaunt's hands, if you think of it being clasped around the neck of Katherine Swynford? If you think of it as being a gift to celebrate the birth of one of the Beaufort children?"

There was little expression behind Genevieve's words, just simple supposition. Yet Aventurine could feel the excitement growing in her own breast.

"So it's not all money," the old woman said at last. "The value lies in the story the piece tells. And there are people in this world—collectors, they call themselves—who would hoard a piece like that, and like this, to keep it and the story away from the public, out of the light. People who want to own the magic. There's a flavor of greed there that's not monetary. It's far more psychological, but it's not about the value of the thing in pounds."

She sounded bitter now, angry, as though someone out there was, even now, plotting to keep Duncan Grant's painting, and the Swynford Jewel, away from the enjoyment and wonder of ordinary people like themselves. As though she had failed in preventing that.

At last Genevieve sighed, gazing up at the beautiful blond man on the tympanum. "He's really something, isn't he?" she observed, cocking her head. There was a gentle amusement in her voice, a soft note Aventurine had only heard on one other occasion.

"Does he look like someone you know?" she asked quietly.

Genevieve's expression closed down quickly, and she was her inscrutable, sardonic self once again.

"Don't be silly. I can safely say I've never known anyone who pranced about the countryside wearing sheep."

Avi laughed again, but another cliché bubbled to the fore. *Wearing sheep.* Perhaps he was the proverbial wolf, then. She leaned forward in her straight-backed chair, staring at the romance novel face. Beefcake Jesus, indeed. Perhaps he really was the devil. He had the same color eyes Neil had had, but beyond that, Grant's figure bore no resemblance to Neil at all.

Aventurine had not heard her move, but when Genevieve spoke, she was so close that her breath moved Avi's hair.

"Stop it, Aventurine," she murmured, her voice so low it might have been a growl. "Just stop it."

Genevieve read her mind, Avi thought. Always, the old woman read her mind. It was uncanny.

"Stop what?" she demanded defensively. Pretense was her only shield.

"You need to banish him from your mind, once and for all."

"I don't know what you're talking about."

Genevieve sat back in her chair and crossed her hands again over the handle of her furled umbrella. The odd lighting carved out her high cheekbones, her aquiline nose. Aventurine stilled in the chair beside hers. "You can't be his victim forever," the old woman said, gazing upward at the rolling field, the further sheep, the shepherd beyond Jesus.

Aventurine felt a momentary flush of fury. "I'm not anybody's victim." Those words were a criticism, and they stung. Perhaps because of the barbs of truth; or perhaps because of the lingering effects of gaslighting. Even in death, Neil still had the power to manipulate, but how did one explain that to a woman who had never found herself in such a position?

Genevieve did not turn her head. Avi imagined her dissecting the painting, each brush stroke, each gradation of color. "You are always *reacting*, Aventurine. When are you going to take control of your own life?"

"That's not fair."

It wasn't. It really wasn't. Aventurine was a writer. A successful one at that. A prize-winning author. She had pulled herself up after the devastation Neil had delivered all those years ago, and was pulling herself up again from the devastation his death had caused. She was the one who had made the choice to help her sister. She had done well, she told herself angrily. *She.* She was the one who had done well.

When Aventurine got back to her room, she threw her things onto the bed and sat down at the laptop. She opened to the page with her two meager sentences, took a deep breath, and set her cold fingers on the home keys. Her head was buzzing, maybe from the gin and tonic, maybe from love and longing and anxiety, maybe from the anger she'd felt staring up at the Grant murals, maybe from the cold wind that nearly blew her back along the Bailgate. She hardly even thought, now—or at least, later, didn't remember thinking.

When she looked up again, it was 3:41 a.m.

She threw herself back onto the bed without clearing away her coat and bag, and within minutes, was in a deep sleep.

Twenty-three

Aventurine took a long soak in the bath, listening to the classical music station on Pandora on her phone. She'd left the computer open on the desk in the middle of the night, and at some point, the screen, along with her, had gone to sleep. This morning she didn't bother to wake it. She'd look at what she'd drafted in her frenzy later. Maybe tomorrow or the next day. It might be garbage, the wanderings of a confused and alcohol-buzzed mind. Or...it might just be good. Salvageable. At least some of it.

But she had written most of a draft of an article, one way or another. And the truth of the matter was simply that there was never any way to revise a draft into something halfway decent—unless one had managed to write a draft to begin with. There had to be something to work with. To build on.

Avi slipped along her spine, dunking her head under the cooling water, rinsing away the last of the shampoo. She came up with more of a splash than she had intended, reminding her of the summer's afternoon spent wild swimming with the Mobius crowd. She laughed aloud. How freeing that afternoon had been! Like a baptism. She smiled to herself as she pulled the plug on the bath with her big toe, then clambered out onto the bathmat. She toweled her skin, now covered in goosebumps, roughly before wrapping the bath sheet around her and going in search of her cleanest clothes.

It was all right. Gio was still attractive, and attracted to her—the thought of his touch brought a visceral reaction. Her sister was and would always be her rock. She had friends—the Breedloves and their bunch, who would always welcome her into their raucous circle, and their adventures, with open arms. And there was Genevieve, who, in the Italian restaurant had come, she was certain, as close as someone like Genevieve would ever admit to loving her.

And now, on the computer, there was a draft.

Which, of course, she had saved in three places, including in the cloud, because no one, *no one*, would ever steal her work again.

Aventurine dialed Henry's number. It rang a few times, then went to voicemail.

"It's Aventurine. Call me back. Any news?"

After a cup of coffee and a pastry, she pulled on her coat and set off down the street briskly. The sun shone weakly, but at least the wind had died away, and the day seemed to hint at warmth. Almost friendly. She slung her bag over her shoulder and pushed her sunglasses up her nose. She had no plan until she reached the top of Steep Hill, and then, thinking about the truncated visit of the previous afternoon, she turned left along Exchequergate. There were few people out, but so late in the season, so early in the week and in the morning, there weren't many. No day trippers. No tourists, unless, upon Genevieve's advice, she counted as one. She might have had the old city to herself.

She entered under the now-familiar scaffolding once again, and went to the desk to show her initialed ticket from yesterday. "The floor tour will be starting in about half an hour, if you wish to join it," the unfamiliar young woman behind the till said; she wore the standard dark colors, and had her chestnut hair tied back in a ponytail. Aventurine realized she really wanted a tower tour, but those, she had read, were only scheduled for Saturdays, and she'd missed her chance this week.

Still, Avi smiled. "I've taken the floor tour already, thanks. It was so informative. Mr. Hallsey led it. Is he on today? I might join him again. I didn't take in half the things he showed us."

The young woman exchanged a glance with the other attendant, a young man seated at the other end of the counter. "Mr. Hallsey isn't in today, actually. He had some—personal business to attend to."

Damn. Henry hadn't called back, hadn't texted. She felt rather like she'd been ghosted. Personal business—had he heard from Nicola? But surely he would have messaged her.

"Everything is open except the Medieval library and the Bishop's Palace next door—those are closed today." She handed Avi her change, her expression one of great excitement.

"I heard." Aventurine leaned in conspiratorially and spoke in a whisper. "No news? What do the police say?"

"Nothing. They're being very closed-mouthed about everything."

There was a slight clearing of the throat, from the other attendant, who looked up, adjusting his glasses to look over them in disapproval. The younger woman passed over a fold-out guide to the Cathedral and smiled nervously, obviously expecting a good dressing-down once Aventurine took herself off. "I don't know if you have one of these."

"Thanks." Guiltily Avi moved away, not wanting to hear the scolding. Instead of crossing under the pillars to the aisle where she'd picked up the tour the last time, she wandered down the nave, to find the tomb of Katherine Swynford and her daughter, under the great carved screen. Some dark wooden chairs were arranged in rows there and she sank into one, the better to examine the sarcophagus from this side.

It was quiet, every sound muffled by the soaring ceilings and the largeness of the space. Aventurine thought of that first afternoon, the strange out-of-body experience she had as she walked toward the center pillar of the chapter house. That beehive-shaped building had gathered sound and enlarged it, so that the atmosphere hummed with it. This was different: the quality of sound and silence was different. Sound was not concentrated, but diffused here. It was impossible to tell where sound came from, or even, oddly, when and by what it had been made. Voices? Footfalls? Around her the stonework seemed to breathe, to be a live thing. Her neck prickled. She wiped at the feeling with the palm of her hand, but it did not lessen.

She looked around swiftly.

There was no one there. Of course there was no one there.

Hurriedly she took out her phone and texted Henry.

Where are you? I'm in the Cathedral.

Clasping the phone between her hands, she turned to look at the Swynford tombs. She had read last night about the brass work Genevieve had mentioned, which had been on the tomb originally, both stylized and representational, with images of both Katherine and Blanche. All gone now, thanks to the Reformation and Henry VIII, when his hired thugs went overboard and stripped away everything of value, everything with even a whiff of Catholicism or money. It seemed a shame that even dead people weren't spared; she'd read, even, that his own elder brother's chapel, in Worcester Cathedral on the other side of the country, had been desecrated, the faces bashed off the saints keeping guard there.

Katherine Swynford, one of the Bad-Ass Bitches of Britain. Aventurine half-smiled to herself, thinking that perhaps she should write a series of biographies, of which Genevieve's would be the first. Or perhaps she could start a band, and rival Gio on the festival circuit: *Aventurine Morrow and the Bad-Ass Bitches of Britain.* It had a nice ring to it. She should run it by Gio the next time she saw him— if she got around to it. Or by Genevieve. Their first recording could be "These Boots Were Made for Walking." She could be on a double bill with Mobius. Maybe Linny would dep for them.

Now she was just being silly.

But it felt pretty good.

Aventurine leaned against the back of the folding chair, her head propped on her hand, and considered. Katherine was safely in possession of her own manor, held for their son, with her husband Hugh's death. She could have retired to the house—Avi closed her eyes and envisioned the gatehouse she and Genevieve had looked at across from the graveyard at the church in Kettlethorpe; then she remembered the pictures she had taken with her phone, and called them up. Yes, Katherine could have taken up residence there and led a tame life, but she knew what she wanted: John of Gaunt, Duke of Lancaster. Avi had never seen any representations of the duke, and even had she, there was no way to tell how accurate they might be. The Plantagenets were supposed to be tall and blond, weren't they? Somehow, though, in her mind's eye, he looked suspiciously like Gio Constantine. Well, if he did, then shouldn't blame Katherine at all for wanting John in her bed.

Again, she took out her phone. This time she texted Gio: *where are you tonight?*

Someone slipped into the chair beside her. She looked up.

DCI Burroughs was regarding her with some interest.

"Returning to the scene of the crime, Ms. Morrow?" he asked.

Aventurine decided to play it deliberately obtuse. "She died of old age."

"Katherine Swynford? In her fifties, wasn't she?"

Avi was surprised that he knew this, and then wasn't sure why she should be. People weren't single-layered. Burroughs wasn't *just* a policeman. "Some would argue that that's old age in the Medieval period."

"Very true." He crossed his arms and leaned back to look up at the intricately carved screen arching above the two tombs. "Disease, childbirth. Yes."

"I understand the Black Death was very popular at that time."

"Touché."

They said nothing for a few moments, and Aventurine took the time to examine him surreptitiously. Very tall, she had noted at their first meeting, and now his long legs stretched out before him, crossed at the ankle. Today he wore a dark suit under his tan coat, though his tie was loosened a bit at his neck. His dark hair tumbled over his forehead, and from this angle, she could see that, like Genevieve's, his cheekbones were high and his nose aquiline. Mentally, she gauged his age: early to mid-forties, somewhere around her own age.

"I was just wondering what the Duke of Lancaster looked like."

Burroughs thought for a minute. "Short, in her 90s, prone to wearing matching pastel coats and hats, and carrying a handbag."

Aventurine burst out laughing. She covered her mouth with her hand. "Not the present one. *Katherine's.*"

He waved a hand. "The Plantagenets were all supposed to be fair, weren't they? Blonde and blue-eyed?" He shook his head. "I remember reading that in a history book. I don't know how accurate it is."

Burroughs was obviously not from Plantagenet stock, though he did have the height and the blue eyes down. Still, she had to concede, he was rather handsome, in an ascetic kind of way. She wondered what Katherine Swynford would make of him. Perhaps she would want to take him to bed as well.

"Why?"

Aventurine shrugged. "Just thinking about their history. How Katherine became John of Gaunt's mistress openly, at a time when that was far beyond the pale, societally, morally—you name it."

"And all those children. Six? Seven?"

Aventurine shuddered. "I couldn't imagine." Just the one was complicated enough.

This was certainly a weird conversation to be having with a detective chief inspector. Aventurine wondered what Genevieve would make of it. No doubt she would highly disapprove of the fact that it was happening in the first place. But what was Avi supposed to do? She could hardly get up and walk away from the man. She could hardly plead the fifth, here in the wrong country, when he questioned her about Medieval history.

"Do you have children?"

What an innocuous question. If the man were capable of an innocuous question. She would not think of Paul. She would not blush.

"No. You?"

"None for me, either." He sighed, still gazing up at the carving. "It's probably just as well, as I keep such odd hours. Getting called out in the middle of the night, for example."

Ah, here we go. Aventurine knew he'd get around to the investigation— investigations?—eventually. There was no such thing as idle chit-chat with this man. At least not when he was on the clock. But when was he ever off it?

"Of course." Her voice was non-committal. Not even sympathetic.

"So you're researching Katherine Swynford." He paused, and she nodded. "I've looked you up. You're a writer."

"I am. I told you."

"Make much of a living at that?" Burroughs didn't sound anything more than mildly curious, in the vein of those who would say *when I retire I'm going to write a book*. Not like he was probing, or anything of that sort.

Aventurine shrugged, keeping her tone non-committal. "Not early on. I kept my job working for the newspaper, for the steady income. But my last couple of books have done well."

The detective nodded again. "But it's been a while since your last book came out."

"True. These things take time." She would not be defensive. She would not be.

"Will this be your next one?"

The Bad-Ass Bitches of Britain. Aventurine almost laughed aloud again. "It might make up part of one. I'm looking at material to see what shape it might take."

Another long pause. She wondered what would happen if she crossed to the sarcophagus and laid a hand on it. She could almost feel the coolness of the stone against her palm. She thought of the wrought iron fencing she had caressed just last week, when Henry had stood across from her, his hand also on the fence. She cast a quick glance to her left. Did DCI Burroughs ever feel the urge to run those long fingers over things, to get a sense of them?

What the hell was she thinking?

What was his first name, anyway? For the life of her, she couldn't remember; and she couldn't picture the name on his police-issue ID, either. Of course, she'd had it flashed at her in the pub, when she wasn't really able to examine it closely.

"Katherine Swynford had all those children." Burroughs was back to that vein again, mining for some kind of ore. "The Swynford Jewel—did you have a look at that in the library? Yes, I remember you did—was thought to have been some sort of reward for having them, or as some sort of talisman against death in childbirth."

"You know I saw it. I told you I did, when you asked me before."

"So you must have noticed the saint. Saint somebody, patron saint of pregnancy and childbearing."

"Saint Margaret of Anjou."

"You researched that?"

Aventurine raised her eyebrow. "The librarian told me. I have yet to have had a chance to research further. So much has been happening."

"Right. Like theft. And death."

She wouldn't be baited. "I'm glad I saw the Jewel before it disappeared."

"For your research."

"For my research." Aventurine wanted to ask about the connection between the theft and the death if any truly had yet to be established. But Genevieve's strictures kept her quiet on that question. *Wait.* She heard the old spy's words in the back of her mind. *People like to talk, if only to fill the void.*

Apparently, however, this detective didn't. He kept his arms crossed, kept his gaze on the carved screen. Perhaps, somewhere in his training, he had his own Genevieve, whose voice replayed in *his* mind. They could, theoretically, spend the remainder of the afternoon just waiting each other out, to no effect at all.

Very well. Yet again Aventurine drew out her phone, but opened the photo app this time. She zoomed in on some detail of the now-plain tombs, and the carving of the arch overhead. If he wanted research, he was going to get research.

Then his cell phone buzzed, and he took it from his pocket. From the corner of her eye, she saw him frown, then he stood.

"I hope you'll excuse me, Ms. Morrow," he said, "but duty calls."

Aventurine nodded, feeling both relieved, and strangely as though she would have liked him to stay. He seemed an intelligent sort; in another time, in other circumstances, she might have enjoyed a conversation with him. One that wasn't loaded. One that wasn't filled with traps.

"I'm sure I'll be seeing you around," she said, a bit ironically, as he tucked the phone away. He had taken a few steps away when she called, "What's your first name?"

He turned back, his glacial eyes hooded. "Dominic. Why?"

"I'm an author. I might put you in a book."

Twenty-four

Feeling unsettled, Aventurine took herself around to Pottergate, where the police presence was smaller than before. She took some pictures of the Chancery, easily recognized by its arched entryway off to one side, and its ornate window bowing out over the pavement. Katherine had rented it from the Cathedral, Aventurine knew, and the Swynford Jewel, according to the librarian, had been found during some renovations. She sighed, wishing she could get inside, but of course it was not open to the public. Still, she made a note on her phone: if she was really going to go through with the Bad-Ass Bitches, she might be able to use her credentials at a later date to convince the powers-that-be to allow a viewing with some knowledgeable historian or architect. And the more she thought about it, the more attractive that project was becoming. For now, though, photographs of the exterior were the best she could do.

There was still evidence of police activity through the gateway that led into the Old Bishop's Palace. She walked hurriedly past. DCI Burroughs—Dominic—would no doubt expect her to return to the scene of that crime, too, and she felt no urge to fulfill his expectations. Still, she was vaguely disappointed to see no trace of him, and she chided herself for that.

Aventurine checked her texts as she wandered along the pavement in the shadow of the Cathedral and out through the arched gateway into Exchequergate. Nothing from Gio. Nothing from Henry.

Are you all right? she texted Henry after a moment. His continued silence worried her.

She slipped the phone into her pocket, but then she thought she saw him. Raincoat, blue suit peeking out. Disheveled white hair. He turned down Steep Hill. His shoulders slumped, and he was looking to either side, perhaps for his daughter.

"Henry!" she called. "Henry!"

He paused for a fraction of a second, turned his head, and then hurried on, as though he'd never heard her.

Aventurine found herself staring after him, until he disappeared among an afternoon tour group.

The good feeling of the morning was completely eradicated. As if to mirror her mood, the rains had started again. Aventurine bought a packet of salt and vinegar crisps at the bar, and then climbed up into the upstairs labyrinth to her room. There she sank down onto the bed and stared at the ceiling.

Her phone screen was blank, no notifications, no texts. It was also at 17%. She plugged it into the charger, and then, setting it on the bedside table, her eye fell on Nicola's copy of *A Year in the Life,* abandoned where she had left it after bringing it from the cottage. She wondered where Mobius was tonight, whether they had a gig. She had a rental car. If they were playing anywhere near, she could get there, surprise them. They'd welcome her loudly, a sister in the cause, as though she'd never left them.

She hefted the book. It was, she thought, a good one, one of the best things she'd ever researched and written. Both the most difficult and the most fun research of her professional career, because, oh, those people could party. She could never keep up, and after a short while with them, she had given up trying. Now she looked at the dust jacket, examining the wear along the edges, before turning to the cover, with the picture of the band in silhouette against the brilliant stage lights. Everything seemed to glow from the backlighting, as though the instruments, and their players, were performing some kind of magic. Alchemy. Which, she thought wryly, they probably were, though relatively few seemed to recognize it.

When Aventurine opened the book, she found it naturally fell to the place where it had lain over the arm of Nicola's chair. The beginning of chapter 21, after a disastrous performance in Leicester, where everything that could have gone wrong *had* gone wrong—so much so that the lead guitarist and the drummer had nearly come to blows. Only when their manager Ruth had inserted herself between them and pushed them back had they stopped. This was the part where, when Peter Breedlove had read the proof copy of the manuscript, he had looked up and grimaced: *bunch of fuck-ups, us.*

Avi sighed and slapped the book closed. She let it fall to the coverlet beside her, but when she did, a piece of paper fluttered out and fell to the carpet. She rolled onto her side and peered over the edge of the bed. Not a piece of paper. A photograph.

She reached down a shaking hand to pick it up, and carefully turned it over.

Gio Constantine's handsome grinning face gazed back up at her.

Aventurine stared down into his blue eyes, the smile on the mouth she knew so well. It was one of his publicity photos, from only a couple of years previous. She felt her stomach flip, had to close her eyes when she imagined his touch. She shivered, pleasurably.

Wait. What was Nicola doing with a photograph of Gio in her copy of *A Year in the Life?* Aventurine's eyes snapped open again, and she read the spiky handwriting across the bottom of the picture, the handwriting she had come to know over the years.

Nicola: all my love, always.

It was signed with his name, and the flourish he always used.

Aventurine felt a sudden wave of nausea.

"Calm down," Micheline said. Micheline, who could always be

counted on to answer the phone when Avi called, or at least get back to her as soon as possible.

"How am I supposed to do that?" Aventurine demanded. She was pacing down one side of the bed, along the foot, and up the other side; then she'd turn and do it all again. Outside, the rain spattered against the windows, a cold and angry sound. "Micheline, I spent the night with him, just the other night."

"And was it good? And did you enjoy it?"

"How can you ask me that?"

"I can, because you were the one who told me, and I quote, to *get a Gio.*"

Avi continued her pace. "I didn't know at the time that he knew our triplet. Nicola. I didn't know at the time that he was addressing pictures to her with all his love."

"What's wrong with that?" Mick countered mildly. "You're the one who told me you two weren't compatible for the long term. You're the one who calls your relationship the *crash and burn summer.*"

"So?"

"So. You don't want him."

"There's want, and there's *want.*"

"Aventurine, stop being a selfish bitch. If you don't want a relationship with this man, and you told him that, you can't be whining because he looks elsewhere."

"Mick—"

"And you can't be whining because someone else looks at him."

"Mick—"

"You know I'm right."

"I'm sorry I called you."

"Because I tell you the truth?"

"Bitch."

"Right back at you."

A long pause. Then they both spoke at once, and sputtered, laughing.

"You first," Aventurine said.

There was the flick and hiss of a match being lit; no doubt Micheline was lighting up another cigarette. "Leaving off your getting your nose out of joint," she said, "I will admit that the timing is still weird."

"That's what I was thinking."

"Yeah, right. But Nicola goes missing, and Gio shows up, and there's a picture that hints at some sort of romantic involvement among her things."

"It could be coincidence—"

"But we don't believe in coincidence." Now there was movement over the line, and Avi realized that Mick, too, was pacing. "You saw her get into a car the day after you saw her arguing with the strange man."

"Yes."

"But you didn't see the driver. Or the make and model of the car."

"I was looking down from a parapet. So no to any of that." Now Aventurine moved to the window and looked down upon the terrace below, where the umbrellas were furled, and the walkway glittered with rain. A gust of wind rattled the window.

"Do you know what color Gio's car is?" Mick pressed.

Aventurine closed her eyes and tried to remember the afternoon at the festival, when she had helped him get his gear out of the boot, to set up for his slot in the program. "Silver," she said slowly. She felt the sun-warmed metal as they had slammed the boot shut. "His car is silver."

"And?"

"The car I saw Nicola get into was silver, too."

There was the sound of her sister, all those miles away, blowing smoke into the air. "This," Michelin said slowly, "is where it gets interesting. You need to get hold of your Genevieve."

155

Twenty-five

A *ldi.*
The single word stared up at Aventurine from the screen of her phone. Nothing else. No further time, no further location.

Now, she read it to mean, as she had no other options. *Same one as last time.*

She trundled herself downstairs to collect the car, and then, finding the address in the Sat-Nav's memory, headed out. Traffic on the Wragby Road was slow, but she made it to the shop without too much delay. Genevieve was not at the bus stop. With no other direction, she parked and went inside.

Aventurine found Genevieve in the meat aisle, critically examining pork roasts. She looked up and shook her head woefully as Avi approached.

"Normally," the old woman said, as though they were in the midst of an ongoing conversation, "I would head straight to the butcher's for this, but Mary Wentworth lives within slightly more straightened circumstances."

"What on earth do we need a pork roast for?"

She shook her head again, and lifted her choice into the trolley, which was, so far, otherwise empty.

"You are a person with little imagination sometimes, Aventurine, I fear." Genevieve moved on. Avi, after a moment, quickened her pace to keep up. "It's late afternoon. We are about to drop in on Henry

Hallsey. What's our excuse? An evening meal. We're bringing our friend tea, because he's worried about his missing daughter."

"And I have something important to tell you about his missing daughter," Avi said. Despite herself, she looked around, her neck prickling vaguely.

"You'd better tell me. But look at the food while you do. Comparison shop." They wheeled down an aisle teeming with vegetables. Genevieve frowned as she examined the apples, piled up in all their glory. "I do wish they wouldn't wrap things in plastic every time they turn around." She sniffed disdainfully.

Aventurine leaned forward to examine a package of mini pears. She didn't look over at the other woman as she related the story of Gio, Nicola, and the photograph.

"This is interesting, and your sister is absolutely right. On all counts. You can't expect the man to stay faithful to a woman who doesn't want a long-term relationship—I would argue that you can't expect a man to stay faithful at all—"

"But–Honoré—"

"We're not talking of Honoré here, Aventurine. Do pay attention." A bag of apples made their way into the trolley. "But it is interesting, that, of all the gin joints in all of the world, Gio had to walk into Nicola Hallsey's."

"And she's disappeared."

"And he might have had a hand in that disappearance." They moved along the displays. Genevieve selected a package of potatoes, and then one of onions. "Does Henry have flour?" For a moment Aventurine thought the question directed at her, but then the old woman shook her head. "No, he doesn't. But he does have butter, and some spices in the cabinet."

"How do you remember this?"

"I searched his kitchen," Genevieve said, as though that were the most natural thing to do when visiting someone's home. She pushed the trolley forward.

"What did you find?"

157

"Butter and spices, foolish girl." Genevieve clicked her tongue. "I really don't like the way this is playing out. Any of it."

She didn't. Aventurine pressed her hand to her forehead. All of it was difficult to believe, difficult to take.

"Let's rephrase that." Slowly they walked toward the front of the shop, and the tills. "What did you expect to find?"

The glance Genevieve cast her was scathing. "Sometimes you make me so impatient, Aventurine. It's not necessarily a case of expecting to find *anything*. But you have to look." She scanned the lines ahead, and chose one toward the middle. "Think about your first examination of Nicola's cottage. What did you expect to find there?"

Aventurine frowned, thinking of her frustration, passing from one room to another, in the other woman's life. Looking at the book-filled self-containment. Thinking of how her own apartment would compare. "I had no idea what I was looking for. That was the problem. I wouldn't have recognized a clue had it leapt out and bitten me."

Genevieve nodded, inching the trolley forward. Aventurine helped unload the few selections, then helped rebag them as Genevieve somewhat shakily completed the transaction.

"Do you have enough, Mary?" she asked, somewhat snidely.

Genevieve smiled gently at her, though her eyes, as always, were hard. "No, don't worry, my dear, I'm fine. If you could just do the heavy lifting for me?"

They left the store, returned the trolley and retrieved the pound coin, and then Aventurine carried the bags to the car. "Heavy lifting," she snarled as she slammed the rear door closed. "I'm always doing the heavy lifting."

Genevieve eased into the passenger seat. "That, my dear, is because you refuse to do the heavy thinking. That's always my burden, isn't it?"

Aventurine snapped her seatbelt into place peevishly, and started the car.

"Besides. Had you stumbled across a clue at Nicola Hallsey's cottage, it would have bitten you, and you would have recognized it."

Aventurine refused to look at her, and instead concentrated on entering traffic at the road.

"It's just that you carried it back to the hotel with you, is all." Genevieve smiled to herself. "And it bit you, didn't it?"

Henry's car was parked before the house.

"He's home, then," Aventurine sighed, thinking of the furtive way he'd pretended not to hear her on Steep Hill, the way he'd turned and hurried away, trying to hide himself among the people on the street. Why on earth had he done that? Why was he ghosting her? She could taste the old anxiety welling up from her gut, and it was bitter. "I'm worried about him, Genevieve."

"I am, too, slightly." The old woman stood beside her open door, looking up at the first floor windows. "But I'm Mary here. Don't forget it."

"Forever?"

"Until I decide not to be."

Which might be today, or it might be never.

Aventurine retrieved the shopping bags from the rear seat, and then approached the door to knock. There was no response. She leaned into the door to listen, and knocked again. No shuffling of feet, no calling out to *wait a moment.* Glancing over her shoulder at Genevieve, she frowned and knocked a third time. Waited.

"The draperies are closed in the front room," Genevieve observed.

"Is he still avoiding me? Us? Pretending not to be here, so we'll go away?" Avi shifted the bags to the other hand, feeling the strain in her elbow. Heavy lifting indeed.

"He might be out for a walk," Genevieve suggested. She took a step back, her hands in her coat pockets, and looked up at the upper story windows as well.

"Or he might be ill," Aventurine suggested. She swallowed. "He's not young. And he's under a lot of stress."

This earned her a speculative look from the old woman.

159

"You wait here," Genevieve said decisively. "Keep knocking."

"What are you going to do?"

She shrugged. "Have a look around the back garden."

Aventurine watched her until she disappeared around the corner of the house. It was sometimes better not to know. Avi was learning at least that much. She knocked again, leaned in to press an ear to the door. When she stepped back this time, she gauged the distance to the front door of the other half of the house. Unless they came out to investigate, there wouldn't be any way for them to see much over here—and the overgrown hedge between their front gardens hid her from sight anyway. Despite herself, she wondered what Genevieve was up to, and was reaching out to knock yet again when the old woman opened the door from inside.

"He's not downstairs." She grasped Aventurine's arm and pulled her in. "Hold on while I check upstairs—though I haven't heard any movement."

The house had an expectant air to it—unless that was just Aventurine. She looked around guiltily, as though an enraged Henry would leap out at them, snarling, ordering them out of his house and out of his life. When she moved, her footsteps echoed, a hollow sound.

"Come along, then," Genevieve ordered, returning briskly down the stairs. "He's not up there, either." She turned and headed back toward the kitchen. When Avi set the two carrier bags on the countertop, she saw the key.

"Where did you find that?"

Genevieve took it up in her long fingers and glared at it, as though it had personally insulted her. "The same old place. When will people ever learn? It was under a stone in the flower border."

Something in Aventurine was relieved to hear it, though, because that meant that Genevieve had not gone out back to pull her lock-picking tools out of her garter. When she lifted her gaze from the key to the old woman's eyes, though, Genevieve's held a challenge. Probably she really *did* have lock-picking tools tucked inside her clothing. Probably she would have taken them out to use them had

Henry hidden his spare key better.

"So what are we doing here?" Avi asked. She hoped Genevieve was not going to suggest that they search the house. She cringed at the thought. And what could they possibly say, should Henry return home and find them tossing the place?

Genevieve went unerringly to the cabinet which held the cookware, and selected a non-stick frying pan.

"You're putting the shopping away. I'm going to start dinner."

"But Henry—"

"Oh, he'll be a bit angry to come home and find us in his house. Especially as he apparently is attempting to avoid you." Genevieve set a chopping board on the countertop, then opened a drawer and withdrew a knife. "But he'll get over it, because we're making him dinner. Hand me two onions, will you? You can put the others in the refrigerator—I don't know how soon Henry might eat them, and they'll last longer there."

"What if—he doesn't come home?" Aventurine bit her lower lip, thinking. His car was here; where was he? What if he had disappeared just as his daughter had? She shook herself mentally. That was unlikely. That was *Twilight Zone* thinking. He had probably, as the other woman had suggested, merely gone out for a brisk walk, to clear his head.

"We'll give him until the roast is done. Then we'll go to plan B."

Aventurine didn't know what plan B was. Let alone plan A.

Genevieve was good at multitasking—or at least directing Aventurine while she herself sliced the onions and put them in the pan on low heat to soften, then peeled and cored the apples.

"Can you butterfly that roast?" she asked.

"I haven't a clue what you just asked me," Aventurine returned. "If it's something to do with cutting it, I don't believe I have the knife-wielding skills you do."

Genevieve pursed her lips sadly. They switched places, Avi cutting the apples into small pieces as the other woman sliced the pork and rolled it out into a thin, flat length. They were spreading the cooked and seasoned apples and onions across the surface of the meat when they heard Henry's key at the front door.

"We're in for it now," Avi murmured guiltily.

Genevieve held up the knife. "I can handle it."

"Don't joke like that."

"What the hell are you doing in my house?"

Henry stood in the kitchen doorway, nearly shaking with rage. This afternoon he looked rumpled, his suit untidy, the shirt beneath wrinkled. His hair was a mess, but perhaps that was from the wind? But the wind had died back earlier. Aventurine closed her eyes for a second, trying to envision him turning away from her in the street. No, he'd not been his usual dapper self, she thought, once again seeing his shoulders slump as he'd tried to creep away. She looked back, feeling a constriction in her chest, a crushing pity. His skin was pasty. Only his eyes retained any spark of life, but it was an uncomfortable spark: they blazed, and shifted about his kitchen, at them, at the food on the counter, at the back door—as though they couldn't light for long on any one thing.

"Henry, you're not well," she gasped, and moved toward him. He swayed slightly, a hand on the doorframe. "Come sit. I'll fix tea."

"We're just cooking up a meal," Genevieve said, her voice changed subtly. She had transformed into Mary again. "We'd wondered when you'd last eaten a decent tea."

Aventurine led him to the table and pulled out a chair. He leaned against it, and did not immediately sit. "How did you get in?" He sounded suddenly frail, almost confused.

"Sit," Avi directed again. This time he sank wearily into the seat. Genevieve had already hit the switch on the electric kettle and pulled the tea things forward.

"Your spare key," Genevieve said. It still lay on the countertop, though edged off to the side. "We thought you were home—your car was here—and Aventurine worried you might have been taken ill."

Well, Avi *had* been the one to suggest it, when he had not answered her knock.

"I'm fine," Henry said, taking a deep breath and attempting to pull himself together. "Just worried. Still." His eyes flickered between them, and then fell away again.

"Still no word," Aventurine said.

"Nothing."

The water boiled, and Genevieve paused in scrubbing the potatoes to rinse the pot, and then fix the tea. She carried it over to set it on the table. "You sit, too, Aventurine."

"The vegetables—"

"Are under control."

Of course they were. Fleetingly Avi thought of Genevieve's mother, the original cook, who had no control over anything save the food she served her family. Aventurine sank down across from Henry, waiting for the tea to steep. She caught Genevieve's eye. *Should I ask him? Should I tell him?*

Genevieve nodded, the slightest of motions.

Aventurine took a deep breath. "Henry, tell me again about— Nicola's love life."

Henry drew back as though she had asked the unpardonable. Which she might very well have. Except that they'd discussed it before.

"I don't see how that's any of your business, Aventurine," he said stiffly. As though he'd not already told her about Justin, as though he had admitted he hadn't simply wanted to drop by his daughter's cottage, in case she had been entertaining a lover.

Aventurine took a moment to pour the tea. She remembered that Henry liked two sugars, Genevieve none. They both took milk. She poured hers last, black as her feelings. Black as her intention toward Gio, should she ever have him within arm's length again.

Dog in the manger, Micheline had called her. *You don't want him, but you don't want anyone else to have him, either.* Her thoughts toward her sister blackened as well.

"Have the police followed up with you, Mr. Hallsey?" Genevieve asked. She washed her hands in the sink before lifting her teacup to her lips. "About your report of your daughter being missing? It's been a week, hasn't it?"

"Nearly." But he did not look at her.

"Have you called them?" Avi asked gently. "And let them know you've heard nothing?"

"No." Henry's answer was terse, the single word like a shot.

Aventurine and Genevieve exchanged looks. The old woman's brow lifted; she'd noted the tone. Outside the window over the sink, the sky had darkened, nighttime drawing down around them.

"They'll ask you that," Aventurine said carefully. "When they really begin to investigate. They'll ask you about her love life, because—a romantic interest—is usually the first suspect."

Henry just shook his head. "But I've told you. She hasn't had a serious relationship for years. Just dates."

"Just dates." Aventurine tilted her head. "Henry. Come on. The first time you told me about her not calling on Wednesday night, you said you thought she might have had a date."

He picked up his teacup and sipped. Then he grimaced and set it back down again. His hands were shaking, and he folded them in his lap. "Yes. I thought she might have had a date. What about it?"

"Then you told me that you didn't go over Thursday morning because you were hesitant in case she'd brought her date home with her."

Henry took a deep breath, but did not look up. He seemed intent upon his hands in his lap. "What of that? She's a grown woman. If she wants to bring a date home, if she finds the person attractive, why is that my business? And why would you think it's yours?"

"Because I think—" and Aventurine faltered, feeling that weird betrayal that wasn't.

"We think," Genevieve said, coming to the table to pour herself more tea and add a dab more milk, "that Nicola went off with someone who was a love interest."

Henry shook his head. "No. It's not like that. She would have told me. If she was going on a trip with someone—like that—she would have told me."

"That's supposing that she went willingly," Genevieve said.

Now Henry's head shot up, and he glared into the old woman's face. *"Who are you?"* he demanded.

The silence grew between them like crystal; Aventurine could almost hear it ring. For the longest time Genevieve just looked down into Henry's agonized face, before coming to a decision.

"I've told you," she said grimly. "My name is Mary Wentworth."

It was not the reply Aventurine was expecting; but Genevieve had been adamant. She was Mary Wentworth until—she wasn't

Then she lifted her chin and narrowed her eyes. "And that, Henry Hallsey, is all you need to know for the time being. Just understand that I'd like to help find your daughter and bring her home safely." She turned to Aventurine. "Show him the picture."

"I—"

"Don't be an idiot, Aventurine. I know you have it with you."

Avi flushed at being figured out so easily, but indicated her bag, still on the end of the worktop. Genevieve handed it over, and under her watchful eye, Aventurine withdrew the photograph of Gio and laid it on the table between them.

The atmosphere was still, definitely, uncomfortable. Resentment, that's what Avi smelled: her own, right now, of Genevieve, probing the sore spot that was Gio; Henry's of both of them—for a reason she couldn't make out. What had happened in two days to turn Henry away from them, and inward? She still couldn't erase it from her thoughts, his pointedly turning and walking away from her in the afternoon. Pretending not to see her, not to hear her. She would have to demand an answer. But right now, Henry was drawing the photo closer with a trembling finger.

Nicola: all my love, always.

Not the way one signed an autographed photo to a mere fan.

The bastard was so handsome, and he knew it. It was just like him to give away publicity photos as love tokens; not of this candid, caught-on-the-fly photography for him. He was ready for his close-up, Mr. DeMille.

"Who is this man?"

Still, oddly, Henry did not look up at them.

Genevieve shot her a look.

"His name is Gio Constantine," Avi said. She too looked again at the portrait, the light glinting off the silver of Gio's hair, the bright smile, his chin tipped to his good side, so his dimple showed. "He's been a friend of mine for years."

"Which is, you have to admit, an odd turn-up for the books," Genevieve observed. "Do you know Gio Constantine? Have you ever met him?"

"Wait." There was a furtive glance from under Henry's brows. "That name. He's—in that book you wrote, isn't he? The one about the band. Mobius. He's a musician, too, isn't he?"

Aventurine nodded. She had been rather restrained in her writing about Gio, since the book was supposed to be about Mobius, not an exposé of her own love-life. But he had slipped in and out of the pages, when they crossed at festivals, just as he had slipped in and out of her bed, in and out of her life.

"I've never met him," Henry said slowly. He picked up the photograph now, and turned it over, but there was nothing on the back. He looked again at the front, studying the words, written with that dramatic flair across the bottom. *Leave room on the prints so I can sign with a dramatic flair,* Aventurine could almost hear Gio say.

"But?"

Henry frowned and shook his head. "I've never heard her mention him, either. I didn't know they were friends."

"Neither did I," Avi said flatly. Genevieve's glance made note of the tone; then the other woman turned back to fill the kettle and flick it on. The tea could do with some heating up.

With the teapot warmed again, and the tea steeped and poured, Henry set the photo back down. "Where did you find this picture?"

"In a book," Aventurine said. She grimaced. "In *my* book. It was face-down over the arm of a chair, as though Nicola had been reading it before she got up and left—to go *wherever.*" She didn't mention that she had carried the book away with her. "The first time I was there. Before I discovered the place had been searched, the second time I was there."

This got his attention. "Searched?"

"Yes. Have you gone over there?"

"You didn't tell me her house had been searched." Henry glanced between them; his expression was horrified, and pained, as though he had been dealt a body blow. "How could you tell?"

"Whoever did it made a mess." Aventurine wished Genevieve would jump in here and help out with the explanations; but she seemed to be limiting Mary Wentworth's involvement. "They stole Nicola's computer. I couldn't tell whether anything else had been taken."

"Why didn't you tell me?" Henry's voice was rising. "Aventurine, I trusted you."

That stung. But she couldn't tell him about avoiding the police, especially after she'd made such a hash of it. "You've had a lot on your mind," she retorted, quoting his own words back at him. "What could you have done? How would that have helped?"

"The police. You could have called the police."

"Henry. Listen to yourself. You want my help, and then you don't want my help."

"I never said that."

"*You walked away from me on Steep Hill today!*"

"I never saw you," he said, but he was looking at his hands again.

"You're a bad liar."

They ate dinner in silence, except for the scraping of silver against plates. As always, Genevieve had outdone herself, especially with the stuffed pork roast. The potatoes and vegetables were roasted and tender, the gravy dark and rich. Out of the corner of her eye,

Aventurine watched Henry pushing his food around on the plate, trying to make it look as though he were actually eating. She knew that Genevieve was watching that, too, and wondered whether she took it as an aspersion on her cooking. Probably not. The old spy did not operate on feeling, but on analysis.

"We'll wash up, Henry," Aventurine said, again feeling the pity stir in her gut for him. Tomorrow would be a week. "You should go call the police again, to see if they've made any progress. At least to put a burr under their saddles."

He mumbled his thanks for the meal, then wandered down the hallway to the front room.

"Make noise," Genevieve whispered.

"Noise?"

The other woman cocked her head toward the front room. Aventurine nodded, and began opening and closing cupboards, ostensibly to look for storage containers. She portioned leftovers into three of them, for three microwaveable meals for Henry, should he not feel up to cooking in the next couple of days. She slid these away into the refrigerator, nearly bare save for what essentials Genevieve had purchased, and then started filling the dishwasher.

Genevieve had disappeared down the hallway, and now returned.

"Is he calling them? The police?"

Genevieve ran the water to cover their voices, rinsing the plates and handing them to Aventurine. "He's not. He's sitting on the sofa, staring at the phone on the coffee table in front of him."

"That's weird." Avi took a handful of silverware and put it in the box.

"It's more than weird, if that's what you call it." Genevieve gave the roasting pan a good scrub under the running water.

"For a man who's making himself ill over his missing daughter, he's not taking the next logical steps." The dishwasher closed now, Avi leaned back against it. Genevieve wiped down the dining table.

The other woman looked up. "Unless his logic isn't like ours."

"What do you mean?"

"I'm not really sure. Yet."

The kitchen clean, they turned off the lights, and moved down the hall to the front room.

"Yes," Henry was saying into the phone. "Thank you." He set the phone down on the coffee table. Then he looked up, but not directly at either of them. "They're still looking into it. They'll send someone out tomorrow."

Aventurine lowered herself to the sofa beside him. She felt him recoil, as though from a venomous snake. "Are you all right, Henry? Something's going on with you, and I'm worried."

"*Something's going on with me?*" His laugh was bitter.

"You know that's not what I mean," she said helplessly. "Something more. Something other. Last week you wanted my help. This week you can't even look at me. I'm—scared, Henry. Frightened for you."

"Don't be. I'll be fine, as soon as Nicola returns home." His tone was dismissive.

Aventurine felt the prick of tears behind her eyes at the rejection. She looked to Genevieve for help, for support, but that woman's face remained impassive.

"It was a lovely meal," he said, drawing slowly to his feet. "I appreciate you two looking out for me. But now, if you'll excuse me, I think I need to get some rest. I—I have to talk to the police in the morning."

A clear dismissal. He opened the door for them, and then, once they were outside, closed it again without further goodnights. They heard the lock turn behind them.

Twenty-six

"Turn off here," Genevieve instructed, when they had taken the corner and could no longer see the house. She indicated a side lane. "Turn the car around, so we face the road. Turn off your headlights."

"What—"

But Aventurine did as she was told. She maneuvered so that they were parked flush against a wall of shrubbery, with a churchyard on the other side. She could see the main road plainly.

"Turn off the headlights," Genevieve repeated. "Leave the car running. Wait."

"I don't understand."

"You will in a minute." The old woman's skin shone pale and papery in the darkness, and she shook her head. "He really is a bad liar, our Henry Hallsey."

"I didn't feel like he was being completely truthful with us," Aventurine agreed grimly. "Not at all what he was like last week. I wish I knew what had happened with him. But at least he called the police."

"No, he didn't," Genevieve corrected.

"But the cell phone—"

"Wasn't connected. Wasn't even on. He didn't turn it off when he set it on the table, and the phone icon was red. He wasn't talking to anyone."

Aventurine sank back in her seat. "He was trying to fool us."

"He might have succeeded with you, perhaps," Genevieve chuckled. "He's got to be a bit better at this to fool me, I'm afraid."

"Because you're a professional."

"And you, my dear, are still a rank amateur."

"I'm trying."

"Try harder."

A long silence ensued.

Finally, Aventurine glanced over at that sharp profile once more. "What are we waiting for?"

A car passed on the main road up ahead.

"That," Genevieve said. "How good are you at following without being seen?"

A second car passed, and Aventurine turned on the headlights and pulled forward, then turned. "I guess we're about to find out."

She tried to hold back and at the same time keep Henry's car in sight. It was easier when there was a single car between them, but as they drew closer to Lincoln, it grew slightly more difficult.

"At least it's not a high-speed chase," she groaned.

Henry actually was a cautious driver, staying well below the speed limit. After a short while, it was a fairly simple matter to figure out where he was heading anyway. Though Genevieve had seemed to know all along.

He pulled his car up alongside Nicola's cottage on the Nettleham Road. Aventurine drove past quickly, before he climbed out and recognized them, then took the next left, parking a bit along from the corner.

"Come on, then." Genevieve was out of the car almost before Aventurine had killed the engine.

Henry had left the door wide open behind him, and they could see him, even from the pavement: the lights of the front room splashed out on the ground before the door. He stood just inside, in the midst of the chaos, his hands hanging by his sides, gazing around as though without comprehension. Slowly he moved further into the room until he stumbled against the chair with the torn cushion, where he sat down and dropped his head in his hands.

"Oh, Nicola," they heard him sob. "*Nicola*."

Aventurine clutched at Genevieve's bony hand.

And then, disaster.

"Good evening, ladies."

Aventurine whirled. She had heard no footsteps. Genevieve turned about more slowly. If she was surprised, she did not let on.

DCI Burroughs stood a few feet away, backlit by a streetlamp. He had his hands in his pockets, shoving back his raincoat, and now he rocked gently on his heels.

"Fancy meeting you here," he said. He stepped closer, and Aventurine could see his face, the calculation in his icy gaze. "Quite the coincidence."

"We were just—"

Genevieve squeezed her hand so hard she thought she felt all the delicate bones snap. She gasped and fell silent.

"Good evening, Inspector," Genevieve said. "It *is* Inspector, isn't it?" Though it was plain that she knew exactly what it was.

"Chief Inspector, actually." The smile showed his teeth, but did not extend to his eyes. "Good to see you again, Mrs. Wentworth."

For a moment they sized each other up. Genevieve said nothing more, just squeezed Aventurine's hand. *Say nothing. Force him to make the opening volley.*

"I'd come to have a look at Miss Hallsey's home—see if she'd come back," Burroughs offered. "Convenient to find you all here." He turned to look in at Henry, still seated in the chair with his head in his hands; Henry seemed oblivious to the conversation happening just outside. Burroughs indicated the open door. "Perhaps we'd better not go inside just yet?"

That was just fine with Aventurine; entering the cottage with the detective to their rear felt too much like being herded into a cage. She steeled her spine and drew her shoulders back in an attempt to match Genevieve's composure, and at the same time knowing she would never be able to, even if she did live to be nearly a hundred.

"Mr. Hallsey?" Burroughs called. "Mr. Hallsey? DCI Burroughs—perhaps you remember me?"

Henry started. He lifted his head, his wrinkled cheeks damp with tears, and stumbled to his feet. Again Avi felt the wash of pity. For a moment he looked cornered, his eyes flitting from one to the next of them. Genevieve made no sign, no doubt waiting to figure out how best to play this hand. Aventurine could feel her own flush creeping up her neck and into her face. She half-wanted to turn to take in Burrough's expression, but, following Genevieve's lead, she did not.

Until he had brushed past her, reaching into his pockets to pull out and don a pair of gloves. His eyes roved over the tumbled furniture and books.

Henry's watery eyes fell on Aventurine's face. "You," he said, his voice low and raw. "*Now* you bring the police. Long after it would have done any good."

"Would you step outside, Mr. Hallsey?" the detective asked. "Carefully, now. Try not to disturb anything." He narrowed his eyes, still scanning the room. "What seems to have happened here?"

"It looks as though the place has been searched," Genevieve said. Shocked, horrified—as though she hadn't walked into the mess just a couple of days previously. "Mr. Hallsey—I know you said your daughter was missing, but this makes it look as though she's been kidnapped or something." She sniffed. "You poor man!"

"You know," Burroughs sighed, crossing his arms and rocking back once more on his heels. "I'm starting to get the feeling that none of you are telling me what's really happening here. None of you are telling me everything you know. And I don't like that. It makes me angry. And it makes my job all the more difficult." His voice remained mild, but there was steel in it. He looked at each of them in turn, but his glance stayed longest on Genevieve. She simply widened her eyes, and returned his gaze with a guilelessness that Aventurine knew she could never emulate—even though, she figured, that out of the three of them, she herself was hiding the least. And knew the least of what the hell was going on. Probably even DCI Burroughs knew more than she did.

"If you don't mind, Mr. Hallsey, I'm going to call for backup here. I think your daughter's house definitely needs going over as a possible crime scene." Burroughs's words, though, were a formality, and they all knew it: at this point, he didn't particularly care whether Mr. Hallsey minded or not. Perhaps, Avi thought, he was rather hoping for Henry to object, just to see what would happen—though for the life of her, she couldn't figure out why, exactly. Burroughs extracted his cell phone from that inner pocket and dialed. He gave a few orders to the person at the other end, then rang off. "There will be a team here shortly," he said. "In the meantime, let's all stay outside, and close the door, shall we? To avoid further contaminating the scene."

Henry's throat was working. He took a handkerchief from his pocket and blew his nose before tucking it away again. "I don't understand."

"Mr. Hallsey, when you first reported your daughter missing—" and here a quick, unmistakable glance at Aventurine—"we sent an officer to do a wellness check." The detective replaced his cell phone, then drew out his notebook and flipped through several pages, leaning toward the streetlight, until finding the one he wanted. "The constable didn't get an answer to his knock, so he looked in the front window, then went around the back to look in there. At that time, this mess—" and now he turned, indicating the door behind which lay the overturned furniture, the books scattered all over the floor—"wasn't in evidence. The constable asked the neighbors whether they'd heard anything, or when they'd last seen Miss Hallsey, but they had noticed nothing untoward. The last time the neighbor in the cottage to the right spoke to her was last Wednesday morning, when he was taking his dog for a walk. About the time when, he says, she usually left for work."

Genevieve tilted her head, frowning as though having trouble following the explanation. All farce, of course. Aventurine knew the old spy was consigning each detail to the massive file that was her brain, organized the better to draw out again when needed. Her thin lips were pursed. Avi said nothing.

"I don't understand," Henry repeated. A broken record.

"None of the neighbors have spoken to Nicola Hallsey since, though they have claimed to have seen her twice in the intervening days."

Shock. Avi jerked around to stare at him, as did Henry. Genevieve continued to frown, a finger curled under her chin.

"She's been here?" Henry gasped. "Nicola's been home and she's not contacted me?"

"Friday morning. And again Sunday."

DCI Burroughs waited, to see if any of them were going to ask the obvious questions, and when they didn't, he shook his head. "So there are some interesting speculations," he said slowly, opening the metaphorical doors invitingly. Still no one took him up on his offer. "She came home, went away again. It was Friday, after all, when the constable did the wellness check—they must have just missed each other. Then two days later, strangely, shortly after the death at the Bishop's Palace."

"You don't think Nicola had anything to do with that," Henry protested, angrily.

Burroughs shrugged. "*You* did. You were the one who charged up to the police cordon and demanded to know whether the victim was your daughter. Why would that be, Mr. Hallsey? I've been wracking my brains about this, and not coming up with a satisfactory answer. Perhaps you'd be so kind as to help me out here?"

"Because she's missing!"

"And yet the neighbors said she was back home on Sunday. In light of all the disparate events over the past week, you have to admit that it's all very suspicious." When no one said anything, the detective sighed again. "Imagine, though, that she comes home on Sunday, and perhaps finds *this*." He indicated the mess behind the door with both hands. "That would certainly get her wind up."

"It would scare me half to death," Aventurine said.

"Unless," Genevieve mused, "she did it herself."

She used that small voice, the Mary Wentworth voice. She made the idea sound awkward, confused, and half-formed.

For a long moment DCI Burroughs simply stared at her. His expression in the half-light was unreadable.

"Why on earth would she do that?" demanded Henry. He kicked angrily at a stone, which skittered away into the darkness.

Burroughs shrugged. "To cover her tracks. A red herring."

"Oh," breathed Genevieve. "Like Agatha Christie uses."

This earned her a brief rise of the dark eyebrows before the detective continued. "If she looks like a victim, no one will look for her as a perpetrator."

"A *perpetrator*?" Henry was furious; he was visibly shaking. Aventurine longed to put a calming hand on his arm, but a quick squeeze from Genevieve's fingers stopped her. She was going to have bruises in the morning, she just knew it. Henry bowled on. "A perpetrator of *what*?"

"Oh, I don't know. How about the murder at the Bishop's Palace?" It was the first time he had used the word *murder*. "How about the theft of the Swynford Jewel?"

"That's absolutely ridiculous. My daughter—"

"It's all supposition, Henry, dear," Genevieve said mildly. She looked up, all pink and white innocence. "Isn't it, Chief Inspector?"

Again, a silence, as he looked each of them over.

"It is," he said at last. "Until you three tell me everything you know."

A van pulled up behind Henry's car, at the front of the cottage. A number of scene-of-crimes officers clambered out.

"Stay here," DCI Burroughs ordered, then moved to confer with his army of evidence collectors.

Aventurine reached for Henry's arm. He moved stiffly away from her, evading her hand. Genevieve leaned into her gently, an elderly lady turning to her for support. Aventurine's head spun, as the white-suited SOCOs moved past into the house, with distress, anxiety, the works. Genevieve still clung to her hand. If *clung* was the word.

Burroughs returned. "Until," he murmured into Avi's other ear on the way by, "or unless—we find out those two times Nicola came home?—that it *wasn't* Nicola."

Twenty-seven

"You seemed to get on with Detective Burroughs quite well, Mary. Like a house on fire. And don't you feed me that *old woman* line again, because I don't want to hear it." Aventurine was driving slowly, down toward the river and Mary Wentworth's home on Chelmsford Street, unable to shake the feeling that they were being followed. "You never did tell me how that interview with the police went," she added accusingly. "You know. When they were checking my alibi for the time of the theft."

Genevieve shrugged, adjusting her seat belt. "It went. I *am* a doddering old woman, and you were kind enough to take me on your drive to Kettlethorpe. I paid for our lunch in gratitude, showed them the card receipt—"

"I know, I know. I would have paid in cash," Aventurine said, again marveling at the old spy's foresight.

"Sometimes you need to leave a trail," Genevieve pointed out easily. "Sometimes it's better not to. It's always good to be able to tell the difference."

There was little traffic, and an open parking space not far from the house Genevieve indicated, where a single light burned in the front window.

"I don't need to leave a trail," she continued. "But Mary Wentworth does. And now, because Mary's a doddering old woman, she needs you to see her to her door, to make sure she gets in all right."

So Genevieve felt it, too.

"In case anyone is watching?"

"In case anyone cares to look at the CCTV footage later, yes." Genevieve raised her eyebrows as she opened the car door. "I don't think your charming police detective followed us down here, but of course, you never know with these people."

These people? "He's not my charming police detective."

"Perhaps not."

She was waiting, and after a moment, Aventurine climbed out to come around and give her a hand out of the car. She locked it with the fob, and when Genevieve fumbled with her own house key, drawing it out of her handbag—Genevieve carrying a handbag was not something Aventurine could quite get used to—Avi took it to unlock the unprepossessing door in the unprepossessing house. When Genevieve touched the light switch, she revealed good, though slightly worn, furniture, with antimacassars on the arms. Everything was meticulously clean, but looked lived in.

"The police came here." Aventurine followed the other woman into the house, and peered down the hallway.

"Had a look around, refused tea when offered, and left Mary to her dithering old womanhood rather quickly." Genevieve smiled, a self-satisfied curl of the lips. "It's a clever disguise."

"You are an old woman," Avi countered tartly. "You tell me that all the time."

"Chronologically, yes. But that's the only gauge that means anything to me." Now she raised her voice slightly. "Can I offer you a cup of tea before you go, dear?"

Aventurine opened her mouth, and Genevieve stepped on her foot. A couple strolled past on Chelmsford Street, holding themselves carefully apart from one another.

"No, thank you, Mary," she replied, as though speaking to a deaf aunt. "It's a little late for me, and I really must be getting back." Aventurine stepped back out onto the pavement. "I'll see you in the morning, shall I, to take you to your appointment?"

Surprisingly, Genevieve leaned forward to press a cheek to hers. "Thank you, dear," she said, straightening and patting Aventurine on the shoulder. She smelled vaguely of lavender, the optimal old lady fragrance. "You really are a good girl. Bring your sister around when she gets here." Then the door closed behind her. Avi heard the snick of the lock. And then the snick of the second one.

Her sister?

Despite downing a couple of paracetamol, Aventurine could not fall asleep.

What had Genevieve meant?

Micheline? But Micheline had said nothing about returning to the UK. She had floated the idea of flying to Italy to meet up with Paul and Lance, but talk of that possibility had petered out: both she and Mick were still tip-toeing gingerly around Paul, and perhaps her nephew had put paid to that idea. Aventurine hoped not, for that would have hurt Mick. The truth of the matter is that none of them had any idea how to deal with the others; the wedge that Neil had driven between them was too big, had gone too deep.

Not for the first time did Aventurine curse the snake. *We have killed the snake, not scotched it,* she reminded herself. Punching the pillows, she rolled over onto her other side.

It was no use. She grabbed the phone and went to speed dial.

Micheline's phone rang and rang and went to voicemail.

"Call me," Avi said, and ended the message. She slumped back among the pillows, which seemingly had gone flat again.

Of course, Genevieve could have meant Nicola. They could have been sisters: they looked alike, they both wrote books, they both quoted Kafka in a self-deprecating manner. But Aventurine was no closer to finding Henry's daughter than she had been last Wednesday. The cataloging of their likenesses only made Aventurine think of Micheline's DNA testing—had there been a response yet? How long did these things take? And Genevieve didn't know about the kits

Mick had sent away in the hopes of finding—*something.* Or maybe she did—the old spy wasn't an old spy for nothing. Who knew what ways she had to find out things? For all Avi could tell, Genevieve had hacked into her phone ages ago, and was privy to every bit of information stored there.

Part III:

Mary

Twenty-eight

Aventurine dutifully reported to Chelmsford Street at nine the following morning. Her head ached, she had bags under her eyes, and she felt as though she hadn't closed those eyes for a moment in the night. Genevieve, looking pink and sprightly—Mary probably got up at the crack of dawn to water her geraniums—let her in and ushered her back to the kitchen.

"I've tea on," she said. "Come on back."

The kitchen was minuscule, and, as used to Aventurine was to Genevieve's custom-designed cook's kitchen, this one was a shock. Used as she was to the green Aga with the many burners, and the two ovens, along with the refrigerator that was large enough, she reckoned, to fit an entire ox, she now stared around her in amazement. Like the front room, this kitchen was meticulously clean, but the appliances were not new, and showed years of wear. As no doubt Mary Wentworth's would, she being a widow on a pension and all.

Curiously, Avi opened one of the upper cupboards, to find only a box of Yorkshire tea bags, and a can of Spam. She closed the door quickly.

"Not much in here," she observed.

Genevieve shrugged. "Emergency rations. I haven't been out provisioning yet. Right now Mary Wentworth either eats out, on the kindness of her friends, or orders meal delivery."

"Uber Eats?" Aventurine couldn't help but laugh, picturing the elderly spy having Wahaca delivered. Or Pizza Express. "But—you're such a good cook."

The look Genevieve tossed over her shoulder was impatient. "Mary Wentworth isn't, necessarily, though."

Aventurine felt shamed for a moment—*not everyone could be a good cook*—and then realized, of course, that the metaphorical floor of this funhouse was tilting again, where Genevieve was in control.

"Who is—who was—Mary Wentworth?" Avi asked slowly. She watched Genevieve check the water level in the kettle, before dumping it out, rinsing it, and refilling it. She flicked the switch, and it lighted blue. Tea was an emergency ration, apparently, and everything—for days, it seemed to Avi—was an emergency.

"Wait here," the old woman said, and left the room. In a few minutes she had returned with an armload of clothing, which she spread across the kitchen table. Then, multi-tasking again, she opened another cupboard to draw out two mugs—the only two mugs, Aventurine noted.

"Mary Wentworth," Genevieve said, "is a state of mind."

Aventurine moved to look out into the nondescript garden, where the grass could have used a trim. Mary Wentworth didn't have a mower, or a string trimmer? "You make it sound as though she's one of a set of multiple personalities."

The old woman shrugged. "That's one way to look at it." She reached for the box of Yorkshire tea and pulled out a couple of tea bags. "She's a persona. A disguise."

"Yours? A cover?"

Again the arch look. "Sometimes mine. Sometimes other people's."

The ground beneath Aventurine's feet was really unstable now. "You share a cover. You and—other operatives."

The water came to a boil in the kettle, which shut itself off. Genevieve poured. "We share the accoutrements of Mary Wentworth. This house. The credit and debit cards. Whatever Mary owns, we use."

"But—" Aventurine's voice was weak, and so were her knees. She sank into a chair next to the clothing on the table, and took a deep breath. "Mary doesn't own anything. Mary doesn't exist."

"Except when we need her."

It was too much. Avi accepted the tea mug, and pushed away a few clothes hangers to give herself space on the table. "And you need her to exist now." She rubbed the crease between her eyes, but this morning's headache remained. "Why?"

Instead of answering, Genevieve opened the refrigerator and brought out a small carton of milk. She opened it, sniffed at it, and jerked her nose away, grimacing. She poured the contents down the sink and ran the water after it.

"If I told you—" She let her voice trail off.

"I know, I know. You'd have to kill me." Aventurine clutched at her mug again with both hands, but it was too hot to hold. "I know."

Genevieve set her own mug on the table, then pulled a soft blue-grey skirt from the pile she had spread there. "In any case, sometimes our Mary has splendid taste in clothes." She glanced at the label. "Max Mara. And these ought to fit you." There was a jacket to match, and a cream-colored silk blouse in a loose surplice.

Aventurine gulped and took a sip from her mug; the tea was still far too hot. "Me?"

Genevieve raised her fine brows. "You. Because it's your turn to be Mary Wentworth."

Aventurine's jaw dropped. "*Me?*" she repeated.

Genevieve took away the tea and thrust the clothing into her arms instead. "Go change. Use one of the bedrooms upstairs."

"But why?"

"I'll tell you when you get back down. Suffice it to say that you have your first assignment."

A pair of impossibly high heels with tell-tale red soles lay on their sides on the table.

"I'm not supposed to wear *those*," Aventurine protested.

Again the shrug. "They go with the suit. How are you with heels?"

"You're going to get me killed. By a pair of shoes."

"There are worse ways to go."

Aventurine stood, taking the suit and leaving the shoes. "Maybe. But I think I'd like to prolong my life just that much longer, thanks."

Upstairs, two bedrooms and a bath. Neither of the bedrooms, strangely, looked occupied, and Aventurine found herself scanning for signs that Genevieve might have actually slept in one. That Genevieve actually slept. She chose the room to the rear, and donned the Max Mara suit. In the armload of clothes was an unopened pair of hose, and with a grimace—when was the last time she'd poured herself into a pair?-—Aventurine slipped those on. Then she turned to look at the mirror on the back of the door, and was astonished. Who the hell was that? Of course, the hair and the face gave her away, but she could see, examining the reflection, why women might be tempted to pay an arm and a leg for this suit. It shimmered over her shoulders and hips, the skirt gliding when she moved: it was amazing how several thousand dollars of tailoring could transform a person. And Genevieve had been right: the suit did fit, surprisingly well. With one last mildly shocked look at the new Mary Wentworth, Aventurine descended again to present herself to the old spy for inspection.

"Silver earrings," Genevieve decided, eying her critically. A case had appeared on the kitchen table, and she pulled out some jewelry. "Chunky necklace. Ring with a big rock. You need to look like a person with more money than sense."

"Would you care to tell me what we're doing here?" Aventurine turned and held her hair up from the back of her neck. Genevieve's fingers were cool against her nape as she did the clasp of the necklace.

A laptop was also open on the table. Now Genevieve indicated the page, with a featured property which had definitely been built—or perhaps restored—by someone with far too much money and far too little taste. "Congratulations, Mary. You've just bought a house for your long weekends."

Avi almost slumped back into her chair, but remembered herself in time, and glided in for a soft landing, crossing her ankles gracefully, before pulling the computer closer. "I bought a house." She scrolled through the photographs: several reception rooms, a kitchen even Genevieve would die for, bedrooms which had furniture arranged in ways that made them look obviously staged. "Why would I have done such a thing?" She fixated on a bath with a free-standing tub, all swooping lines, but so high she'd need a stepladder to climb in and out of it.

Genevieve had disappeared into the bathroom here, and now returned with a full makeup kit.

"Who knows why the rich do these things? To throw house parties, I assume, for their other rich friends."

The front elevation showed a curving drive that circled around a fountain—dry in the picture—with a naked cherub apparently meant to dump water from the jug he was holding awkwardly over his shoulder. The expression on his face made Avi want to punch him.

Genevieve dumped the makeup out onto the table. A tube of lipstick rolled off onto the floor, and Aventurine stooped to pick it up. When she opened it, she found the red to be the same color as the soles of the Leboutins. She capped it again quickly.

"I still don't get it."

"Sit back. I need to do your face."

Aventurine jerked away from the hands approaching with the foundation sponge. "What are you doing? You don't wear makeup. Do you even know what you're doing?"

Genevieve snorted impatiently. "Listen, sister. I've been doing makeup for myself and others since before you were born."

"But you don't wear any."

How many times would Avi see that Gallic shrug? "One of the perks of being as old as I am. Now hold still. I'm going for the casual yet elegant look. I don't want to accidentally draw on wings that swoop halfway to your temples."

Makeup, then hair.

"Go look in the mirror," Genevieve instructed at last.

Aventurine did not move from the chair. She didn't quite dare, in case the illusion of the new Mary Wentworth shattered with the movement. "Not until you tell me what this is all about."

Genevieve was packing the foundation and eyeliner back into the case. "After you go have a look."

The reflection, with its red mouth, drew a gasp. "Oh, my God, Genevieve, you've turned me into Taylor Swift." Avi dashed back to the kitchen. "Can I go out like this? I can't possibly go out like this." She grasped the back of the kitchen chair for support. Before her, the computer, and the impossibly high bath: she felt the distinct need to climb into it immediately.

"Put on the shoes," Genevieve instructed. "You've got an appointment with a security company, to wire up your new estate. Because that's what rich people do." She tidied up the table, closing down the laptop, returning the makeup kit to the bathroom. "We've been going at this from the wrong direction for far too long."

"Why me? Why not one of your other—people?" Aventurine checked the on-board Sat-Nav, and signaled to take the next left. "I mean, we've already established that I'm a rank amateur. Shouldn't you have a professional for this?"

The look Genevieve tossed from the passenger seat was inscrutable. "Perhaps it's time that you stepped up into the pro circuit." She sighed. "And as for me—I've always had to work with whatever tools were to hand."

"I'm a tool."

"We're all tools."

They were heading north toward Burton. Genevieve had looked up the street map, and the street view, before heading out.

"None of this, Aventurine, is official business," she continued, apparently relenting. "None of it is. I thought I'd made that clear. So I don't have the resources you imagine at my disposal. I have to improvise. I have to use what I find convenient."

"And that's me."

"I consider your training part of the challenge."

Aventurine didn't know whether to be gratified or frightened.

She parked the car away from the front entrance.

"Remember," Genevieve said, eyeing her critically. "You'll need to play that up. You're a *nouveau riche* American, who's snapped up a drafty old country manner and dropped another load of money tarting it up. Give them bait they'll overcome any reservations to bite." She handed Avi the smart hat nearly the same color as the suit, and a pair of oversized Jackie O sunglasses. Aventurine couldn't help but feel her appearance absolutely screamed money. She tucked the black Valentino bag over her arm, threw up a quick prayer to whatever god oversaw deception, and swished down the pavement to push open the door.

A buzzer sounded jarringly. The surprisingly young receptionist glanced up, her eyes widening as Avi stepped into the front office. The glance took in the bag, the shoes, the entire package, and the woman drew in a sharp breath. She peered closer at Avi's face, then shook her head.

So chic, Genevieve had said.

So not me, Avi had replied helplessly.

That's because you're not you. You're Mary Wentworth. The new and improved version.

Now Aventurine cleared her throat gently. "Good morning," she said, in a voice as regal as she could muster. "I need to speak to someone about installing a security system in my house?" Big, she thought. Brash. She swept her sunglasses off her face and dropped them into her bag, then drew out a business card and handed it to the woman.

"Mary Wentworth," she introduced herself. "Miss Hallsey was recommended to me by a business acquaintance."

The young woman took the embossed card and gazed down at it. *Paula Edwards,* read the nameplate at the front of the reception desk. She didn't look old enough to be a Paula.

Aventurine removed the swing coat Genevieve had insisted she wear, and folded it over her arm as the receptionist scurried behind a smoked glass partition. Avi glanced around the tastefully subdued outer office, trying to look bored. After a moment or two, she let out a long-suffering sigh, and checked the time on the chunky bangle watch on her left wrist—just as the receptionist returned, followed by a tall man in a dark suit.

Aventurine froze.

Him. The man from the terrace.

Did he freeze as well? His eyes rested on her face—*Nicola's face*—no, *Mary Wentworth's face*—but only briefly, before a smooth hardness dropped over his expression. Only those eyes seemed wary.

"Miss Wentworth," he said, holding out a hand.

After a beat, she handed him her coat. He quickly passed it off to Paula, who had fallen back uncertainly, without looking. "I'll just hang this up," the receptionist murmured. Neither acknowledged her.

"It's *Mrs.* Wentworth, actually," Aventurine corrected, in her bored drawl. She knew he'd look to her left hand, where Genevieve had insisted she wear a gleaming wedding pair.

"Of course. My apologies." He tilted his head, allowing a slight frown to show between his brows. "I'm Magnus Etheredge. I'm sorry, but have we met before?"

Aventurine looked him up and down, appraising him coolly. "I don't think so. I might have remembered." She sighed again, looking at her watch once more, as though this chit-chat were wasting her valuable time. "Actually, I was here to see a person called Nicola Hallsey. She was recommended to me as someone who could help with the security system for my new home in Torksey. Is she available? I've a few more appointments this morning, and I'm afraid I don't have much time."

At the sound of Nicola's name, Magnus Etheredge's eyes narrowed, but at the mention of the village of Torksey, they widened again. Genevieve had said that would perk him up—*look rich, talk rich,* she had advised dryly. *People will believe anything if you act privileged and bored enough.*

"Miss Hallsey is not available this morning, Mrs. Wentworth," he said apologetically. He swept a hand toward the inner office. "Perhaps you might come have a seat and tell me what your needs are. As the owner of the firm, I'm sure I can be of help."

Aventurine knew she had to tread carefully here. Again she looked at her watch, and adopted a slightly annoyed look. "When will she be back?" she asked. "I'm sure I don't want to waste your valuable time. And she did come highly recommended." She tried to give the impression, with her tone, that his *valuable time* was not quite as important as her own *valuable time.* It was a delicate balance.

There was a slight hesitation. "No, that's fine," Etheredge said after a moment. "Miss Hallsey is—on extended leave. Family business, I understand."

"Can you get in touch with her?"

A shadow passed behind his eyes. "No, I'm afraid not." Then back to his urbane self. "Please. Come into my office. Miss Edwards will bring something to drink. Do you take coffee? Tea?" He took her elbow, and it was all Aventurine could do not to flinch. He did not even deign to cast a glance at poor Miss Edwards; she might have been a fixture, not a human.

"Coffee, please," Avi said. As though to ask otherwise of her American-ness was a social gaffe of the first order.

The office was on a corner, with windows to two sides; as they overlooked not some magnificent skyline, but the parking lot of an industrial estate, the effect was lost. The furnishings gleamed, though. Etheredge held a richly upholstered chair for her, before circling behind his broad, and nearly empty, expanse of a desk to seat himself. He tented his fingertips. "You're American."

"I am, originally." Avi hoped her drawl would place her somewhere in the vague Southwest; she tried to appear bored with the question. "Married over here, now widowed over here." No doubt with loads of money; the clothing, she knew, screamed it. Probably this version of Mary Wentworth had married an elderly man with a minor title and a large offshore bank account. Slowly she arranged herself in the chair, crossing her ankles, which the heels emphasized. She adjusted the heavy necklace at her throat, and noted with gratification the way his glance sharpened with every movement: she could almost see cartoon dollar signs—pound signs—rolling behind his eyes. *Work on high maintenance*, Genevieve's voice instructed at the back of her mind. Aventurine examined her ridiculously red nails.

Magnus Etheredge made a noise which was no doubt supposed to be sympathetic, but which sounded, to Avi's ears, more like the licking of chops. He was a type, she realized; or perhaps she should say he was interested in far more than her alarm system: his not-so-well-hidden focus was on a woman who had the wherewithal to require an elaborate alarm system.

"You said the firm was recommended to you by someone?" Etheredge leaned forward now, hands clasped on his desk blotter. Clear of papers. Though a computer was at his left elbow.

Aventurine raised an eyebrow, assessing him and being fairly obvious about it. *There are many ways to bait a trap.* She let her gaze linger on his hands—no ring on his finger. "Specifically, my acquaintance—an old school friend of my husband's—mentioned this Miss Hallsey." She smiled, but at his hands, not at his face: make of that what he would. "But I'm sure you'll be able to take care of *all* my needs equally well."

"If not better," he suggested.

She could almost hear the trap snap shut. She opened her bag and withdrew the sheaf of house plans Genevieve had given her, just as the receptionist tapped and entered with the coffee tray.

If nothing else, Magnus Etheredge *did* appear quite knowledgeable about the installation and maintenance of an alarm and security system, and seemed more than a little excited about the plans for the enormous property. He spoke of the need for cameras at particular angles and distances from one another; his finger traced from window to door on the plans of the huge house while he explained. Something in the back of Aventurine's mind snagged on his level of enthusiasm: was it because of the fair amount of income providing security to such a house would bring to the company, or was it because of the rich, widowed (and no doubt lonely) client, who would need his services—his personal touch? *Magnus indeed,* she thought dryly, allowing him to invite her back to examine the banks of monitors in the cavernous room beyond the offices, where the real work of security systems took place. He kept a sure hand at her elbow as he guided her, and it was all she could do not to cringe, remembering the way she had seen him put that same hand on Nicola Hallsey, that evening on the hotel terrace.

"Any breach of security sounds an immediate alarm, both at the property itself, and at the monitors here at the facility. We are then able to initiate contact with our client, and with the appropriate emergency services." His voice continued on, and she had to lean in to hear him. There were a handful of security personnel in uniforms seated at various consoles, and it said something to her that he did not speak to any of them, though a few looked up at their entrance.

He walked her back to the office. That tiny frown between his eyes was back; he'd better watch out, or he'd have permanent wrinkles in his handsome face. "Are you certain we haven't met before?" he asked, standing uncomfortably close.

Aventurine did not move away, though her instincts told her to run. *Play that by ear,* Genevieve had said on the drive over. *See if anyone pegs the likeness.* It was unlikely, the old spy had told her, because the outside trappings can convince anyone to ignore what they might actually know. Now Avi once again raked what she hoped was a provocative glance over him, from head to toe, lingering, as though she liked what she saw. "I don't think so. I'm sure I would have remembered. Why?"

Etheredge shook his head, meeting her smile with a pseudo-sincere one of his own. "You just look like—someone I used to know."

The past tense was somehow chilling.

"I hope she was—interesting." She rested her gaze on his mouth.

"Not as interesting as you, Mrs. Wentworth."

Her skin was crawling. She turned toward the door, moving slightly away, knowing that if he touched her again, he'd feel only the icy coldness of her skin. How did Genevieve do this?

Well, she obviously didn't anymore, which is why she had sent Aventurine out in her place.

At the door, Aventurine handed him another business card, this one with a cell phone number printed on it. He held her hand a bit longer than necessary as he took it.

"I'll run you up a quick estimate and get back to you," he said. She noted that he slipped the card into his pocket, rather than handing it to the secretary. "Of course, it would be better if I might come out to the property and have a look around. Measure properly. You understand."

Aventurine did understand, and she was repulsed. He was too like Neil to be true. She slewed him a look so sharp it should have required first aid, but he did not even seem to notice. Slavering jaws, she thought; she suspected he viewed the entire transaction as a wolf would: easy pickings, in his view. Stupid, vain American woman with more money than sense. Though whether his goal was access to her wealth through her house or through her person, she wasn't sure. Probably both.

All this ran through her mind as she lifted her chin and smiled. "That might be a marvelous idea. I'll check with my agents and see about a good time. Call me when you've run up some numbers, and perhaps we can make a date of it."

Etheredge held the door for her, and she felt his eyes on her back as she drew out her cell phone and dialed while she walked away. Carefully, so as not to trip over the damned heels. When she turned the corner, she leaned against the wall, closing her eyes and breathing heavily. Then she stripped off the shoes and ran barefoot along the pavement until she came to the place where Genevieve had started the rental car's engine.

Twenty-nine

For a long moment Aventurine leaned back in the passenger seat, eyes closed; beneath the hand she pressed to her chest, she imagined she could feel her heart fluttering, a tiny terrified bird trapped in a cage.

"Well?" Genevieve demanded.

"Drive," Avi ordered. She did not stop to wonder what the old woman was doing behind the wheel.

Genevieve put the car into gear without further question, and Aventurine was grateful. She kept her eyes closed until the movement of the car made her feel vertiginous.

"Don't go straight to the hotel," she said, as they approached the Bailgate.

A slight flick, and the sound of the directional. Genevieve took a right. She glanced up into the rearview. "You think we might have been followed?"

"I don't know, and I don't care, either."

She liked that Genevieve didn't question the gut instinct.

"That bad?"

"Worse than that bad." Aventurine took a deep breath, her heart still pounding unsteadily. "He's that guy. Magnus Etheredge is Nicola's guy from the terrace." She wiped a hand across her face, forgetting the makeup.

"Did he recognize you?"

"Not as me. But as someone who looks very much like Nicola."

"We expected that. But not for this reason. Shit."

"You wanted that to happen." The vulgarity both surprised Aventurine and didn't; no doubt with her early life and upbringing, and her work among agents for so much of her life, Genevieve was versant with all sorts of colorful vocabulary, in all sorts of languages. Yet Avi very rarely heard those words from her.

"But not for that reason."

"The only time he would have seen me—being me, and not all tarted up as Mary Wentworth—before this morning would have been that one time in the beer garden, and he was far too busy trying to strong-arm Nicola to pay attention to some middle-aged woman hiding behind a book, or tripping him up with a chair." Aventurine moved to wipe her brow, but remembering the makeup, stopped herself just in time. "Still—"

"We should have thought about the possibility that the man you saw would have been a co-worker. Her boss." Genevieve's voice was rife with disgust. She had turned the car, at last, into the car park behind the hotel, and now backed easily into a slot between a Mazda and a Mini. She turned off the engine and passed over the keys.

"He did ask a couple of times whether we'd met. He mentioned my resemblance to *someone he used to know.* Used to. Past tense." Aventurine did not mention the clenching of her stomach each time, when she was certain her cover had been blown, or when he touched her or looked at her in that over-familiar way. She didn't mention how she had channeled a certain sixteen-year-old operative to lift her chin and brazen it out.

"What did you do?"

"Deny, deny, deny. Behave in a way as far from naturally as possible. Throw out Mary Wentworth's exclusive expensive address. Lay the plans to that behemoth of a mansion across his desk, and play the rich, sex-starved widow to the hilt. Come on to him a little bit."

"Good girl."

Aventurine was surprised at how good the approbation felt.

"Did he fall for it?"

"Honestly, darling," Avi drawled. "They always fall for it."

Genevieve laughed darkly, and patted her knee once. "You're learning. Well done that, woman." Now she took the black handbag, and dug around inside until she found a cell phone. She handed it to Aventurine. "Call him," she said.

Avi clicked the phone on. It was, of course, the burner with the number on Mary Wentworth's business card. Of course. "Now?"

"Now. It'll keep him off balance."

"And tell him what?"

"Tomorrow morning. Say—eleven. Not too early, in case you're the sort that wakes at the crack of ten. Tell him you'll meet him at the property."

"But—" This was moving too fast. "How are we supposed to get in? Do you have keys?"

Genevieve smiled craftily. "Keys? Who needs keys?"

Aventurine could only hope Mary Wentworth had another Max Mara suit hanging around.

Thirty

A fter they'd slipped the car into the far garage bay and pulled the door to—*should have rented a Porsche*—Aventurine tented her hand over her brow to look out onto the unfamiliar countryside spread out below them. Even at this time of the year, there was a golden sheen to the day. The house was sited at the crest of a hill, overlooking rolling pastureland; sheep, or maybe goats—Aventurine couldn't really tell from this distance—dotted the faded grass. Sheep, she decided: nobody would keep that many goats.

Genevieve handed her the strappy heels. "Come on, then. We've only got about half an hour to acclimatize ourselves before our Magnus Etheredge arrives."

"Whose house is this?" Avi called to the retreating back, before throwing up her hands. She followed Genevieve toward a rear door, all planks and iron fittings, and set deep in the mellow stonework. Beside the door was an incongruous electronic keypad, and with a gloved finger, Genevieve punched in a code. There was a slight buzz, and the door opened to her touch.

Keys? What keys? Aventurine knew better than to ask.

"I haven't the slightest. We're only borrowing it, anyway."

How had the old spy got hold of the entry code? Aventurine shook her head. It probably was better not to know.

The back entryway was bare. Aventurine followed Genevieve past the kitchen, where a deep green Aga held pride of place, and into a long hallway that led past innumerable rooms to the front door with its sidelights of colored glass. At the foot of the staircase, a statue of a naked nymph cavorted on the newel post. Their footsteps echoed on the hardwood, a hollow sound of a house unlived in. She wondered how long it had been on the market, how long since it had been staged and shown by an estate agent. There had been no sign at the gates down at the road.

The thought caught her by surprise: what if there was a showing, while they were in the house? What if the estate agent came by to check on the place? What if there was a caretaker?

The perspiration was gathering at her hairline, and she touched the back of her hand gently to her skin, so as not to disturb her newly reapplied makeup.

"Relax," Genevieve ordered. She moved into a large and echoing reception room to her left, off which debauched a solarium as big as Nicola Hallsey's entire house. A glass-topped table and a steel-framed chair were the only furnishings here. "Everything's been taken care of. We're quite safe with the house all day. No one will come near."

"I'm still not sure what I'm supposed to do here," Aventurine protested. "What I'm supposed to say."

Genevieve turned. "Get him to talk. Get him to say something about Nicola. Maybe something about the Swynford Jewel."

Avi's surprise must have shown on her face, for the other woman clicked her tongue impatiently. "Come, now, Aventurine. Use your brains. Even your friend the detective knows there's a connection."

"He's not my friend," Aventurine replied automatically. "And it could be all coincidence."

Genevieve's expression made her wish she hadn't spoken. "In this world, coincidence doesn't exist. Nicola is missing. The Jewel is missing. The common denominator is the security company."

"Magnus Etheredge." That made it sound so obvious. "But what about the dead woman? Where does she fit in?"

"We don't know yet." The old woman frowned. "So far we haven't been successful in finding out. I haven't been successful at protecting the Jewel. You haven't been successful in finding Nicola. We haven't been very successful here at all."

"But perhaps Mary Wentworth will be."

"Yes. So put on the shoes."

They heard the whisper of tires on the gravel in the front of the house. Genevieve drew the heavy drapery away from the window with the tip of a finger.

"A Mercedes," she observed. "E Class convertible. Our Magnus must be doing well out of that security business." She let the curtain fall back into place. "I'm going to make myself scarce."

Aventurine found herself clenching her fists; she straightened her fingers and took several deep breaths, telling herself to relax. But she didn't like Magnus; she loathed him. He hit too close to home. "You'll be close by?" She couldn't keep the anxiety from her voice. She pressed her lipsticked lips together.

Genevieve's glance was somehow both calculating and sympathetic. "I'll be close by." On the way out of the room, surprisingly, she touched Aventurine's cheek. "We'll make an operative out of you yet." Then she disappeared.

The doorbell chimed, deep within the house. Aventurine squared her shoulders and crossed the hardwood foyer, the Leboutins clicking. When she opened the door, Magnus turned toward her, away from the rolling pastureland that spread out before them, no doubt put on just for their enjoyment. His smile widened, and he lifted the aviator glasses from his eyes.

"Mrs. Wentworth," he said. "This house—what a magnificent setting."

She held the door open for him. "Thank you. I think I'll be comfortable here, once the decorator and the furniture arrives." She sighed. "And once I've hired some help."

Etheredge nodded. He tucked the glasses into an inside pocket. He was standing very close, though still looking around the foyer, the stairway with its wrought iron rail curling away to the right and the upper floors. "You're not living here yet."

Aventurine shook her head. "No, no. It's not really habitable yet. So many things to have done—the security system being one." She glanced around, once again adopting that air of vague annoyance. "I'd offer you a cup of tea or a drink or whatever you Englishman want at this hour, before we start, but I'm afraid there's only the one chair, and no one to serve us." She attempted to wear the arrogance of someone who couldn't possibly imagine pouring tea or lifting a decanter herself. It was, she was relieved to find, hard going. She wasn't really a lost cause after all.

"Of course. Could we start—on the ground floor?" His voice was smooth, the corner of his mouth turned up in a private sort of smile, as though he were making an inside joke.

Aventurine took one last obvious look at the Mercedes convertible in the drive, then raked her eyes over him: suit, cufflinks, tie tack. Evaluating. She reeled her own smile out slowly.

"Of course," she echoed, her smoothness matching his. She closed the heavy door and led the way further into the house.

As they ascended the sweeping stairway, Aventurine slightly ahead in order to entice him with the red soles of her shoes—did he even know how much Leboutins would set a person back?—she took a deep breath, then asked, "What about the theft in the Cathedral?"

She sensed him pause for a fraction of a moment before his footfalls resumed. "What about it?" His voice held a slight note of wariness.

"Well, isn't your company providing security?" She tried to balance her own tone on the fine edge between challenge and bored arrogance. "I'd like to think I was hiring a company who could avoid that sort of—difficulty." *Who could just do its job.*

They had reached the mirrored landing, and she saw Magnus's annoyance smooth over quickly, into handsome blandness.

"A technical lapse," he assured her quickly—too quickly? Was he uncomfortable, or just annoyed at her question? "A concatenation of unfortunate mishaps. We're cooperating fully with the authorities to determine what happened."

"Unfortunate mishaps? That resulted in the theft of some supposedly priceless artifact?" She sniffed disdainfully. "What about my belongings? What if something like that were to happen here?"

As though Mary Wentworth's belongings were far more important than *some supposedly priceless artifact.*

"It won't." Etheredge seemed to be trying to find a secure footing from which to defend himself. He spread his hands wide, and smiled reassuringly, his canines gleaming. "First, that was a one-off. The odds of that one camera failing at that time were extremely long. Second, this is a residential set-up, which is very different from the security protocols at the Medieval Library."

Still Aventurine narrowed her eyes. "I certainly hope so. I'd hate to choose your company for security, and then find my valuables have all been stolen."

She might have overplayed it, but Avi thought the situation was easily saved: it was fairly obvious that Magnus Etheredge's cupidity was overriding his caution. He'd push to close this deal, she knew, because Mary Wentworth, to him, was just another dumb blonde rich widow mark. She shrugged and smiled, and led him along the landing, opening door after door. In each, he paused, made a note or two in a small black notebook, snapped a picture with his over-large cell phone.

At last he paused in the bedroom of the master suite, barren save an ornate mirror over the fireplace. "You really do look like someone I used to know," he murmured, staring at their side-by-side reflections. "It's uncanny." He edged closer, and once again Aventurine felt her skin crawl; it was a marvel that he couldn't feel the waves of revulsion rolling off her. He frowned as though trying to remember, trying to *see,* the fine lines appearing between his eyebrows, marring the perfection of his tanned face.

"As I said yesterday: I hope she was interesting." Aventurine let her gaze linger on his reflection a bit longer than was necessary. Well, feigning interest *was* necessary. Just as this dialogue—so false, so forced: how could he not sense it?—was necessary to this game she was playing. She touched her fingers, with their improbably scarlet nails, to his sleeve. "Is she still—important to you?"

Magnus half-turned, letting his own hand cover hers. His black eyes traveled over her features, lingering on her mouth. "Oh, no. She's no longer in my life. You're vastly more interesting."

Vastly more wealthy, she read. Well, he didn't really know.

Suddenly his hand was sliding up her arm, past her shoulder, to cup her jaw. He leaned in. He was going to kiss her. *Oh, God.* She'd played her hand too well, too quickly. Aventurine froze. Was she supposed to do this? *This?* To make him talk? To trick him into letting her know where the Jewel was? Where Nicola was?

She's no longer in my life.

Aventurine shivered. Had Magnus done something to Nicola? Had he perhaps killed her, just as he had perhaps killed the woman at the Bishop's Palace? But Nicola had climbed into a silver car, not a sleek black convertible. Possibly Gio's car—but she banished that thought quickly. She only knew that Nicola was missing, and the possibilities were nearly endless. Aventurine closed her eyes, knowing her expression would betray her fear.

The younger Genevieve would have kissed Magnus.

The younger Genevieve might have done so much more, to get what she wanted from him.

And then the younger Genevieve might very well have slit his throat. The older one definitely would have.

Every nerve in Aventurine's body screamed against this, as she felt his warm breath along her cheek.

Then came the crash.

Aventurine sprang away from him. "What the hell was that?"

Etheredge pushed past her and into the corridor. She followed, to where he paused at the head of the sweeping stairway. At the foot, the grand front door stood open, and the statue of the nymph lay on the floor near its pedestal.

"Stay back," he warned. "There might be someone in the house."

Aventurine followed him down anyway. "It was just the wind," she protested. "It had to be just the wind."

"No wind opened that door," he said grimly. "Far too heavy." He glanced at her quickly. "Someone opened it hard enough to knock that statue down."

Leaning against the balustrade, she watched him search, opening one door, then another. "Hello?" he called. "Who's there?" His voice echoed in the emptiness.

But Aventurine knew he wouldn't find anyone.

Because Genevieve was far too wily for that.

Thirty-one

"Tell me I don't ever have to do that again," Aventurine shouted down the stairs of Mary Wentworth's terraced house.

In the back bedroom, she pulled the pins out of her chignon, to let her hair fall around her chin where it belonged. With a makeup remover wipe, she scrubbed the layers of Mary's face from her skin. Then she changed hurriedly out of the black Max Mara suit, hanging it up next to the blue one in the wardrobe. She felt a thousand times more human in the jeans and sweater, and she knew her aching feet would be so much more grateful in Converse than in Christian Leboutin. Genevieve looked up from the phone in her hand as Avi pounded down the stairs.

"Fish and chips," Aventurine said. "Stat."

Genevieve grimaced in distaste. "I'm envisioning the horrifying state of your arteries. You'll die young, from a heart attack."

"At least I have a heart," Avi shot back.

"Touché." The old woman raised an eyebrow. "Perhaps that's why I didn't die young."

"You can have a salad or something." Avi slung her bag over her shoulder and headed for the door. "Right now, I need sustenance. And a beer. Several beers. I've put in a hard day's work, trying to be a snake charmer." The thought of Magnus Etheredge's leer, the touch of his hands, made her break out in a sweat again.

"Okay. But take your phone."

When Aventurine turned, Genevieve held out what was recognizably her iPhone. The burner lay on the table before her. Despite herself, Avi patted the side pocket of her purse, which was, of course, empty.

"You were looking at my phone?" she demanded.

Genevieve shrugged that annoying shrug. "It was on vibrate. I just needed to see whether it was Magnus. Whether our trap was sprung."

"And was it?" Aventurine couldn't keep the peevishness from her voice. She jammed the phone into her bag, then pulled it out again, opening the screen with her fingerprint. "Oh, you couldn't open it. And he'd have called the other phone anyway. "

Again the shrug. "Your password is too easy, Aventurine." She slipped past to open the front door. "Let's go down to the river."

They found a pub at Brayford Pool with wide windows overlooking the docks on the far side. They placed their orders, and Aventurine found herself brushing back her windswept hair as she sipped at her pint. Outside, gulls strutted on the pavement as though they owned the place.

"I can't believe you opened my phone."

"I told you. I had to be sure our trap had sprung." There were mischievous creases at the corners of the old woman's eyes. "Don't worry. I didn't read any texts from that handsome Gio."

That didn't explain what the old spy was doing in her phone, when she had the spare on the table in front of her. Aventurine shot her a look that would have killed anyone else. But Genevieve was made of sterner stuff.

"Much better looking than that Magnus. Magnus, indeed." The old woman shook her head. "Talk about compensation. I bet his name is really Marcus, and he changed it to make himself feel better."

Aventurine couldn't help but laugh. The bitter got up her nose.

"I don't know what it is with all you young people and sex," Genevieve continued. "Really hasn't interested me since menopause. It's all so awkward and messy."

Avi thought of Gio, and smiled, then felt a pang.

"Sex or no sex, we've got no useful information from Magnus yet anyway."

Genevieve's expression was arch. "Probably because of no sex," she said. "I probably frightened him off with my imitation of a ghost." She winked. "A bit of door-slamming, a bit of art-toppling—"

"If you can call that art. But at the very least, you managed to back up his selling point that a home security system was an absolute necessity. I mean, really: you can never tell what sort of hoodlums are wandering about the countryside, breaking into mansions."

The plates came, and Aventurine, finding she was starving, tucked into her cholesterol-laden dinner. Across from her, Genevieve had chosen soup, and now gazed toward the outside, wearing that far-away look of concentration she donned when trying to figure out the seasoning in her food. So very rarely did Avi see the old woman still, feeling her way gingerly over her thoughts, that she stopped now and watched, fascinated.

"If you're going to observe your mark, you need to do it a bit more surreptitiously," Genevieve said, without looking over.

"Do you have eyes in the back of your head or something?"

"No. But there's plate glass. And this place is full of mirrors. For some reason, most places are—it's as if people think they'll just disappear if they can't see themselves." Genevieve lifted another spoonful of soup to her lips. "And this could use more seasoning. People also think they'll die if their food actually tastes of anything."

"You're a bit testy."

"We haven't found out anything useful. Of course I'm testy. We have to think of a way to push harder. Make something happen. Make someone spill what they know."

"Magnus Etheredge?"

"And Henry Hallsey. And Gio Constantine. And if need be, DCI Burroughs. There has to be a way to get to him." Her glance now was direct, and speculative.

Aventurine held up her hands, a fork-speared chip waving in the air. "Oh, no. Don't look at me. I've tried to seduce enough people for one day." She glared. "And you were the one who just said that sex was awkward and messy."

"You can always take a shower afterwards." Genevieve spooned some more soup. "A little water clears you of this deed."

Aventurine stared across the table at Genevieve. The other woman gazed back steadily, her head tilted, her eyes unblinking. She reminded Avi of nothing so much as those gulls outside—what were they doing this far inland, anyway?—strutting about on the cobbles, fixing their beady demanding eyes on anything that might be comestible.

"I'm an object lesson for you," Genevieve said, a note of amusement in her voice. She lifted her water glass. "After all, your book about me—isn't it better to see me in action? Isn't it better to be inside the story, rather than outside, having me repeat it to you later?"

"You still don't tell me everything," Aventurine complained. "Half the time I don't know why we're doing what we're doing. It's hard to be inside the story when the narrator is untrustworthy."

Genevieve took a sip and set the glass aside again. "If I told you everything, I'd have to kill you."

The old joke. "But—I'm just a writer. A *non-writing* writer." She grimaced; it hurt. "I've never had any aspirations to be an operative. Not like you." She dropped the fork to her plate with a clatter, and ran a frustrated hand through her hair. She felt hot and sweaty, despite the cooling temperatures, and the wind skittering a discarded paper napkin along the pavement outside. She probably looked now as far from the sleek and perfectly dressed Mary Wentworth as was possible, but despite what the old woman had said, she couldn't see her reflection in the window to be sure.

Genevieve only shrugged. "Oh, I never had any of those aspirations, either, all those years ago. I never woke up one day and wondered what it would be like to be a spy in occupied France." The waiter zoomed by, measuring their progress with a practiced eye, then was off again. "I just wanted out of the life I was living, and probably would have grown up living, and when I saw the advertisement in the newspaper, I showed up."

"But you stayed."

Genevieve seemed to be considering as she delicately spooned up a piece of chicken from her broth. "I found it suited me. The waiting. The planning. The trying to put myself into someone else's head, in order to outsmart them—that takes a certain level of empathy, and an enormous knowledge of psychology: both how they think, and how they feel. And then always came the action."

"Always the action."

"Always."

"And you are enjoying yourself now." Aventurine picked up the bottle of vinegar and looked at the label without really seeing it; instead she saw the ghostly film of parachutes falling in the darkness. Outside, a gull opened and closed its beak angrily, recognizing food it could not get to.

"Of course I am." Genevieve smiled, and seemed momentarily as far away as Avi's imaginings, in her reminiscence. "I keep telling you I'm an old woman, Aventurine. Opportunities like this don't come by as much as they used to. And now I must, for the most part, do the planning and have you be my surrogate in the action department."

Now she seemed sad. Aventurine thought again how this strange jewel theft seemed well below the usual level of Genevieve's operations. Perhaps she did have to dial it back because of her advanced age, because whatever nebulous and secretive part of the government no longer had the use for her that they had formerly.

"Wait." Aventurine paused in the splashing of vinegar over her remaining chips. "Are you really—*freelancing* here?" She couldn't help feel there was something missing. Something Genevieve knew, but Avi didn't. Oh, hell, there were probably tons Genevieve knew but Avi didn't. She shook her head to clear it. Unsuccessfully.

Once again, alone back at the hotel, Aventurine sat down at the desk, opened the laptop, and began writing, picking up where she'd left off the other night.

As dawn approached, she awoke once again, stretched across the bed in her clothes, with no real idea of how she'd got there.

Thirty-two

She slept through breakfast. Hell—she checked her Fitbit and found the battery dead; she flicked a key to bring the computer back to life, and saw she'd missed lunch, too. Again.

There was a knock at the door as she was brushing her teeth. She rinsed quickly. The knock came again. *Not* the insistent pounding of a police raid, if television dramas were anything to go by.

"Who is it?"

"Hi, honey, I'm home!"

Aventurine closed her eyes and leaned against the door for a moment. The voice. *That* voice. *That* man.

She shivered, not meaning to, and not wanting to. What she wanted was to punch him in the throat, knee him in the balls. At the same time, she wanted to have some wild, abandoned sex with him. He was keeping things from her, things which he absolutely *knew* she was trying to figure out. He held the key, and he had lain there, in that bed beside her, pretending he knew nothing.

What would Genevieve do?

Two courses of action: the punch, the sex. Which one would get the answers she sought? *That* was the course Genevieve would follow. But how was one supposed to know which one that was?

"Are you going to open the door?"

Aventurine took a deep breath, cleared her expression, and unlocked the door. She would make Commander Smith proud if it killed her.

"I'm sorry—I was brushing my teeth," she said.

Gio grinned at her and pushed into the room, then kicked the door shut behind him even as he cupped her face between his hands and kissed her. She couldn't help it: she responded.

"Mmm," he murmured against her mouth. "Minty fresh."

"I texted you," Avi said. *The other day. Before she knew.*

"I'm better in person than in text."

And he, damn his eyes, absolutely was.

Despite her misgivings, she luxuriated in his touch, in his kisses. She ran her hands along his bare skin and up into his hair; spent, he buried his face in her neck.

"Avi," he whispered.

"Not Nicola?" she asked.

In her arms, he stiffened immediately. Slowly he lifted himself up onto his elbows, to look down into her face.

"Don't go there, Aventurine." His voice had hardened. His eyes were flint.

"Why not? You obviously have." She stared up at him, afraid that she had now overstepped the fine line that defined their relationship, and that what they had been to one another for all these years was damaged beyond repair. "And we don't keep secrets from one another. Or do we?"

"You haven't a clue what you're talking about," he said. He pulled away from her abruptly, swinging his feet to the floor.

Aventurine struggled up and pulled the sheets around her protectively. "You're absolutely right, Gio, I don't." She looked at his back, wanting to count his vertebrae with her fingers, knowing she might never be able to do that again. She took a deep breath and pressed forward. "But you do, and you could enlighten me."

Gio grabbed his underwear from the floor, pulled it on, and then reached for his jeans. He straightened and turned, doing up his belt.

"Or not," he said, his voice ice cold. He said nothing else as he slipped on his shoes, pulled his shirt over his head, and then, picking up his jacket, slammed out of the room.

That was brilliant.

Genevieve wouldn't cry now, Aventurine told herself fiercely. She wouldn't.

Genevieve would follow him. Aventurine dressed faster than she ever had, grabbed her bag, and flew from the room, pulling on her own coat on the way downstairs.

Aventurine reached the rear door just as Gio was backing his silver car out of the slot behind the hotel. She ducked behind the gate to the beer garden, then hurried, bent nearly double, to her own rental car. Thank God for Genevieve and her foresight in backing in! She waited until she saw which way he had turned at the road before pulling out.

'How good are you at tailing another car?' the old spy had asked the other night. It would be trickier in the daylight, but she had the advantage in that Gio did not know she had rented a car, and could not know the color or make she was driving. She just had to make certain that she didn't get close enough to allow him to recognize her in his rearview mirror.

She cursed herself for not thinking to pair her phone with his, so she could use the Find-My feature. But then again, why would she ever have done such a thing, even thought to do it? It was not as though they'd ever been in a relationship that would require that kind of—connection? *Surveillance?* It had come in handy with Paul and Lance in the summer, but this? This was something out of the ordinary. No, this was just plain weird. She wished she had Genevieve with her: weirdness was that old woman's forté.

Up ahead, Gio slowed for a traffic circle, then eased out. Aventurine gripped the wheel and joined the traffic, following him off at the third exit. Another car had fit itself in between them, and for the time being Avi breathed a bit easier.

She wondered, as she followed, trying to keep that other car between them, how long Gio would remain unconscious of his tail. He had slowed down, ironically, as he left the outskirts of the city. It was as though, as his anger eased, so did his foot on the gas pedal. After a few miles, she realized that some of the scenery was beginning to look familiar. Hadn't she and Genevieve passed this way on the road to Kettlethorpe? As she drove on, she became more and more convinced that they had. But why would Gio be heading out there?

"Hey, Siri," she said. The cell phone was in her purse on the seat beside her. "Call Genevieve."

The phone, connected by Bluetooth to the car speakers, rang and rang, until the old woman answered. No trace of the quavery Mary Wentworth this morning. "What's going on, Aventurine?"

"I'm in a low-speed chase. I think we're going to Kettlethorpe."

"Who is we? Who are you chasing?"

"Gio."

For a moment she saw again the iciness of his gaze as he drew away from her in bed, and she swallowed.

"I asked him about Nicola."

"Oh, dear. Nothing like flushing the secrets out into the open, is there? I take it that didn't go well." Was that sympathy in Genevieve's voice? Probably not.

Flushing secrets. Like *flushing sewage.*

"Aventurine. Listen to me. I need you to be careful. Very careful."

"It's Gio."

"Who might be responsible for Nicola's disappearance. Who might be dangerous."

Up ahead, Gio had flicked on his left directional. The car between them pulled out and around, leaving no cover. Aventurine slowed, and then turned when she thought enough time had passed. She wished desperately that it was a dirt lane, instead of this narrow paved one; a bit of dust thrown up between them would definitely help hide her. As it was, she hung back as far as she dared.

"Where are you now?"

Aventurine reminded herself to breathe. "We're in the lane to the church, in Kettlethorpe."

"What the hell?" Obviously this was not what Genevieve had expected. "There's nothing out there, Aventurine. *Be careful.* There's next to no help to be had should you need it."

Avi hoped to God she wouldn't need help. This was Gio. *Gio.*

Who had looked at her with such coldness, as though he didn't even know her.

Gio.

He turned just past the church, and continued on down the road. Again Aventurine slowed, and then turned once she felt he'd moved far enough on. Then she was stymied by an enormous tractor, which had pulled out into the lane between them.

"Damn it all to hell!" she shouted, pounding the steering wheel with her fist.

"What's happened?" Genevieve demanded. Avi had forgotten to hang up the call.

"There's a tractor between us. I can't see him. He's getting away."

Along the line she could hear the sound of Genevieve's exhale. "Thank God."

"What do you mean? *He's getting away!*"

"That's exactly what I mean. Aventurine, leave it. It's too dangerous. You don't know what you'll find when you find him."

"That's what I have to find out," she ground, and hung up the call.

After an eternity, the tractor pulled off the lane and into a fallow field. Aventurine stepped on the gas, picking up as much speed as she dared among the ruts, but there was no sign of Gio's car ahead. No dust, no tail lights, nothing.

"Damn it all!" she shouted again, pounding the wheel again in frustration.

Avi slowed to a normal rate of speed, not wanting to drive herself off the road in her fury. Gio must have simply outdistanced her: there were no turnoffs here, no other lanes, simply fields to either side. Up ahead, a copse on the left. She scanned the road, the fields, the trees. No sign of him. Had he figured she'd been following? Had he taken the piece of luck that was the tractor to pull away while there was nothing she could do about it?

She pulled into a layby and scrabbled to find her phone. Data was slow, but she managed to call up her location on the maps application. Swiping at the screen, she enlarged it. Yes—there was another lane, just a couple hundred yards down this one. He had to have turned down there. Aventurine enlarged it further, and dragged it to follow the faintest of lines—until it petered out at what looked like a small building, on the bank of an equally small waterway. Quickly she tapped to the satellite view. Yes, there was something there. House? Barn?

Got him.

Genevieve's words in her head, she quickly texted her location and the link to the map, then pushed her way out of the car. She wouldn't drive down: far too risky. She could be seen; she might get stuck. No, she'd walk.

Good thing she wasn't wearing those Leboutins. She shut the door behind her and locked it.

Thirty-three

Aventurine could see flashes of Gio in his green jacket through the trees, like parts of a Picasso painting: an arm here, a torso there. Those leaves which hadn't already fallen were turning, and in the nostalgic slant of autumn sunlight made them glow a brilliant golden. Ordinarily she would have stopped to appreciate the colors, but now she only cursed inwardly, glaring down at the leaves littering the path into the trees. How was she supposed to follow Gio with any kind of stealth? He was up to something, sneaking off like this, and she knew she had to find out what that was. She'd already passed his car, pulled off to where the lane narrowed to little more than a path.

It occurred to her as she slipped carefully from tree to tree that he, too, was moving with an economy of motion foreign to him: walking with care, furtively almost, as though trying not to draw attention to himself. It helped that today he was dressed in subdued colors, greens and browns to help him blend in. It was as though he'd planned the camouflage. He absolutely meant not to be seen—which was also foreign to him.

Impatient, Avi stepped on a twig; the snap it made was the sound of a shot. She pulled back behind a giant oak and held her breath. He would be looking over his shoulder, she knew. Aventurine stayed frozen, as she had done playing statues in the cemetery with Micheline when they were young. She waited without breathing for

219

the faint sounds of Gio's continuing on. Perhaps he would think it an animal. A deer, a fox—what animals prowled this woodland? She had no idea. It sounded as though he took a step or two back towards her. She clenched her eyes closed and leaned into the tree, her breathing stilled, as though any of that would have any effect. A pause. Finally his steps moved away in the leaves. Only then did she exhale.

Aventurine counted to ten before she peered around the tree trunk. She could not see Gio clearly, but she could make out his movement through the woods. She calmed herself and followed.

The path took a slight dogleg to the left, and for a moment she panicked. Then she rounded the turn and saw Gio clambering over a stile, beyond which she could just make out a low-roofed building. A cottage, the one which had shown up on the satellite view. Aventurine slipped forward to the next tree, where the ground was soft from the off-and-on rain of the past several days. The bark of the trunk was wet under her hands as well. She peered around silently.

The door of the cottage opened.

Aventurine's breath caught.

Her doppelganger stepped out into the dying sunlight of the afternoon.

Aventurine's heart dropped.

Nicola. At last. *Nicola.*

There could be no mistaking her, even at this distance. It was as though Aventurine were looking at a reflection, or looking at Micheline.

She might have gasped. She didn't know. She felt dizzy, as though she'd been whirled around and thrown down in the middle of this glade, where everything swam. Gio. Nicola.

Gio held out his hands.

Nicola tripped across the small clearing and took them in her own. Gio bent down and kissed her, first one cheek, then the other.

Then he straightened, and, without releasing Nicola's hands, turned his gaze back down the path from which he'd come, in the general direction of the tree behind which Aventurine cowered.

"You might as well come out," he said now, that voice carrying through the afternoon. "Come out and meet Nicola."

She could hear her heart pounding, the blood rushing in her ears.

Aventurine took a deep breath and stepped out from her hiding place.

Part IV:

Circuit

Thirty-four

Outside the window the wind had increased, and now rain spattered against the glass; leaves which had held on to this point now fluttered down from the trees like snow. Aventurine wasn't cold, though; far from it—standing as she was near the fire Gio had lit. Her shock and fury still burned beneath her skin. She could feel Gio's and Nicola's eyes on the back of her neck, in this room that served as both the cottage's living room and kitchen.

"What about your boss?" she demanded of Nicola. "Magnus Etheredge? What about him?" The name tasted foul on her tongue.

The pause was so long that Aventurine finally turned away from the small window to glance between the two. Gio stood with his arms crossed, his eyes locked on Nicola, who gripped the back of a leather library chair with both hands. She met Gio's gaze momentarily, but then looked away.

They both spoke her name at once. "Aventurine—"

"I saw you with him, you know," she interrupted. "That last afternoon, before you *disappeared,* Nicola? At that beer garden." Avi too crossed her arms, and lifted her chin, challenging.

Nicola's eyes flickered up and away. "You saw us. Did you see him threaten me, then? Did you hear him?"

"I didn't hear anything but you saying *no.*" Aventurine swallowed then, realizing what she'd said. Nicola had said no, and had wrenched her arm—and her person—away. Avi closed her eyes, and felt herself sway for a second. The moment on the terrace suddenly was juxtaposed with that moment outside Neil's car in the Polygon in Southampton. *No.* Met by that laughing attitude of superiority, that mocking familiarity. "You were lovers," Avi said, but the anger was draining away, despite her clawing to maintain it: it had given her strength. In its place, the self-loathing at having become involved with the absolute wrong person. "You and Magnus Etheredge."

"Because he was using me," Nicola said, and the bitterness in her voice burned like acid.

"Using you." It was all too familiar. Magnus hadn't looked like Neil, but in every other way—his actions, his assumptions, his presence—he had been Neil reincarnated. Still, standing here at last in this dim front room, with the crackling of the fire and the pounding of the rain on the roof, facing the mirror image Aventurine had been looking for for days, she could not let it go. "Using you."

"To get to the Swynford Jewel."

Wordlessly, Gio pressed a tumbler of scotch into Nicola's hand. In the flickering lighting she looked ghostly, ethereal, her skin pale, her hair gold and sparking, a halo encircling her head. But on closer inspection, the dark circles beneath her eyes were evident.

Gio handed Aventurine a tumbler as well. She looked into its amber depths, and, her stomach churning, set the glass on the mantelpiece. It was getting too hot to be comfortable next to the fire, and she moved closer to the small window, where the old panes rattled in the frame against the wind.

There were just too many questions.

"How? And more, why?"

Nicola made a restless motion with her free hand, the slightest flutter which jarred. She took a sip from the scotch, and even in the dimness Aventurine could see her grimace before she took another drink.

"He has a buyer. Some oligarch art connoisseur." She shook her head. "Someone with a weird John of Gaunt fixation. I don't know. But in his twisted logic, he needed me for the heist."

"You?"

For the first time Nicola looked stricken.

"He wanted *you* to steal the Jewel?"

"Not me. Dad. And he could only get to Dad through me."

"Nicola," Aventurine said, the name still tasting of dull fury in her mouth. "You have to let your father know you're all right."

Nicola pressed a hand to her cheek. Were those tears in her eyes? Gio placed a comforting hand on her shoulder, which was not shrugged off. Aventurine felt her anger, ebbing and flowing with her confusion, revive.

"Dad," Nicola breathed. She looked up, almost pleadingly. "All I wanted to do was to protect him."

"By disappearing?" Aventurine looked around in disgust at the cozy front room of the cottage, the fire in the grate, the golden light it threw dancing on the plaster walls between the dark beams. On the sofa, a throw blanket tossed aside, a book open and face down over the arm.

Nicola opened her mouth to protest, but Gio cut in.

"Avi, you don't know what you're talking about. You've got no idea what's going on here."

Aventurine whirled on him. "You're right, Gio, I don't. But I'm beginning to figure it out, and I'm not liking it at all."

"Avi—"

"Shut up, Gio. Just shut up." Aventurine pulled out her cell phone: a couple of bars of weak signal, but signal all the same. She pressed her finger to it to unlock the screen, and held it out to Nicola. "Call him."

Nicola drew away from her outstretched hand as though from a venomous snake. "I—can't."

Aventurine set the phone on the table and leaned back, crossing her arms once again. "You'll let him worry about you like this? For God's sake, Nicola, he thinks you're dead." She felt like spitting. In her mind's eye she could see him crumpled on the destroyed chair in his daughter's cottage, his head in his hands; she could hear him crying out her name in anguish. How could this woman be so cruel? "Listen. I don't care about your love life. I don't care about your hiding out with Gio in this little love nest in the woods. You two can just go back to fucking your brains out, for all that matters. But let your father know you're safe. *That's* all that I care about. Your father. Henry."

Nicola raised those tear-filled green eyes, in that all-too-familiar face, to meet Aventurine's gaze. "You don't think I care?" she hissed. "He's *all* I care about. The *only* thing I care about." She glared. "Don't you get all high-and-mighty on me. They threatened him though me, so I disappeared. Don't you get it? If they couldn't find me, their threats couldn't work."

They?

"Magnus?"

"That damned Jewel. On display in the library. I was supposed to shut down the security system so Dad could steal it." She gulped. "Dad—if I didn't do what they wanted—he was going to *meet with an accident.*"

Thirty-five

Still confused, Aventurine ducked into the bathroom and locked the door behind her. She had a moment of misgiving: suppose Gio and Nicola took this opportunity to slip out to Gio's car and take off again? But somehow she thought they probably wouldn't. Their cover was blown. Their secret was out.

She leaned against the rolled edge of the old tub and called up Google maps again, to pinpoint the location. Then she texted a screenshot to Genevieve with a terse message. *Here. Bring Henry. Hurry.*

The reply pinged in only a matter of seconds. *OMW.*

Where the hell did she learn this stuff?

When Aventurine returned, Gio and Nicola were seated next to one another at the battered table to the right of the fireplace. Two tumblers and the bottle of single malt stood on the scarred surface between them. Wordlessly, his handsome face a black thundercloud, Gio stood to retrieve her own glass from the mantlepiece. He set it before a third chair, and waited for her to seat herself before he took his own place. Her heart contracted before she hardened herself. Nicola had both her hands wrapped around her glass, her face in profile as she stared out the window. Without thinking, Aventurine traced a finger along the fine ridge of her own nose.

Outside, the rain continued fitfully. The noise was loud against the roof.

Avi slumped in her chair.

Slowly Nicola turned to study her. Gio dropped his gaze to the scotch before him, as though considering; he placed his palms on the table to either side of the tumbler, instead of drinking. In the odd light, his hair appeared more silver than Aventurine remembered. *You're getting old, Gio,* she thought meanly.

"Who owns this cottage?" she asked. Out of all the things she wanted—needed—to know.

Nicola jerked her chin in Gio's direction. "He was good enough to let me use it."

"I didn't know he owned another property." A stupid observation. Apparently she didn't know very much about Gio at all. He didn't look up.

But wait. *He was good enough to let me use it.* Those had been Nicola's words.

Still Gio said nothing.

"His aunt left him to it. Isn't that right, Gio?" But when Gio steadfastly remained silent, Nicola shrugged. "Or something like that. Anyway, when I asked Gio for help, he suggested this place. They wouldn't link it to me. They wouldn't be able to find me here."

There it was again.

"Who are they?" Aventurine asked. "You keep calling them *they.* The people who were going to make Henry have that accident. The people who were threatening you. I thought it was Magnus Etheredge."

Nicola sighed impatiently, as though trying to explain to a particularly young child. She took a sip from her scotch, and made a face.

Why drink it if you don't like it? Aventurine lifted her own tumbler to her lips. It was particularly smooth, heathery. Gio, at least, had always had good taste in single malt. She set her glass down, and saw Nicola watching intently.

"The people who wanted the Swynford Jewel." Nicola took another drink. "The ones behind their front man, Magnus."

"And how did he become mixed up with this nebulous *they?*"

Again the impatience, demonstrated with a flick of the hand. "That's what he does, don't you see? If someone makes it worth his while. He's peculiarly placed, in the security company."

"But surely people have to notice. You know. When things of value go missing from places his company is supposedly providing protection for." Like the ugly mansion of Mary Wentworth. Whatever she might own of interest to some sideline client of Magus Etheredge.

On the table, her phone vibrated, and Aventurine risked a split-second glance at the screen. Micheline.

"Go ahead," Gio said. "Answer it."

She picked it up, and resumed glaring at the pair of them.

"I've got it, Aventurine," Micheline said, without preamble. "And you're not going to like it."

For a moment the cogs in her mind refused to engage. They made such a perfect couple, Nicola and Gio, sitting shoulder to shoulder in the chairs across from her. Except that Nicola should have been a bit older. Ten years older. Aventurine's age. Even as she glared, the bastard rested his hand on Nicola's arm. Yeah, he was like every other stereotypical man, Avi thought bitterly. Trading her in for a new model. She almost snorted aloud. Same make, newer model.

"What is it?" she said into the phone. "What?"

A deep breath. "The DNA results came back."

"And?" Aventurine focused her attention on Nicola. Her—their—doppelganger.

"She's in the database. And we share DNA. Enough to make her our grandmother, our cousin, or—our half-sister."

Stunned, and at the same time feeling blindsided by inevitably, Aventurine could not find the words to answer her sister. Finally she found her voice. "Listen, Mick, I can't talk right now. Let me call you back, okay?"

"Don't worry," Micheline said. "I'll be right there."

And hung up the call.

Aventurine dropped her phone back onto the table with a clatter, and stared dumbly at her grandmother, cousin, or—*half-sister.*

Thirty-six

Again Nicola had turned toward the window, her fine profile toward Aventurine.

Which one was it, then?

Was their father also Nicola's?

Or was Henry Hallsey their father?

She did not have time to reason it out, nor to ask the questions.

"Gio," Nicola said sharply. "There's someone in the garden."

Gio cursed. He whirled on Aventurine. "Were you followed?"

If he only knew. If he only picked up the phone and looked at her texts, the screenshots she'd sent to Genevieve.

"Get into the lav," he ordered Nicola. "Be ready to climb out the window. You know where the car is." He tossed her the keys.

The other woman slipped away from the table and melted into the shadows. Aventurine heard the squeal of hinges, and the snick of a latch.

A knock at the door.

"I hope you know what you've done," Gio snarled, before getting up to answer.

Aventurine took a drink from her tumbler, and then, after a moment, slugged the entire thing down. She would probably need the sustenance. The false courage. Whatever the hell it was.

Genevieve pushed past Gio and into the cottage. "We've brought pizza," she announced. Henry, looking mulish, followed her in. He carried three boxes in his arms, but dumped them quickly onto the table before scanning the room.

"Henry?" Aventurine gasped. She hadn't thought he'd come; she wondered what twist of the arm Genevieve had employed to get him here.

Apparently Nicola hadn't closed the bathroom door all the way, for now it opened and she eased out. When Henry's eyes fell on her, standing in the dim corner, he let out a strangled cry and stumbled toward her, his arms outstretched. It was almost painful to watch.

Aventurine turned away from their tearful embrace, to find Gio watching her. She glared until he looked down.

"What have you for plates and silver here?" Genevieve asked him briskly. She flipped the lid open on first one box, and then the next. The scent of pepperoni and tomato sauce filled the small room. She then moved to pull open the cupboards on either side of the sink, searching for dishes. "Two dinner plates," she observed. "Two dessert plates." Her up-and-down gaze measured Gio. "Quite the cozy set-up you have here. Two of everything. A cozy love nest. I take it there's only one bedroom?"

"I slept on the couch," he protested. "And it was damned uncomfortable." Then, with a glare, "Who the hell are you, anyway?"

"Oh, for God's sake, Gio," Aventurine muttered. She went to the open door and looked out into the dripping evening. No one else in the overgrown garden that she could see; Genevieve wouldn't have been followed—she'd be careful of that. They were alone, for the time being, anyway.

No. There was someone else out there.

"Holy Mary, it's wet out there," said a familiar voice. A figure stumbled in, and pulled off the hood of her rain jacket.

Micheline.

"You said you'd be right here," Avi managed.

"And here I am."

"God damn it, this is weird," Gio said, his eyes flitting between the three of them.

234

"Shut up, Gio," Mick said.

Fortunately there was a stock of paper towels, so they ate off those, huddled round the kitchen table. Except for Genevieve and Henry, of course; the old woman had claimed the plates for them. Outside, the wind and rain were picking up again. Henry sat next to his daughter, every once in a while reaching out a frail hand to touch her arm, her shoulder. *I'm sorry, Dad,* she had whispered while they were in each other's arms. *I'm sorry. There was no other way.*

Now the story tumbled out. How Nicola was to cut the security apparatus from the company headquarters for just long enough to allow Henry, in the building, to snatch the ruby and effect his escape; then she was to have flipped the network back on.

"A matter of minutes," she said. "It was a stupid plan. At least for me. If anything went wrong, they'd make their escape, and I'd be left holding the proverbial bag. I refused, of course."

"It was Magnus Etheredge putting this pressure on you." Genevieve delicately said nothing in front of Henry about how the pressure was applied, but the long look she gave Nicola made it plain she knew about her lover.

Nicola, for her part, tipped her chin defiantly. "Yes."

"Magnus Etheredge?" Henry asked. He had made little inroad on the single slice of pizza on his plate. "Oh, Nicola, this wasn't—your new beau? The one you'd had a couple of dates with?"

"Oh, Dad." Nicola covered his hand with her own. "It was stupid. I was lonely. He—took advantage of that."

"But you could have told me."

"Dad. The car accident? The person who hit your car and drove off?" She sniffled slightly. "They told me—Magnus told me—that they could do more, that they could do worse."

"What do you mean?"

Gio had turned on a few of the wall-mounted lights around the room, but they made little inroads into the dimness of the cottage.

Still, Aventurine could see the tears standing in Nicola's eyes. She caught herself feeling pity for her fear, but then she felt Gio's eyes on her face, and Avi steeled herself again.

"Dad, they threatened your life if I didn't help with their plan. If I didn't get you to help with their plan. So I—ran. Gio helped."

"And you didn't let me know."

"I couldn't let you know. I'm sorry, Dad. So sorry."

Henry's throat worked, and he squeezed his daughter's arm. "It's all right. I have you back now." His voice was raw, and he blinked several times.

Aventurine caught Micheline's eye. *Half-sister.* But now was not the time to be throwing that bit of information into the bull ring. She made a quick face, and Mick nodded. When Avi looked past her, Genevieve was studying them both.

"And then they searched your house, looking for you," the old woman said, picking up the conversational thread. "I presume these people weren't able to find a clue to your whereabouts."

"Only because I found it, and took it away before they had a chance," Aventurine said. She couldn't keep the bitterness out of her voice. Under the table, she felt her sister's knee press against hers. Her bag was on the floor next to her chair; she grabbed it and pulled out the photo of Gio.

All my love.

"This is how I figured it out," she said, looking up at Gio from under her brows.

"But the cottage." Gio was the one to finally swing the fractured conversation back around to the search. "Somebody actually broke in and tossed the place?"

"It was awful, Nicola," Henry said. "All your things. All your books."

"Was anything taken?" Gio asked. "Could you tell?"

"The laptop," Henry supplied. "That's the only obvious thing."

Nicola had pushed her plate aside. She glared at Aventurine. "You were in my house. You took this picture out of my house."

Aventurine held up her hands. "Hey. Your father asked me to see if there was any clue to your whereabouts. Your father gave me the key. I was doing him a favor, all right?"

"Dad—"

"I'm sorry, Nicola. I was frightened. I was only doing what I thought was best, what I thought would help. I'm sorry if I did wrong."

The younger woman put her arm around her father's shoulders and squeezed. "It's all right, Dad. I'm just sorry you had to go through that. I'm sorry I put you through that."

Aventurine sat back, something niggling at the back of her mind.

Micheline was the one who saw it first, the one who asked. "Was there any sign of forced entry?"

"I gave Aventurine a key," Henry said.

"No." Micheline was frowning. "Avi, when you went to the cottage and found the mess. Was the door jimmied? Was there a broken window?"

Aventurine met her twin's eyes. "No. Nothing like that."

"So whoever tossed the place either had a key—"

"Magnus?" Avi interjected.

"I never gave him a key," Nicola protested.

"—Or had some lock-picking tools," Genevieve said. She too held up her hands. "But it wasn't me."

Aventurine and Micheline both snorted.

"Who the hell *are* you?" Gio demanded again. "I know, I know, you said you were Mary Wentworth, but who the hell is Mary Wentworth?"

For a moment, no one spoke.

"Mary Wentworth," Avi said at last, "is a state of mind." Then she covered her face with her hands, laughing hysterically.

Thirty-seven

No one seemed hungry. There was quite a bit of pizza left, and Micheline boxed it back up and put it in the refrigerator.

"You two might need it later," Mick said guilelessly, and Aventurine couldn't help but admire her aplomb.

Genevieve leaned back in her seat, her palms flat on the table. "All right, then," she said as Micheline returned to her chair, "let's hash this out." She turned on Nicola and Gio, one armed camp on one side of the table. "Did you two conspire to steal the Swynford Jewel?"

The question was so unexpected that Aventurine—and everyone else—reared back; it was as though the old woman had tossed a venomous snake onto the table. Or a live hand grenade.

Nicola's lips thinned. "No."

Seemingly taking courage from her, Gio laughed uneasily. "I'm just a traveling musician. Conspiracy to theft is not really my thing."

Aventurine slewed him a glance. *Conspiracy to hide a woman away in a cottage in the woods, though: that was more like it.*

"Why am I answering to you, though?" Nicola demanded. "I don't know who you are. I don't know who you *think* you are, and why you should elect yourself chief prosecutor."

Genevieve remained unfazed, though her steely eyes glinted. "Not prosecutor. Investigator, if you will." She looked at each of them in turn. "It won't harm anything at this point to tell you that I was—hired—to prevent the theft of the Swynford Jewel, and I failed in that charge." For a moment she was silent. Her mouth worked, as though she were chewing over that failure, and found it both an unfamiliar and unpleasant taste. "Thus it has become somewhat personal for me to discover what happened."

Beside her, Henry grew still. Gio, on the other hand, leaned back and laughed.

"An octogenarian investigator, hired to protect a treasure. That's like the plot of a movie." He crossed his arms. "Go on, pull the other one."

Never had Aventurine felt more like punching that smug smile right off his face.

But Genevieve only smiled. "Nonagenarian, actually. But what would you know about it? You're only a traveling musician."

The legs of Gio's chair hit the floor with a thump.

"However," Genevieve continued, pointedly turning her attention away from him, "I think we should consider the remainder of the options, if we can sort them out." Her sharp eyes scanned Nicola's face. "You didn't conspire to steal the Jewel. Your boss, however, did."

Nicola nodded, her expression stony.

"You wouldn't comply with his plan. When he pressed, threatening your father, you effected a disappearance, in an attempt to protect your father."

"That's correct."

Aventurine felt a shudder from Henry. He reached out a hand to Nicola's arm once again, as though reassuring himself that she was actually there. That she had actually been found.

"Yet once you disappeared, the Jewel was stolen anyway."

"I had nothing to do with that. I didn't even know it had happened until Gio came back with the news."

Again Avi felt the waves of longing and anger: Gio had come back from spending the night in her bed. Back here, to this cottage in the woods, to Nicola. Under the table she felt Micheline's hand on her knee, felt the reassuring squeeze. Micheline might not agree with her choices, and the resulting feelings, but Micheline understood. She put her hand on her sister's.

"I have no reason to believe you," Genevieve said, "but I have no reason not to."

"Well, thanks for that, anyway." Nicola's voice was bitter, and her expression defiant and challenging.

The old spy sailed on as though Nicola had not spoken. "So if you didn't carry out their plan, someone else did, and I suggest we try to figure out who that might be."

Aventurine sat up, trying to remember DCI Burroughs's words. "There was a glitch in the security tapes, the police told me. Only a matter of seconds."

"And the alarm didn't sound, isn't that correct?" Genevieve prodded.

"And there was no forcing of the case: whoever did this had a key."

"Lots of keys floating about here," the old woman mused,

There was a long uncomfortable silence.

Unable to sit still any longer, Aventurine stood to fill the kettle at the sink and put it on to heat. There were teabags in the cupboard.

"And who could gain access to all of those keys?" Genevieve asked mildly. A rhetorical question.

Aventurine fell back into her chair.

There was a long indrawn breath from her left.

"Dad," Nicola breathed, horrified. "Oh, Dad."

Henry's eyes locked on hers. He reached a shaking hand to the breast pocket of his blazer and withdrew his always-jaunty pocket square. Which wasn't really a pocket square today, but a full-sized handkerchief. This he lay on the table between them and slowly unfolded it. As he peeled back the cloth, the light from the wall lamps struck the ruby embedded in the gold jewel, and it sparked with the deep red fire of some dystopian Christmas present.

Aventurine gasped. She could not tear her gaze away. Her hand sought Micheline's once more.

The Swynford Jewel.

She had last seen it safely locked within its display case in the Medieval Library, winking up at visitors. The pendant reputed to have been given to Katherine Swynford at the birth of one of John of Gaunt's Beaufort sons. She leaned forward to look at the likeness of St. Margaret of Anjou, holding the infant. The gold gleamed.

"Oh, Dad," Nicola whispered again. This time she sounded on the verge of tears. "You didn't."

"Henry," Genevieve said, her tone matter-of-fact. She leaned back in her chair and clasped her hands together, as though in prayer. "You really *are* a fool."

Father and daughter held each other's gaze for a long agonized moment, until at last, Henry dropped his face into his wrinkled hands and let out a sob.

Thirty-eight

Aventurine made tea, though she no longer felt any urge to drink it. There was milk in the refrigerator; she checked—it hadn't gone bad, at least—and set the carton on the table between them, niceties be damned. She took one of the mugs, and left them to fight over the second.

"I had to, don't you see?" Henry said. Nicola was holding his hand as though the hand of a drowning swimmer. "You didn't come home, Nicola. No one except Aventurine seemed interested. The police were no help. Then that woman—was killed—at the Old Bishop's Palace. And your house was ransacked."

"We don't know that there was any connection," Genevieve pointed out. "Unless you know something we don't?"

Henry shook his head. He ran a hand up into his sparse hair, which made it stand up like that of a madman. "They told me to look for signs, if I didn't believe they had Nicola."

"Dad—"

"I didn't know, did I?" he cried in frustration. "*I didn't know!* You were missing, these people told me they were holding you hostage, and you'd be freed if I cooperated."

"Who were these people?" Aventurine interjected.

"Obviously our friend Magnus, who knew you were in hiding, and whoever he's working for," Genevieve said thoughtfully. "Opportunists, aren't they? Taking advantage of the cards where they fell, as it were." She looked at Henry, and there was a certain pity there, at the same time there seemed to be appreciation for Magnus Etheredge and company for their wiliness. "He realized your weakness, and exploited it."

"Is he responsible for the death of the woman at the Bishop's Palace, do you think?" Micheline asked. She was frowning, her chin propped on her fist, her eyes glued to Genevieve's face. The woman who had rescued Paul—rescued all of them—and Aventurine knew her sister viewed Genevieve as her personal heroine. Whatever Genevieve said would be true; whatever Genevieve directed would be done.

"Could be." The old woman narrowed her eyes, then lifted her tea, having claimed the second mug. "It's frustrating: we have so many suppositions, because we have so little to fill in the gaps in this story." Her eyes again went to Henry, and the Jewel that winked blood-red on the handkerchief before him. "So you nicked it. How'd you manage it?"

The old man shifted uncomfortably in his chair, his mug of tea untouched before him. "They gave me a time. Just after four, when the complex closed. I had been up to the Library, and I—just hid. When the coast was clear, I texted a number they'd sent me. Then I had exactly five minutes." He looked at Nicola, and then dropped his eyes. "It was the worst five minutes of my life. But if I did it, I'd get Nicola back. I'd get you back."

"The key, though," Aventurine pressed.

"It was dropped through the mail slot at home that morning. I don't know—they must have had access, made a copy somehow."

Genevieve nodded. "He could have made a wax impression when he was consulted on the security set-up, I suppose. Etheredge. That would have meant he was playing a pretty long game."

"The whole plan seems like a long game," Aventurine agreed. She blew on her tea and took a sip; it was still too hot. But Genevieve would insist upon boiling water, even for tea bags, and Avi had learned. "Grooming Nicola, setting up timings, moving Henry like a chess piece when Nicola fell through."

"Dad, they wanted you involved, and I tried so hard to protect you. And I failed in that." This time the tears leaked from the corners of Nicola's green eyes, tracing their way along her cheekbones.

"It's not your fault," Henry whispered. "I should have known better. I should have seen through them."

"But wait."

It was Gio who spoke finally; his voice was puzzled. Aventurine studied her hands and did not look up.

"This." Gio pointed an elegant finger at the golden trinket. "They want it. Now you have it. How were you supposed to make the drop?"

Henry seemed to be having difficulty speaking.

"Dad," Nicola murmured. "What were you supposed to do with it?"

"Day after tomorrow. My next day at the Cathedral. In the south tower. I was supposed to make a drop after the afternoon roof tour."

Genevieve shook her head in admiration. "Brazen, that," she said. "That Magnus and his friends have balls, that's for sure."

"I don't need to now," Henry said, holding out his hands in confusion. "I know they don't have Nicola now, so they can't hold that over my head."

"But you've still stolen a valuable historical artifact, Henry," Aventurine said. "What are we going to do about that?" When she lifted her eyes, she was shocked to find Dominic Burroughs's features superimposed over Gio's. The way his icy eyes narrowed, the way his expression indicated he suspected her of wrongdoing, regardless of what she had to say.

"We could call the police," Micheline said. "Tell them the whole story."

Genevieve patted Mick's hand gently, and the familiarity made Avi momentarily jealous. Unreasonably so. She sat back.

"Oh, Micheline," the old woman said. "You're so naive." She shook her head. "The police won't believe us, will they Aventurine?"

Despite herself, Avi felt her face flush. "No. DCI Burroughs will not believe us."

"And as I've told your sister, Micheline, it behooves us to stay as far away from the police as we can. For all of our sakes, but especially for—the sake of someone in particular." *Paul.* She didn't have to say the name.

"Who might that be?" Gio asked.

Genevieve stared him down.

"Can we just—drop it off?" Henry suggested. "Anonymously?"

Nicola sighed. "I don't think that will just make all of this go away, Dad."

"It certainly won't make Magnus Etheredge go away," Aventurine said dryly.

"Especially if he's working for a buyer."

"No. That's the sticking point, isn't it?" Genevieve frowned, her expression that of a person who is picking through the chaff, looking for that one kernel of an idea. She pushed back from the table slowly, and carried her cup to the sink. Then she returned and sat down again, and tapped her finger on the scarred wood of the old table.

They waited.

When she looked up again, she rested her dark eyes on Nicola. "What if we used their own plan against them?" she mused.

Nicola raised her eyebrows. A question.

"What if—we broke in, and *just put the Swynford Jewel back?*"

Thirty-nine

Cacophony.

"*Who the hell are you?*" Gio exclaimed again, shoving away from the table somewhat dramatically.

Only Nicola kept her level green gaze on the old spy.

"This will never work," she said.

"It has as much chance as any other suggested plan," Genevieve said calmly. "If not more."

"But how?" Aventurine demanded. She hated to agree with Nicola, but she couldn't help it. "It's too risky."

"Come now, Mary Wentworth," Genevieve chided her, with that dark gleam in her eye. "Don't quail on me now."

"I'm not quailing. I'm being practical. What you're suggesting is not practical."

Micheline put a calming hand on Aventurine's shoulder. "Let's listen to her," she urged. "Let's hear Genevieve out."

"*Genevieve?*" Henry echoed. Then he snapped his mouth shut. The old woman met his eyes, and then after a moment, nodded.

"Sit down, Gio," Aventurine ordered. "Don't be an ass."

He looked insulted, but righted his chair and sat back down. "Go on, then," he invited, waving a hand at Genevieve. "The floor is yours."

"Don't be an ass, Gio," Nicola said.

"All right. If the drop is to be the day after tomorrow, we don't have much time. Tomorrow night will be optimal." There was calculation in her dark eyes. "Tuesday night. Yes. There will be fireworks."

"What's Tuesday?" Micheline asked.

The others around the table looked at her, some in surprise, some in pity.

"Guy Fawkes Day, my dear," Henry said, leaning over to pat her arm reassuringly. He no longer looked bemused; he seemed somewhat deflated, as though he had accepted his fate, whatever that might be at this point. "Remember, remember, the Fifth of November."

Aventurine hadn't really looked at a calendar in days, perhaps weeks, hadn't connected the days to the dates since she'd landed at Heathrow.

"We could use them," Genevieve continued, "as cover."

"But what if no one is blowing them up near our target?" Gio asked. He leaned back, draping an arm around Nicola's shoulders; she waited a moment before she pulled away. At first he looked surprised, then pained; but then he winked at Aventurine and laughed under his breath. She turned away sharply.

"We blow them up," Nicola said, meeting Genevieve's gaze levelly. The old woman nodded. "If we have to, we provide our own cover. No one will think any different of our fireworks."

"Who gets that job?"

Genevieve looked at each of them in turn, and then her gaze flitted back to Gio. "You, I think. In case there are any police patrols around. Everyone else here has come under police scrutiny at one time or another in the past week or two. Thus anyone else might attract unwanted attention."

"What about you?" Aventurine challenged. "What about Mary Wentworth?"

"They won't be seeing me at all," Genevieve said slyly. "I'll be going in."

The air in the small room changed.

Gio had found a piece of shelving paper from somewhere, and

had dug a pencil out of a side drawer. On the table between them, Genevieve sketched out a general plan of the Cathedral precincts. Then she placed an initial for each of them.

"Nicola, here, at the security company." The letter *N* in the corner of the page, somewhere north of the Cathedral. Next to that, an *H*. "Henry, you'll be outside, keeping the engine running. Be looking at a paper map, trying to fold it up, perhaps. Play on being the doddering old man. Nicola, you go to the office itself. Wear black. Stay out of the light as much as you can."

"No. I'll go into Apex with her," Henry protested. He clutched his daughter's hand so tightly it was a wonder the bones didn't crack.

"Dad," Nicola breathed, a warning.

Genevieve shook her head. "Henry, don't be any more of a fool than you already have been. Nicola knows what's to be done and how to do it. She can slip in, disable the system, rearm it, and be out easily, without your encumbrance."

Henry sank back in his chair. Aventurine did in hers, too, though the criticism wasn't directed at her. It was still harsh.

"Nicola, when we get into position, Micheline will text you something innocuous. Ask if you have anything for a hangover, for instance. Once you're in and the system is deactivated, reply that you'll bring it around."

"And if I can't get in?"

"You'll text that you have no remedy, and we abort."

Nicola and Mick nodded. "Where will I be?" Mick asked.

"Here." Genevieve marked an *M* at the Exchequergate. "You'll be keeping an eye at the front. We'll have approximately eight minutes to complete the objective. Once I'm out, Micheline will send Nicola another text along the same lines. Nicola, you rearm the system and get out to the car. We want you and Henry away from the area as quickly as possible."

This time Henry made no objection.

Another mark, this time a *G*. "Gio, you set up at the Pottergate, across from the Adam & Eve, and set off all the fireworks your heart desires. We want you to attract all the attention down there. All of it."

"Where am I to get this firepower?" he asked. "Don't get me wrong—it sounds like a lot of fun. I just need the explosives."

When Genevieve turned her lined face to him, her dark glance was withering. And wither Gio did, Aventurine was happy to see. "I'll see that you have what you need."

"And me?" Aventurine asked.

The old woman looked her up and down appraisingly. "You're coming with me. You'll be my lookout. Are you up for it, then, Mary?"

Aventurine glanced around the table at the others. Their faces shadowed, they looked, as she felt, nervous but resolute. She clenched her hands in her lap. This must have been what it was like, all those years ago, when Genevieve and her cell had laid out their plans for destroying bridges, and factories, and any other targets the SOE deemed worthy of destruction. This adrenaline rush. Which would have carried them through the danger to the other side. Please God it did so here. Because as she watched the plan roll out on the paper beneath Genevieve's pencil, Aventurine knew that, whatever danger there was, the old spy was including her in the most of it—which was as strong a sign of trust as anything could be.

"I'm ready," she said.

Part V:

Operation Beaufort

Forty

They parted company near midnight, with directions to make their several ways back to town—Nicola would stay at the cottage with Gio—and regroup the next evening. Genevieve, after burning the shelf paper in the fire and stirring the ashes, left with Henry, who looked back reluctantly at his daughter; Micheline and Aventurine would return in the rental.

"Avi—" Gio took a few steps out into the darkened clearing after them. Mick took one look and slipped off, following the flashlight beam from her phone.

Aventurine looked down at his hand on her arm. If he slid it down until their hands clasped and then pulled away, it would be like that gorgeous evening in Clerkenwell: the most perfect thing, the thing that had left her least satisfied. But she wouldn't think about that. "Go back inside, Gio," she said, extricating herself.

"Avi," he said again, but she'd moved away, toward her sister. "I've been sleeping on the couch, Aventurine," he repeated. She did not turn around.

When she caught up to Mick, and they'd picked their way along the path to the point where they could no longer see the cottage if they glanced over their shoulders, Micheline let out a long sigh.

"This has got to be the weirdest situation you've ever gotten me into, Aventurine," she said.

Micheline had managed to book a room just down the hall.

"It had twin beds," she said as she fished the key out of her purse. "The man at the desk—"

"Pete."

"Yeah, that's the one—he kept looking at me strangely?—said he'd send someone up to put them together to make a double for me. I hope he's done it. I'm beat."

Aventurine followed her into the room and shut the door.

"Listen, Mick," she said. "What the hell are you doing here?"

The room was very much like her own; when she crossed to the window, she could see down into the beer garden, closed down and lit now by only a few security lights. She grimaced, wondering what security company the hotel employed.

"You don't want me here?" Micheline was leaning toward the mirror, taking her silver hoop earrings out.

"I didn't expect you here. You didn't tell me you were coming." Aventurine paused. "But Genevieve knew. I didn't know you were here until you texted the DNA stuff—you did that from the car, didn't you? You showed up with Genevieve and Henry, and I had no idea you were even in the UK. I thought you were coming over for Christmas with Paul and Lance."

Micheline turned her back to Aventurine and held up her hair from the nape of her neck. "Undo this necklace, will you?"

Avi did, and set it on the bureau next to the earrings.

"You've been keeping in touch with Genevieve."

For a moment Micheline did not answer, did not turn. She bent to strip off her shoes, and tossed them into the corner near the bathroom door.

"More than with me, I think. Haven't you?"

There was a sudden tension that Aventurine didn't understand, and certainly didn't like.

"Of course I have," Micheline said at last. Her suitcase, a much larger one than Aventurine's small blue one, sat on the rack, and now she unzipped it. Without looking up, she rooted around amongst the rolled clothes until she pulled out a white nightgown sprigged with tiny blue flowers. She sat down on the bed, clutching it to her breast, and looked up. "Aventurine, she knows things. She knows people."

Foreboding. Avi licked her suddenly dry lips.

"What things, Micheline?" Aventurine asked. "What people?" She wasn't sure she wanted to know.

Now Micheline was crying, the tears tracking down her cheeks, which were much thinner than they used to be. There were the tiniest of lines around her mouth, from her resumed smoking habit.

"Avi," she sobbed, "I miss him. Dreadfully."

Shep.

Aventurine dropped to her knees and took her sister's hands in hers. These seemed thinner, too, bonier; the wedding set was loose on her left ring finger.

"I know, honey," she whispered. "I know."

"And I need to know what happened," she gulped. "I need to know what happened to him that night on the boat. I need to know why he never came home to me, Aventurine."

Avi nodded, rubbing her thumbs over the backs of those hands.

"And I asked Genevieve—"

Oh, no.

"—to help me."

It was nearly three when Aventurine awoke. She and Micheline had been curled around one another, Mick's head on her shoulder. She might have been imagining things, but she was sure her shirt was damp from her sister's tears.

"I'm going to my room," she whispered.

Micheline muttered something, and her eyes fluttered open, unfocused.

"Goodnight, Aventurine," she said. "I love you."

"Love you, too, Mick."

In her room, the bed was still a tangle of sheets. She swore under her breath, then stripped off her clothes and wrapped herself in the blankets. Damn Gio to hell. One of the pillows still smelled vaguely of him, so she threw it across the room in the dark.

Then she lay on her back, spread-eagle, staring up at the faint and wavering lights reflected across the ceiling.

Wondering about Nicola. Their half-sister.

Half-sister.

What were the other possibilities Micheline had listed? Grandmother, cousin, half-sister. Grandmother obviously impossible. Cousin no more likely, as both Michele and Daniel Morrow had been only children.

And which was their father—Henry Hallsey, or Daniel Morrow?

Maybe Nicola knew.

But Aventurine was damned if she was going to ask.

Micheline had been able to find the match because Nicola had taken a DNA test as well, at some point. So perhaps Nicola *did* know. Aventurine ran over the entire afternoon and evening in her head, playing it back and forth like an old eight millimeter film. *Dad,* Nicola kept calling Henry. Was it because she knew positively, or was it out of habit, an unwillingness to hurt Henry with the truth of her paternity, if in fact he was not her father?

And what of Mick and Avi's father? If he was their father. Did he know he wasn't? Or did he know he had fathered another daughter out in the world? One of those things had to be true. But which one?

Her head was spinning and her stomach in knots. Too much. It was all too much at once. The DNA match. Micheline's going to Genevieve for help with Shep and the *Máquina de los Vientos,* and both of them keeping that a secret from her. Henry stealing the Swynford Jewel—and tomorrow they'd attempt to return it. Gio and Nicola, either sleeping together or not.

Aventurine tossed onto her stomach. Got up to use the bathroom and got a drink. Rearranged the remaining pillows. Got up again to take some Tylenol.

Toward dawn she finally fell into a sleep plagued with bad dreams.

Forty-one

They were back at the cottage.

Aventurine, Nicola, and Genevieve all wore black, as befitting the parts they would be playing. The rest wore street clothes, just a handful of regular denizens on Guy Fawkes Night. The air was cold, but there was no sign of rain.

"Thank God it's not a Friday," Henry said. "It'll cut down on the pub crowds. We won't be dealing with too many hoodlums."

Not that there were pubs in the precincts themselves, of course— just the Magna Carta to one end, and the Adam & Eve to the other. Aventurine supposed that they had to cut Henry some slack, as undercover operations were probably not within the realm of his experience. She glanced around at the others: probably not within the realm of their experience, either, if one didn't count Genevieve.

"Just the yobs like me who like to blow things up for Guy Fawkes Night," Gio said cheerily.

Genevieve made a small impatient movement. It was interesting to watch her in mission command mode: how her attention became streamlined, until it was laser focused.

"Everyone has their roles," she cut in. "We'll spread out around the Cathedral at midnight. I want everyone in position at 00:55, to move at 1:00." She looked around the table at each one in turn, her gaze evaluating and cold. "You should all know now what your responsibilities are. But if you have any questions, this is the time to ask."

257

"I'm just the lookout," Aventurine said, already feeling the adrenaline in her bloodstream. "What am I looking for?"

"Anything." Genevieve met her eyes levelly. "You'll know it when you see it."

"And I should do what?"

"You'll know that when you see it, too. Just keep anyone away from the library and the cloisters, if Gio is unable to attract all the attention to his station."

This was not reassuring. Aventurine supposed that this was what it had been like in the circuit, in occupied France: expect everything, be prepared to deal with anything. Improvisation. This was the kind of thing that led up to Genevieve's first kill at sixteen. Avi hoped to God things didn't go to that extreme. She had no knife anyway, and that was probably a good thing. She'd probably just stumble in the darkness and fall on it.

They spent an uncomfortable hour waiting, and Aventurine, for one, was glad when Genevieve at last looked up at the clock on the mantle, set down the book she was reading, and stood up. Avi got to her feet, took one last sip from the water bottle she'd brought, and pulled her jacket around her. Black, for camouflage: she zipped it to the chin. Gio handed her a black watch cap, and she tucked her hair up under it; hard to camouflage the pale blonde unless she dyed it, which she hadn't been about to do.

"Phones?" Genevieve barked. "Battery power?"

Of course they'd all been under strict orders to charge their cell phones before they'd met up. Even so, Aventurine glanced down at hers anxiously. Ninety-eight percent. Good for the night ahead; good for the duration of *Operation Beaufort*. She tucked it into her jacket pocket.

"All right." Genevieve once more tapped the piece of paper on which she'd initialed their positions again, before balling it up and shoving it into the fireplace as she had the other; then she touched a match to it and watched it burn to ash, before raking those around with the poker. "When you're at your posts, text *Fawkes* to the group." She turned her steady glittering eyes on them, examining them one by one, and Aventurine realized again how much she was enjoying this. "Good luck, circuit."

They headed out into the night: Henry and Nicola in his car; Gio and Micheline in his; and Genevieve and Aventurine in the rental. The two women waited two minutes by Genevieve's watch after the others' tail lights had disappeared, and then headed back to the Bailgate, and the hotel parking lot.

"Here," Genevieve said, pulling a flask out of her pocket and twisting it open. "False courage." Avi was surprised that she had it, and more surprised when she opened it, for Genevieve didn't drink.

"I'm driving," Aventurine reminded her. *In the dark, on the wrong side of the road, on the way to do something which, though perhaps not immoral, was definitely illegal.*

"Of course."

They hit a sleeping policeman with more force than Avi should have. Genevieve slopped the whisky onto Avi's sleeve and pant leg, and the pungent smell of single malt filled the car.

Aventurine swore. "Brilliant." She slowed down, to make sure she gave no cause for any patrol car to stop her, because with this smell, no one would believe she wasn't a DUI in action.

Smiling gently, the passing lights picking out the planes of her face, Genevieve capped the flask again and tucked it into Aventurine's pocket. "Now you smell like a Bonfire Night reveler. Just take a quick swig when we leave the car in the lot, and your disguise will be complete."

"I'm wearing all black. I'm not supposed to be seen."

"We cover all the bases, Aventurine."

Avi shook her head and slowed to take the turn.

Aventurine's palms were sweating, despite the cold, inside her gloves. She wiped them uselessly down the legs of her black jeans, then pulled her jacket more tightly about her. The wind was picking up; leaves skittered along the pavement before her as she turned the corner in the darkness.

In her jacket pocket, the flask felt heavy, and she reached in to touch the cold metal with a finger: a talisman. She half-laughed, but choked back the sound. If Genevieve knew how close to hysteria she was, the old woman would be beyond disappointed. "I'm trusting you," she had warned. "Don't let the circuit down. Don't let Mary Wentworth down." Strangely, she'd touched a gloved finger to Avi's cheek before setting off ahead of her. "Don't let *me* down." *Anything for you, Commander Smithson,* Aventurine had thought.

To her right the Cathedral loomed. From further down Steep Hill toward the new city, she heard the pop and whistle of firecrackers, and then someone set some off closer, somewhere up ahead. Gio, probably. Doing his part somewhere near the Adam & Eve. Attracting all the attention to that end of Pottergate.

Her phone buzzed. She cupped it with her free hand to deaden the light of the screen.

Fawkes.

She counted the replies, then added her own.

Then they were in position, in the shadow of Priory Arch.

She texted Nicola.

Do you have any Paracetamol?

After a moment, the answer they'd been waiting on.

I'm checking the medicine cabinet now. Aventurine swallowed a giggle.

"Go," she whispered to the catlike darkness just ahead of her.

Genevieve pulled a black bandanna around the bottom of her face; only her glittering eyes showed. "Eight minutes," she replied. "Then take off."

Then Avi was alone. She reached into her pocket, drew out the flask, and took one last long drink, waiting for the rush to hit her bloodstream.

Eight minutes.

Forty-two

In the frigid darkness, Aventurine regretted not wearing a heavier jacket; but she wore what Genevieve had provided. The spy had insisted on all black, which made sense for the three who needed not to be seen. But it would have to be *cold*, colder than any night so far this season. Wasn't adrenaline supposed to keep a person warm? Avi imagined the teenaged Genevieve on her first mission, in the freezing darkness of occupied France: had she been warmed by excitement? Aventurine pulled her collar up further, to keep the night air from her neck. Again from somewhere downhill she heard the crackle of fireworks, though she saw no light show. These were answered from the end of Pottergate. *Good job, Gio.* She shoved her gloved hands into her pockets. She could see her breath.

A pair of slightly drunken young people of indeterminate sex wandered past, leaning heavily into each other. Weaving.

"Got a light, mate?" one called to her shadow, waving an unlit cigarette about ineffectually.

So much for not being seen. "Sorry, no," she said, and walked purposefully away toward Eastgate. Once she was sure they were out of sight, she turned back to her post at the stone entryway. To wait. Looking over her shoulder into the Cathedral yard, and Genevieve, in there, somewhere. No alarm had sounded. That much was good.

Aventurine wanted to check the time, but was nervous about the light on the face of her watch. Should this be taking so long? In her pocket her phone buzzed, and she drew it out, cupping a hand about the screen, and leaning into it.

4 mins.

She noted the time: 1:14. Then she deleted the text and shoved the phone back into her pocket.

Something snicked on the pavement to the other side of the stone gate.

A footstep.

The shadows moved. Separated.

DCI Burroughs stepped closer. He too had his hands in his pockets. In the strained lighting, his face was pale, his dark hair blue-black.

"Miss Morrow," he said dryly. "Returning to the scene of the crime?"

She stepped away from the wall, unsteady in her surprise. *4 mins. You'll know it when you see it.*

"You always say that," she replied, and her voice was unsteady, too. Do *the unexpected. Say the unexpected.* Genevieve had advised that at one point. She smiled. "I'm so glad to see you."

He raised his eyebrows.

"I took a wrong turn. I can't find the hotel." That sip of whisky was roiling in her stomach now. Maybe she'd be sick at his feet. That would be a diversion.

"You've been out?"

"And I'm lost." She raised her voice a little, sounding querulous, questioning. As thought the hotel had packed up and moved of its own accord while she had been drinking in the town. She looked around, held up a hand. "I went wrong somewhere. Somewhere on Steep Hill."

He wore a half-smile, and his pale eyes glittered. "I bet you did."

3 mins.

The round bulk of the chapter house was just behind his shoulder. Beyond that, the cloisters and the library.

"Are you on your own?"

"I met some people. But they stayed down the hill." Aventurine sounded peevish, as though confused about anyone abandoning her. She thought quickly, took a step backward. Then, hand flailing, she stumbled slightly

Burroughs reached out quickly for her arm, to steady her. "Easy, now."

She felt his gaze on her face, and tried to let her eyes wander drunkenly. "I'm fine," she said with some dignity. "Thank you. If you could just point me—" she looked around vaguely, frowning—"to where the hotel is. I won't bother you anymore."

More fireworks further down the road. She jumped, thought she saw some flashes. She wondered how much more firepower Gio possessed.

2 mins.

"Let me escort you," he offered. He did not release her arm. He studied her, as though trying to make up his mind about the level of her drunkenness. The verity of it. "It's just around the corner of Eastgate and along the way." His glance slipped to the Cathedral, looming to his left, the precincts a play of shadow and light.

Still more fireworks. Someone shouted. Aventurine's stomach was churning now. Genevieve would be out in a matter of moments, and it was imperative that she get the detective as far away as possible.

"I'm fine," she repeated defensively, and managed to stumble again. Then she giggled, for good measure. This time DCI Burroughs held her up with both hands. Aventurine placed one of her palms against his chest, pretending to steady herself. "Okay. Not really fine. Mostly, though." She giggled again, a high-pitched sound.

1 min.

There were no more fireworks, no more explosions. Perhaps Gio had run out. Perhaps he had been run off by a night patrol.

The seconds were ticking down. Aventurine tried to see beyond Burroughs's shoulder. A movement. Anything to indicate that Genevieve was making her escape. Something. Shadows shifting. A slight sound. *Come on,* she urged silently.

Aventurine leaned toward him. He smelled slightly of cloves. She took a deep breath, and then remembered herself quickly. "All right," she murmured, slurring slightly. "Take me home, Mr. Detective." Then she giggled and covered her mouth with her hand, as though having said something slightly naughty. She attempted to turn him back toward the Eastgate.

There was the slightest of rattles, stone against stone.

Burroughs tensed, his face turning slightly.

Aventurine locked a hand behind his neck, and pulled his mouth down to hers. She was suddenly grateful for that last parting shot from the hip flask, because she knew he'd taste the whisky in her mouth.

He seemed surprised by her kiss, and his body stiffened—and then he almost, *almost,* relaxed into it. As though enjoying it. As though he might actually have thought about it. Before. Already. Avi realized she was enjoying it herself. She pressed closer, whispered his name against his mouth.

Had Genevieve done this? Had she enjoyed it? Had Mata Hari enjoyed it? At the same time Aventurine felt slightly dirty, she felt a *frisson* of excitement.

And then DCI Burroughs pushed away. The cold air was a shock.

"Come on, then," he said, holding Aventurine away, his hands firm on her upper arms. His voice, usually like ice, cracked. "Let me get you as far as the Bailgate. You'll know how to get back to the hotel from there?"

It might have been a question. It might have been a statement.

Aventurine giggled again, and then hiccupped, tasting the whisky, wondering whether she might be overdoing the drunk act.

"Don't sick up on me now, Aventurine," Burroughs warned.

It was the first time he'd used her given name. And in what a context. At least he was still fooled. She slewed her eyes over his left shoulder, where the shadows reassembled themselves without a whisper. Unless she was imagining things.

"Which way?" she asked, leaning into him.

Gently he turned her in the direction of the eastgate, and, after a moment, tucked her arm through his to steady her. She stumbled a little, as though on slippery ground, and then allowed him to guide her along the pavement.

Half of her needed to stay at her post, waiting for the signal from Genevieve. The other half needed to get the detective away. But overriding it all was a vaguely formed desire to get him back to her hotel room, even though, she knew, she had ruined her chances anyway, because of her ostensible drunkenness.

Damn it. She screwed that one up on all fronts. Unless she hadn't.

Stay away from the detective, Genevieve had warned. Aventurine presumed that that meant *don't sleep with the detective.*

Damn it all to hell.

Forty-three

They were splitting up, Gio heading back to Kettlethorpe, Genevieve to Chelmsford Street, Henry—who was, surprisingly, looking much more energetic than he had for days—back to his semi-detached house out the Wragby Road.

"You should come home with me," he said to his daughter. "Your place isn't fit for habitation."

But Nicola only shook her head. "You don't know where I am yet," she reminded him. "You won't know for a while, and then you'll have to be surprised and disappointed and a little angry at my heartlessness in running off for a tryst without telling you." An ironic smile played around her lips. "Better I go home, Dad, and lie low for a day or two before miraculously reappearing."

"You could come back to the cottage with me," Gio offered, sliding into his car.

Nicola cast Aventurine a glance, which Avi returned stonily; Nicola laughed a little. "No, Gio, I don't think that's a plan. But thank you." She leaned in through the window and kissed him on the cheek, and then he was off. They watched his taillights fade out of sight.

"At least let me drive you home," Henry suggested.

"No, Dad." Now Nicola kissed his cheek as well. "That won't work for the plan." She smiled fondly. "I'll just walk. It's not far."

When it was just the three of them, Micheline smiled. "We'll drive you home, Nicola," she said.

Nicola looked from Mick to Avi and back. "No, that's fine. It's really not far."

"It isn't, Micheline," Aventurine added. "I've walked there a couple of times." She turned a matching smile on Nicola. "We'll go with you, to make sure you get there safely."

She shook her head again. "No, really, it's fine."

Aventurine clapped a hand to her chest. "Oh, no, you have to let us. Don't forget—someone matching your description was nearly assaulted, and then went missing from this neighborhood."

A long pause. Nicola then raised her chin. "All right. I don't know what it is you two want from me, but we might as well get it over with."

"Good girl," Micheline said, opening the passenger side door. Avi didn't know whether she was addressing her, or Nicola.

The house was still a mess when Nicola unlocked the door and led them inside. She barely even looked—shock, probably—but stepped over the books to replace the gutted cushions in the chair and on the small sofa.

Micheline moved to Nicola's wide mirror, spiderwebbed with cracks, and stared at her broken reflection. Aventurine took a place behind her left shoulder, and, after a moment, unable to help herself, Nicola joined them. Her jaw was set stubbornly, her lips thin: a look Aventurine recognized so well, having seen it in tandem for her entire life. A line of blonde women, with similar haircuts, eyes the same emerald color, cheekbones the same shape. Parallels, but at the same time, skewed, like a Picasso painting, by the broken glass.

"We need to talk about this," Micheline said.

"I don't know the answer," Nicola protested, throwing up her hands. There was a crease, all too familiar, between her pale brows. She would have to watch that, Aventurine thought meanly, or in ten years' time, it would be as pronounced as that of Micheline and herself.

"But you knew," Aventurine said. "At least, you knew about *me*."

"I didn't." But Nicola's glance gave her away, darting to the reflection of the bookshelves, empty now, their contents strewn over the carpet.

Slowly Aventurine drew the copy of *A Year in the Life of Mobius* from the pocket of her bag, retrieved from the car. The copy she had found open over the arm of the easy chair, the first time she'd entered this cottage. She turned it over slowly so her face—their face—stared upward from the back cover.

"Are you looking for this?"

Nicola reached out a hand, but then apparently thought better of it, letting it drop to her side.

"You knew," Micheline echoed, watching Nicola's reflection in the glass.

"I thought it a coincidence, that's all." But there was a strange sort of hunger in her eyes as she looked down at the author photo. A longing.

"There are no coincidences." Aventurine might have been Genevieve, speaking her cryptic pronouncements.

"And I did a DNA test. Several of them." Micheline shifted and put a hand on Avi's shoulder. They both faced Nicola. Twins. Singleton. Three. "I found you on one of the sites. Identified genetically as grandmother, cousin, or half-sister."

"You are our half-sister," Aventurine drove home.

"That's impossible," Nicola said sharply. But again, the tell. She dropped her eyes. She, like the pair of them, would have made a terrible poker player.

"Is it?" Aventurine ran a fingertip over her face on the back cover of the book. "I think it's not. I think you came across this book, and you went looking for us. At least, for me. There were just too many similarities between us. Our appearance. That we both write books." Avi didn't add *that you slept with Gio, almost as though you were trying to* be *me*. But she tasted those angry words at the back of her mouth. "You wanted to find out."

"Why didn't you ask your father?" Micheline demanded.

"Look." Nicola threw up her hands again, and dropped into a ruined chair. She ran her fingers through her hair distractedly, and Aventurine shivered at the familiar gesture. "Look. It's not something you ask your father, is it? 'Hey, Dad, did you have an affair before you met Mum? Or did she have one after you married?'" When she looked up, her expression was agonized. "Listen. I love him. Those questions would hurt him terribly. Destroy him, even."

"Especially that second one," Aventurine said dryly. She had felt Micheline's hand tighten on her shoulder at the first one. Difficult to have Nicola put that fear into words for either of them.

Nicola glared at Aventurine. "Yeah. That second one. My father adored my mother. Worshiped the ground she walked on, and all that. You've seen the picture." She gestured to the photograph Avi had retrieved from the floor. "That question would kill him, so I sure as hell wasn't going to ask it, all right?"

Aventurine and Micheline shared a look.

"Besides," Nicola protested, continuing on as though she no longer had control; she plucked at the stuffing exposed by the cut fabric of the chair. "It's not something you just *do*. You don't just ask your father whether he's had an affair, whether you have siblings you know nothing about. That's—that's simply not done." She lifted her eyes now and glared at them. Aventurine caught her breath—Nicola's expression, her mannerisms, were all Paul. Their son. Their nephew. "Or do you?" Nicola demanded. "*Have you?*"

That was the conundrum. Micheline released Aventurine's shoulder and sank into the chair opposite Nicola. "We never have," she said. She clasped her hands together between her knees.

"Then how could you even—"

"Nicola," Aventurine interrupted impatiently. "Our parents have been dead for years. Neither of us knew you even existed, until last week. We could hardly ask a question like that." She refused to sit down, refused to give in. "But you, Nicola. You knew of my existence, even if you didn't know about Micheline. You had my book, with my

269

picture. You were hiding out in the woods with Gio, my former lover. And you did your own DNA test—Micheline *found* you—so perhaps you were looking for some evidence." Avi crossed her arms and met Nicola's glare with one of her own. "So don't feed us that indignation, okay?"

Nicola was the first to drop her eyes. Aventurine knew she would be. Avi could sense Mick, in the chair to the side, softening toward her; but Aventurine still didn't—still couldn't quite bring herself to trust Nicola.

"All right," Nicola whispered at last. "I knew there was something uncanny. You and I—we had so much in common. Not just our looks. Something told me that it couldn't be a mere coincidence. I saw the author photo on Amazon. So I bought a book. And I was confused, all right? So I started looking you up."

"So how did you find Gio?" Aventurine couldn't trust him, either. And it said something that Nicola never denied sleeping with him. Trading Avi in for a younger model, indeed, as he had apparently done. "I haven't mentioned him except in passing in *A Year in the Life*. We were never an item for public consumption."

Nicola shrugged. "I didn't find him. I went to a festival, and afterwards, in the beer tent, he called me by your name. He was really taken aback when he discovered his mistake."

But he'd recovered quickly, apparently.

"Well," Micheline sighed, "for better or worse, this is where we are. And Genevieve expects we'll make this work for us tomorrow. Today. This afternoon." She stood, stretched, yawned. Then she looked pointedly at Nicola. "But this isn't over yet. Sister."

"Don't call me that," Nicola hissed.

Aventurine followed her twin's lead. "This afternoon. At the Cathedral at 2:30. Don't let us down, Nicola."

Forty-four

No one seemed to pay Henry any mind—a dapper man in a blue suit with a tour guide's sash across his breast—as he ushered them into the arched doorway of the south tower at two-thirty in the afternoon. He closed the door behind them and followed them up the stairs. "Be careful," he whispered, and the words followed them round and round up into the tower.

Aventurine clutched at the rope and leaned against the wall to her left, staring upwards at Nicola's legs and back; somewhere up above her climbed Genevieve, and she wished fervently for the old woman's strong legs. How the hell did she do it? She could hear Micheline behind her, the labored breathing her smoking engendered as they climbed. Fortunately they did not have far to go—relatively speaking—only as far as the southwest chapel, a square room they tumbled into through a narrow door.

There were chairs ranged against the west wall, and Aventurine sank onto one, her legs quivering, her heart pounding. She leaned her head back and tried to catch her breath; above her ranged the red-velvet colored ropes of the Cathedral bell ringers. Micheline sat next to her. Avi checked her wire, and saw Mick do the same. Only Nicola, some ten years their junior, and, as far as they knew, not a smoker, seemed unaffected by the climb. Henry pulled the door closed behind them; he did not flip the light switch. Genevieve was not in the chapel.

"I hope they're on time—he's on time," he said, his voice hushed. "I wouldn't want to be caught up here by the Domus Supervisor. He might have something to say."

"Where'd she go?" Micheline murmured, her hand at her heart.

A door to the side opened. Genevieve looked out at them. "Henry, there's another way down from here, isn't there?"

He nodded. "You can pass through there, across to the north tower, then above the nave and come down in the transept," he said. "Dark and dusty and narrow, with beams that will take your head off if you're not careful. But yes. That's the way the roof tours finish up. Why?"

Genevieve nodded. "Always good to have a second escape route, should things not go to plan. You know the way out? You'll have to lead us." She looked around the inside of the tower chapel, the terrible concrete reinforcements, at the bell-ringers' ropes, and the red-clothed communion table. Then she looked at the rest of them.

"Who starts?" she asked.

"I do," Nicola answered.

"Good. Aventurine, through that door. Don't close it all the way. Micheline, Henry, you come through here with me." She thinned her lips. "Scare the hell out of him, girls."

Avi cast a look over her shoulder, to where Nicola was crouched down behind the table, then slipped through the door, moving up two steps, and pressing herself against the wall. It was a bit dusty, and she felt the tickle in her nose, but she couldn't sneeze. Couldn't make a sound. Not only did she not want to ruin the plan; but she didn't want to lose her balance and go tumbling, round and round and round to crash at the foot of the spiral staircase.

Then she waited.

Aventurine heard the muted creak of the door below, and a slight thud as it was pulled back into its stone jamb. Then measured steps, approaching upwards. She strained her ears, and heard the breathing of someone who felt the workout of the climb, just as she had done.

She pressed further back into the darkness.

Magnus Etheredge, dressed casually in jeans and a dark sweater under a glistening raincoat, emerged just below her, and paused, his hand on the door to the chapel. He looked around—Aventurine held her breath—and then pushed the door open and slipped inside.

She moved down the few steps until she was at the door, still open a crack. She could just see him as he turned, scanning the room. Then he froze, his eyes locked on Nicola, a silvery shadow behind the communion table.

"You threatened me," Nicola said, her voice low but clear. She stepped forward into the faded light from the high window. Her words echoed between the stone walls. "You threatened to harm my father if I didn't get him to help you steal the Swynford Jewel."

"You," he hissed, taking a step closer.

"Me," Nicola said. Her expression did not reach her eyes.

In the subdued lighting, his face was cruel and angular. "But you ran away," he sneered. "Disappeared."

"And now I'm back." Her own expression was hard. Aventurine couldn't help but admire her coldness.

"Why?" Magnus took another step closer to her: a power move. "What are you doing here?"

Nicola laughed. The sound echoed. "What do you think?"

Another step forward. Nicola did not flinch. "Perhaps you couldn't get enough of me. Is that it?"

"Perhaps I've come to make the drop."

Nicola drew out a package wrapped in one of Henry's white handkerchiefs. She set it on the red cloth before her and smiled, an ugly expression.

There was, surprisingly, a crack of thunder. Aventurine jumped, and knocked into the door. She grabbed the handle to steady herself, to keep the door from swinging open. Magnus turned.

Nicola was gone.

"Oh, no. You're not that special. I've had enough of you already."

Etheredge whirled to the voice and found himself looking at

Micheline. She, too, stood with her feet apart, her arms crossed. She shook her blonde hair back.

"Who are you?" Etheredge demanded. "Who *are* you?" His expression went blank as he looked away from Mick to the communion table where Nicola was no longer, and then back again.

Micheline shrugged. "Nicola."

He shook his head, and then reached his hands out as though to grasp her, to shake her. He took a step in her direction. She did not move. "You're not. You're not her."

Another peal of thunder, this time accompanied by a flash of lightning, and Aventurine slipped into the room as Micheline slipped out across from her.

"Oh, but I am," Avi said. She crossed her arms and tossed her hair over her shoulder.

Magnus whirled so quickly he nearly fell.

"You threatened me," she said.

"You're not Nicola," he protested.

"We're all Nicola," she whispered.

"No. Mary Wentworth. One of you is Mary Wentworth."

Aventurine adjusted her own crossed arms. "We're all Mary Wentworth," she said. "There is no Mary Wentworth."

Nicola reappeared. Crossed her arms.

Aventurine smiled, a hard twist of the lips.

"Stop playing games," Etheredge snarled. "Where's Hallsey? Just give me the Jewel."

Micheline stepped back into the small room. "Where's Dad?" she asked, looking at Aventurine.

"I don't know," Nicola said.

Magnus whirled to each of them in turn.

"What are you trying to do?" he shouted.

"Is it bothering you?" Aventurine asked.

"Is it working?" Micheline asked.

Aventurine took a step toward her twin. Nicola moved around from behind the table.

Another peal of thunder, closer now.

Magnus Etheredge suddenly launched himself at Nicola, knocking her to the floor, wrapping his hands around her neck.

Aventurine leaped toward them, grabbing at Magnus's jacket, his shoulder. His grip was too tight, his body too heavy. Nicola had her hands on his wrists, trying to pull them from her throat, but her face was reddening. Suddenly she let go one hand and flung it out toward the communion table. She mouthed something—her gasping made it possible to hear it.

Jewel?

Aventurine reached up and grabbed the handkerchief-wrapped packet and threw it to Micheline. "Run," she shouted.

Mick turned back to the door she had come from and bounded through it.

"Bitch!" With a final slam of Nicola's head against the floor, Etheredge scrambled to his feet to follow. Aventurine hurled herself toward his legs, and, just as the first time she'd seen him, she brought him down awkwardly.

"Run, Nicola!" she yelled.

Nicola, gasping for air, staggered to her feet and fled after Micheline.

Etheredge hit her on the side of the head, and Aventurine rolled away, her vision momentarily black. She reached for his leg again, and when he fell this time, he clutched at the communion table and pulled it down onto himself.

Aventurine struggled up and followed Nicola, pausing only to pull the door to.

Five of them up there, in the narrow passage before the accusing eyes of Bishop Remigius.

"Hurry," Genevieve called over her shoulder. "Follow Henry."

Did someone look up at them from the nave, far below? The one quick glance Aventurine managed made her head swim. She swiveled her eyes to Nicola's back. How long before Magnus Etheredge regained his feet and followed? He would follow, Aventurine knew: he was a type, like Neil, and no one woman—or two, or three—would defeat him. And he thought they had the Swynford Jewel.

Just ahead of her as they pushed through the door into the north tower, Nicola was clutching her throat and wheezing. Aventurine banged the door shut behind her, just as Magnus opened the far door with a thud.

Through another door, over some steps, and they were in the clerestory above the north aisle. The wooden walkway through here, with rough wooden railings, was as narrow as Henry had warned, maybe two planks wide, and uneven where one board ended and another one began. They moved as quickly as they could, cautious on the treacherous footing. Though Avi thought she could make out bulbs and fixtures on the beaming overhead as she ducked under them—Henry had been right about knocking her brains out up here—they were not on, and the only light came through the lancets to their left.

Magnus was through into the clerestory.

Aventurine pushed Nicola on ahead, and risked a look over her shoulder.

Turning, she ran right into a low stone arch. Her foot caught, and she stumbled.

It was enough. Magnus was upon her immediately.

He pulled her roughly to her feet, one hand holding her wrists, the other arm around her throat. His laugh was ugly.

"Which one are you, now?" he snarled into her ear. His breath was hot.

"Avi!"

Micheline's voice, somewhere ahead.

Aventurine struggled against Magnus's arms. He jerked her head back.

"*Not* Nicola," he said. "*Not* Mary." He raised his voice, calling along the walkway. "I want the Jewel." He tightened his arm at her throat again, and Aventurine couldn't get a breath. "Just give me the Jewel."

Through the stone archway, she could see Nicola, shadowy, and beyond her, the pale hair of her twin. Micheline took a step toward her along the walkway, and a hand appeared on her shoulder: Genevieve's.

The blood was screaming in Aventurine's ears, and her vision was fading in and out. Below them in the nave, a chorus of children's voices, loud and then becoming less distinct as they moved away. Aventurine pulled a wrist from his grip and grabbed at the arm at her throat, Could she kick him? Elbow him? She swung a leg back, and only dealt him a glancing blow with her heel.

"Give me the Jewel," he said again.

Nicola stepped forward. In the dim light through the archways, her face was pale, ethereal, her blond hair a nimbus. She could have been an angel.

"Or what?" she demanded, her voice hard. An avenging angel, then.

Aventurine felt him turning, looking to the side, and behind.

There was no way out but back. Something of that must have occurred to Etheredge: a hostage situation, but to what end? The realization seemed to infuriate him. He dragged Aventurine backwards, to a side way built for access to the lancets.

"I'll hurt her," he said. "I've done it before." *The woman at the Old Bishop's Palace.* Avi hoped the wire was still intact. His voice was rising. Aventurine willed someone below to hear him, willed someone to look up into the clerestory and see—what? A man's back. What would they think? A workman? But everyone who worked under the Domus Supervisor wore a yellow safety vest. She struggled against him, tried to turn so that someone might see—her. A captive. Held hostage to whatever plan Etheredge might have.

"Then what?" Nicola demanded. Her voice was still hard, absolutely rife with contempt. "Throw her off, Magnus. Throw her over the railing—"

A distressed cry, possibly from Micheline.

"—And you've got what?"

She held out a long-fingered hand, the small wrapped parcel resting on her palm.

"Not this," she said.

Another jerk of his arm, and Avi saw stars.

"And then you've got to escape."

"And one of you," he returned, "has a broken neck." He took another step back.

Someone had to see them from below. Someone *had to.*

A standoff. Nicola glared at Magnus, her eyes glittering in the light from beyond the lancets.

"How much is she worth to you?" Etheredge demanded.

"Aventurine—" Micheline's anguished voice. Etheredge laughed.

"Just give it to me," he repeated.

"Catch," Nicola said, and tossed the tiny parcel.

Marcus Etheredge let Aventurine go to reach for the handkerchief. She nearly fell, had to reach for the rough railing for support.

Nicola grabbed her arm. "Come on," she ordered.

Part VI:

The Badass Bitches of Britain

Forty-five

In the confusion, Henry led them down to the transept, and out through the service entrance. Everyone in the Cathedral, after the initial scream, had followed the sound into the aisle, or so it seemed.

"Give me the wires. Then split up," Genevieve ordered. "Go to ground, all of you. And most of all—" and she looked pointedly at Aventurine, who was still shaking, "*keep your mouth shut.*"

Stuffing the mini-recorders into her pocket, she strode off up Eastgate.

"I'm going to Herefordshire," Aventurine said, pausing before the door to Micheline's room at the hotel after a quick supper. "Come with me."

"Now?" Micheline had her hand at Avi's elbow, a solicitous gesture which Aventurine appreciated. She pitched her voice low, though there was no one else in the corridor. "Avi, it's late."

"Tomorrow. My hotel reservation runs out then. I'm going to keep to the original plan: anything else would look suspicious."

Micheline nodded. "I'm going to sleep. I've had enough," she said. Her embrace was quick, but hard. Then she turned into the room and closed the door behind her.

When Aventurine turned the key to her own room, the house phone was ringing.

"It's the policeman," Pete the bartender said, without even a greeting.

Aventurine yawned. "You must be getting sick of this," she said dryly. "Is he standing right there?"

"Pretending not to listen."

"Damn it," she hissed, then sighed. No nap for her. "Tell him I'll be down in a minute. And thanks." She dropped the headset back into the cradle and picked up her hairbrush. She looked a fright. She leaned forward to examine her face in the mirror: there were purple circles beneath her eyes. She grimaced and slapped on some lipstick. At least, looking like hell as she did, it would be easy to keep up the charade of last night, and pass as hungover now.

One last glance at the time on her watch. A little after eight. He'd probably come straight from the Cathedral, straight from Magnus Etheredge's broken body. She took a deep breath, but it wasn't calming. She wished she still had Genevieve's hip flask, but probably the entire contents, hair of the dog notwithstanding, wouldn't help at this point.

Keep your mouth shut, she reminded herself. She wondered how long it would take Genevieve to splice them out of the recordings and forward Etheredge's words to the police.

DCI Burroughs had chosen the same table, in the corner near the window. Fortunately, it wasn't crowded tonight, though she'd rather expected more people to be out, discussing the afternoon's event at the Cathedral. Tonight he had a pint before him, which he turned lazily on the coaster. He didn't appear to have drunk any. He stood as she approached.

"Ms. Morrow," he said by way of greeting. Formally. Warily. He indicated the chair across from his own.

Aventurine had not expected to be betrayed by her own reaction; she felt the heat rush up into her face. She prayed he wouldn't notice in the intimate lighting. "Call me Aventurine," she said. "Everyone does."

Except policemen.

Well, he'd called her by her given name last night, when he was responding to her kiss. She felt the flush under her skin again. She dropped her eyes, and her gaze fell to his hands, long-fingered, nails neatly trimmed. A mistake: she found herself wondering what those hands would feel like against her skin. She slumped gracelessly into the chair.

"Can I get you a drink? Coffee?" Burroughs raised a hand toward the bar, where Pete was just knifing off a pint. Then he folded his hands together; the movement was almost languid, as though he knew quite well the effect he was having on her.

There was the tiny pulse of a caffeine headache at her right temple. She rubbed at it, and squeezed her eyes shut for a moment. What the hell—she wasn't going to sleep anyway. "Coffee, I think, today."

He laughed shortly, but not unkindly. "It's almost night time, Aventurine."

She really liked the sound of her name in his mouth.

"That late?" Of course it was that late. The Bailgate, outside the window, was dark, only illuminated by the streetlights.

Burroughs's dark brows drew down as he watched her. He did not lift the pint to drink, but began, again, to turn it on the coaster.

They remained silent until the coffee came. Aventurine busied herself with the cream, but left the sugar packets on the saucer.

Still he watched her, until she couldn't bear it any longer. She rubbed her temple. "Stop it. I've got a hangover."

The detective nodded gravely, but still said nothing.

"What?" she demanded, flustered.

Burroughs shrugged. "Nothing. Except that I wonder if that's really the case."

This was the proverbial slippery slope, then, the sheer iciness of which made her know that she had to be extremely careful. She could feel Burroughs's gaze upon her, and she knew that, should she look up, she would meet the speculative glance of his cold blue eyes.

"I don't know what you mean," she protested. "I'd had a few, down in the town. I'm a bit hazy about the rest of last night. I mean, I got so turned around coming back up Steep Hill that I had to have you walk me back to the hotel."

She risked a glance at his face. A mistake. His mouth quirked at the corner. She caught her breath, looked quickly away again.

"You're babbling," he said. "I wonder why."

"Because I'm embarrassed," Avi shot back, squeezing her hot face between her hands. "I'm embarrassed, because I was drunk and I—"

"And you—?"

"You know what I did."

He laughed. "I know exactly what you did, Aventurine. And I responded. Exactly as—dare I say it—you planned?" He pushed the pint glass aside, and turned his attention to the cardboard coaster, rolling it back and forth on its edge with his long-fingered hands.

Aventurine's eyes shot to his face, which gave nothing away. She quickly dropped her gaze again, and picked up the spoon to stir her cup. When she finally lifted it to take a sip, the coffee was scalding on her tongue, and she winced. "I'm embarrassed. Because I was drunk. Because I threw myself at you like that." She swallowed. "Do you think I'd lie to you?"

This elicited the ghost of a mile, which quickly disappeared again. "About this? I'm not sure. In general? Oh, yes."

Again Aventurine slumped back in the chair. She was too exhausted for this. "Thanks for that, anyway." She turned away to look out into the Bailgate, where the post-holiday street was sullen and empty, like her mood. She could see his reflection, a phantom in the wavy glass: she saw him, at last, lift the pint and take a long pull of the ale. "I thought police officers weren't supposed to drink on duty."

"I'm not on duty." He took another long drink, then set the glass down.

"Oh, ho! A social call." Aventurine slewed a glance in his direction. Despite herself, she felt her gaze linger on his mouth. *Overtired,* she chided herself. Quickly, she turned back to the window.

"I came to make sure you were all right, after your adventures of last night."

His voice was neutral.

"No, you didn't."

He laughed again. She liked that sound.

"Do you think I'd lie to you?"

Touché. Aventurine didn't bother to answer. Again she felt the flushed creeping up from her throat.

Burroughs held up a hand. "Sorry. I shouldn't have said that."

Aventurine drank some more coffee. Her head seemed to be clearing, the ache in her temple dulling. "Let's start this again, shall we? You tell me why you came to see me when you're not on duty."

Burroughs was silent a long time, long enough to compel her to meet his blue gaze, which didn't seem all that icy this evening. "I wanted to know whether you'd heard the news."

"About?" *Play ignorant. Say nothing.*

"The Swynford Jewel."

She looked up. He was ticking off his fingers.

"The reappearance of Nicola Hallsey."

Avi took a breath.

"The death of Magnus Etheredge."

"Who's that?"

DCI Burroughs was watching her closely. She concentrated on wiping her expression clean of anything save puzzlement.

"You don't know the name?"

"Should I?"

"Seems he's a security consultant of some manner. Runs an agency out toward Riseholme."

"Where's that?"

Burroughs waved a hand vaguely in a direction that might have been north. "The company that was providing security for the Swynford Jewel. He died in a fall this afternoon. In the Cathedral."

"That's awful!"

Those eyes, on her face. She forced herself to meet his gaze.

"It is, yes. Awful," Burroughs repeated, lifting his glass. "And coincidental."

Aventurine emptied her coffee, and set the cup down, trying to keep her hand from shaking. *Disinterested,* she heard Genevieve say. Genevieve, who was probably well away from Lincoln already, probably safely ensconced in her darkened library, petting her bad-tempered tabby cat, editing the recordings. Cutting herself a slice of homemade Victoria sponge.

She gestured to Pete, wiping down the bar, for more coffee. Definitely not going to sleep tonight. She rubbed her temple again. Hungover. Headachy.

His pint was gone. He gestured to Pete as well.

"The Domus Supervisor doesn't know what Etheredge was doing up in the clerestory to begin with—he wasn't scheduled to do any checking on the security system. Even though there appeared to be yet another glitch late last night—camera and alarm down for a few minutes, that sort of thing."

"*That sort of thing* sounds a bit serious, doesn't it?"

She gripped her hands together beneath the table. This was, she realized, possibly the most dangerous conversation she'd ever had in her life. *Keep your mouth shut.* Hard to do that, when the detective seemed intent on engaging her in this loaded tête-à-tête.

Burroughs didn't answer.

Pete appeared with more coffee, and a full pint glass which he traded for the detective's empty one. Then he slipped away again.

"And also, speaking of coincidence, your friend Henry Hallsey called the station this afternoon," the detective said slowly. Changing the topic, or at least changing the angle of approach. She could feel his eyes on her face, studying. "He wanted to let us know he'd heard from his daughter, and that she was all right. She'd taken a few days out of town for a romantic tryst." The words were not a question, but Aventurine could sense the question behind them.

"Just like you police thought," she said. Avi rolled her eyes. "I'm so mortified, for making such a fuss."

"Oh, your friend Henry is, too. He just kept apologizing, the duty sergeant said."

A long pause.

"That doesn't explain, of course, the destructive search in Miss Hallsey's house."

He seemed to expect something of her.

"No, it doesn't." Aventurine shook her head. Puzzled. Not an act.

Burroughs continued on. "Unless someone took her absence as an opportunity to break in and toss the place, hoping for something to steal."

The laptop. But Aventurine said nothing. She held onto the puzzled expression for all she was worth.

"Makes you wonder, doesn't it?" he mused. "A person who works for a security company, not using one of their security systems. You'd think she might."

"Too expensive?" Aventurine suggested. "Unless she gets an employee discount, or something?" She shrugged. "I really don't know how these things work."

The noise in the pub was increasing; a few more people had entered, shaking off the rain.

Might as well bite the bullet.

"What about the Swynford Jewel?" Aventurine poured more milk into her coffee cup, watching the swirls for a moment before taking a sip. "I mean, you said there was news. Have you cracked that case, or something?" This would be where Genevieve's—Mary's— expression would be guileless, deadpan. Again, Avi concentrated on keeping hers smooth and empty.

Burroughs's blue eyes were steady on her face. "It's back," he said. His voice was non-committal.

"Just—back?" Inject mild shock and confusion here, she told herself: a delicate balance. "What do you mean, *back?*"

"As though it had never disappeared at all," he said. "Or as though it had only been on a brief holiday and now it's come home."

A romantic tryst?

It was all Aventurine could do to keep from bursting out laughing. Hysteria. Exhaustion. Instead she hurriedly took another sip of coffee. She sloshed it onto the table when she set the cup down again.

287

"I'm not following you."

There was still something controlled about his movements, as though he were holding back. DCI Burroughs leaned into the shadows in his chair and lifted the pint to his lips, taking a long drink while staring out into the darkened street. "I said there was another glitch in the security last night? Everyone was busy out on the town for the Bonfire Night shenanigans, and by the time we got to the Medieval Library, the security system appears to have righted itself."

She opened her eyes wide. "Are you telling me that—the jewel was stolen—and then returned?"

"That's exactly what I'm telling you."

"But that makes no sense," she protested, frowning. "Unless—"

"Unless?"

Aventurine met his gaze, still wide-eyed. She wondered whether he could hear her heart pounding. "Unless someone stole the original and—I don't know—returned a copy?"

His slow blink was like a cat's. If cats had blue eyes. "Believe me, we've thought of that."

Avi continued on, as though he hadn't spoken, as though she was thinking aloud. "But that wouldn't make sense, would it? If you were the thief, and going to go to all that trouble—to break into the library and do the switch—wouldn't it make more sense to do it all at once, instead of waiting almost a week to break in a second time?" She rubbed her forehead, still frowning. Let him think she was trying to figure it out. Let him think that was made difficult by the hangover. "Wouldn't the whole idea of a fake be to exchange them and hope no one would look too closely for a while? To hope that no one would notice until you'd got away?"

Burroughs lifted his brows and nodded. "One would think."

"And you had the Jewel checked, though? It *is* the real one?"

"It is the real one."

"Then I guess I just don't get it." Aventurine blew on her coffee, and sipped again. Just right. She took another sip.

"No, I didn't think you would," Burroughs said evenly. He too lifted his drink, and gazed through the amber liquid at the light. "And if you did, you wouldn't let on."

Aventurine felt her heartbeat stumble for a moment. *What the hell was that supposed to mean?* But when she flicked her gaze to him, she found that he was looking at her over the rim of his glass as he drank slowly.

The elephant in the room was now a woolly mammoth, tusks and all. Dangerous in so many ways. She drank her coffee slowly. Outside, three men stumbled past, singing "You'll Never Walk Alone." Burroughs, too, had fallen silent.

He knows, she thought. *I don't know how he knows, but he does.*

The coffee mug emptied for a second time, she set the cup down. No sloshes this time. She used the napkin to wipe her lips, and found, to her surprise, that her fingertips lingered there.

His eyes were on her hand at her lips. There was the tiniest of smiles on his own mouth. She flushed hotly.

"I think," he said slowly, rising to his feet, "that I have been outwitted." He drew out his wallet, and set some notes next to his now-empty pint glass. "Just as the police in York were, back in July."

Then he disappeared into the Bailgate.

The rain was picking up again. In her purse, her cell phone vibrated with a text. She pulled it out.

The eagle has landed.

Acknowledgments
and a Note

Thanks are owed to so many for their help and inspiration on this one.

To the Tiffany Farm Writing Retreat in the Green Mountains of Vermont, for granting me two weeks to write and revise deliriously. And for the bears!

To Joshua Wright, who cat-sat Toast and Editor Cat, so I could spend the time in the UK and in Vermont.

To the unnamed floor guide at Lincoln Cathedral, with whom I discussed chapter houses, Katherine Swynford, and the Beefcake Jesus in the Duncan Grant Chapel; his question to me that afternoon—*What were you looking for in our Cathedral?*—both took me by surprise, and led to some serious think-work on many levels.

To Sue, the roof guide at Lincoln Cathedral, who asked me, amidst the great beams between the vaulting of the nave and the inside of the roof, whether it might be a good place to set a scene in an adventure story.

To Alison Weir, whose *Mistress of Monarchy* is an excellent resource about Katherine Swynford, one of the Bad-Ass Bitches of Britain; and to Anya Seton, who is often the first source for Swynford fans, with her novel *Katherine.*

To Phil Lawrence, who quick-marched me up to the top of Steep

Hill in Lincoln *twice*, took me to tea, and then later found me the Hamlet teapot.

To Julia Hawkes-Moore, for humoring me with our Houses of the Day. It's always good to keep an architect among friends.

To Lesley Collett, who answers questions of an archaeological nature whenever I ask. It's also good to keep an archaeologist among friends.

To Ian Blake, my Urban Exploration Friend, who doesn't mind walking around and looking at things; and who understands my need to touch them. Who helps with research. And who sings on traffic islands, which is an added bonus.

To Eddie and Cynthia and Deirdre, who believe in Aventurine, even when she doesn't believe in herself.

And always, to Rebecca Bearden Welsh and Brenda Sparks Prescott, because Simply Not Done believes in me, even when I don't believe in myself.

P. S. There is no Apex Security and Alarm. To the people in charge of security at various locations atop Steep Hill: sorry.

About the Author

Anne Britting Oleson lives and writes in a small town in Central Maine. A frequent traveler to the U.K., she has published six previous novels, including *The Springs* (Encircle Publications, March 2023), and the first Aventurine Morrow Thriller, *Aventurine and the Reckoning* (Encircle Publications, January 2022), as well as four poetry chapbooks. She has three children, five grandchildren, and two cats. Anne is currently working on her next Aventurine Morrow novel. Follow Books by Anne Britting Oleson on Facebook and @ annebrittingoleson on Instagram for the latest news.

If you enjoyed this book,
please consider writing a review
and sharing it with other readers.

Many of our authors are happy to participate in
Book Club and Reader Group discussions.
For more information, contact us at info@encirclepub.com.

Thank you,
Encircle Publications

For news about more exciting new fiction, join us at:

Facebook: www.facebook.com/encirclepub

Instagram: www.instagram.com/encirclepublications

Sign up for the Encircle Publications newsletter:
eepurl.com/cs8taP

Printed in Great Britain
by Amazon